con

Hiss and Tell

Claire Donally

BERKLEY PRIME CRIME, NEW YORK

THE BERKLEY PUBLISHING GROUP
Published by the Penguin Group
Penguin Group (USA) LLC
375 Hudson Street, New York, New York 10014

USA • Canada • UK • Ireland • Australia • New Zealand • India • South Africa • China

penguin.com

A Penguin Random House Company

HISS AND TELL

A Berkley Prime Crime Book / published by arrangement with Tekno Books

For information, address: The Berkley Publishing Group,
a division of Penguin Group (USA) LLC,
375 Hudson Street, New York, New York 10014.

ISBN: 978-0-425-27606-8

PUBLISHING HISTORY
Berkley Prime Crime mass-market edition / May 2015

PRINTED IN THE UNITED STATES OF AMERICA

10 9 8 7 6 5 4 3 2 1

Cover illustration by Mary Ann Lasher (B&A Reps).
Cover design by George Long.
Interior text design by Laura K. Corless.

To the married members of the family:
Charlie and Betty, Frank and Nancy, Chris and
Maureen, and to Mom. If she hadn't met Dad,
where would any of us be today?

And, as ever, sincere thanks to Larry Segriff of
Tekno Books and Shannon Jamieson Vazquez
of Berkley Prime Crime. Without their input
and chastisement, where would any of
these books be today?

1

He didn't know how long he'd stood in the cover of the bushes at the rear of the house. But it was long enough to convince him that the place was empty.

So he strolled across the yard. No hurry, anyone who might look would instantly recognize that he belonged here. Of course, the door barred his way. But he knew that wouldn't be a problem. He'd been practicing.

A little finagling with the latch, then a quick jump to catch the top of the door, and it swung open without a struggle or a noise. All it took was a little twist, and he was inside.

The kitchen was warm—it had been a sunny day—and there was no sign of anyone in residence. A quick prowl of the ground floor quickly enlarged the no-one-home zone. Even so, he moved silently, listening for any telltale noises. As he stood at the foot of the hall stairway, he heard the gurgle of running water above. That brought him upstairs at a run; quietly, but quickly.

As he stood in the hall, he also heard a snatch of song under the rush of the water. But he followed the scent of perfume into her room. Just as he expected, she had her fresh clothing laid out on the bed. He reached out and snagged one of her underthings—absurdly tiny, sheer and lacy.

He was just raising it to his nose for a whiff when something happened he couldn't have planned for: the phone rang. An instant later, she burst into the room, headed for the phone. She had a towel wrapped around her head . . . and that was all.

They stood frozen for a long moment, him with the frilly little nothing still dangling, her with her bare skin pink and still damp from the water.

And then she moved, tearing the towel free and throwing it at him.

He yowled in surprise, his attempt to dodge sending him tumbling to the floor, with barely enough time to get his feet under him. But he could move, too, darting to squeeze under the bed where she couldn't get at him easily.

His quick action—not to mention his lashing tail—stirred up a cloud of dust under there that made him sneeze. But he hunkered down on all four paws, staying put and warily keeping a lookout for any more possible attacks.

I don't know why she overreacted like that, he thought. *Maybe she's embarrassed about having so little fur.*

*

Sunny Coolidge stood on the deck of the cabin cruiser, enjoying the sailing. Although she hadn't set off feeling very laid-back, after dashing out of the shower to find her cat Shadow playing with her underwear. He hadn't appreciated getting attacked with a damp towel and had taken cover under the bed, leaving her with a heck of a job coaxing him out.

Sunny had felt rushed and frazzled by the time Will had picked her up, and he'd just laughed when she told him what had made her late. "I always had him pegged. You're sheltering a peeping tomcat." She'd finally relaxed now, though, and they'd ventured far enough from land to feel a rhythmic swell in the ocean, the remains of a storm considerably farther out to sea. It was enough to impart a rocking feeling to the vessel and made Sunny glad that she was a good sailor.

If only I could be sure that Ben Semple is as good a skipper, she thought as she watched the man at the wheel. Dressed in a pair of Bermuda shorts and a long-sleeved shirt to avoid sunburn, he looked about as non-nautical as a person could get. A long-billed Kittery Harbor Police baseball cap completed his ensemble, and he wore it down low over his eyes as he scanned the waters around them.

Will Price must have been reading Sunny's mind, since he came over and draped an arm around her shoulders, grinning. "Don't worry. We've got at least three GPS gizmos on board to get us back safely."

Sunny had less faith than Will in navigational systems. She couldn't help thinking of a cartoon her dad had shown her of a car going off a cliff while the GPS voice droned, "Recalculating . . . recalculating."

"I'm just wondering if heading for the Isles of Shoals might not be a little too ambitious for Ben," she whispered. "You said that on your other trips, you always stayed in or near the river."

The river was the Piscataqua, which divided Maine and New Hampshire. On one side was Kittery Harbor, Maine, Sunny's hometown. On the other was the city of Portsmouth, in New Hampshire, where Will had previously been posted. Nowadays, both he and Ben were constables in the Kittery Harbor police, but Will was aiming for a promotion—he was running for county sheriff. Last night he'd been speech-making at a homeowners' association meeting in one of the new developments at the edge of town, and Sunny had sat there trying to look loyal and gracious, while Tammy Wynette sang "Stand by Your Man" nonstop in an irreverent corner of her brain.

Today represented a rare break in routine or campaigning, a chance to kick back and enjoy themselves before Labor Day arrived to put an end to summer. "I remember when my dad first took me out to the Isles of Shoals. We went with one of his fishing buddies. I thought it sounded like a fairy-tale place, someplace where we might see mermaids sunning themselves on the shore," Sunny said.

"Huh," Will said. "As a kid, I always thought that was the place where all the foot-care stuff came from."

"Different spelling." Sunny glanced at Will, not sure whether he was kidding. He had an oddball sense of humor.

"We might see some seals over on Appledore Island."

"Which was not named after the guy who taught Harry Potter," Sunny said, trying to get ahead of Will. "I guess I should be glad you didn't bring up Smuttynose Island."

Will shrugged. "I was just thinking of things that would be nice to see, like the lighthouse on White Island."

Sunny sighed. Maybe she was just making things harder than she had to. For a small town like Kittery Harbor where the pickings were slim, Will was prime boyfriend material—tall, dark (especially with his summer tan), and yes, handsome, with regular features and a pair of gray eyes with odd-colored flecks. He'd rate as decent male companionship even in New York City, where Sunny had gone in search of a journalism career before returning home to help her dad when he got really sick. His health had recovered, but alas, her New York City newspaper career hadn't, so Sunny had stayed put.

"I haven't seen any of this," the fourth passenger on the boat joined the conversation. "So you guys will have to point everything out to me."

Sunny wasn't sure which pride and joy this little voyage was supposed to show off—the boat Ben had devoted a big chunk of his salary to getting, or the girlfriend he'd also acquired this summer. Robin Lory was a nice, uncomplicated girl from a little town up in the woods who'd been excited to get a job running a cash register in one of the stores lining the interstate north of Kittery Harbor—outlet-land, as the locals called it. The store was local, however, a bakery with a wonderful line of pastries and, yes, donuts. Sunny had to hide a smile at the spectacle of a cop falling for a baker's assistant. Still, Robin was cheerful, bubbly, and she'd certainly pepped up the usually stolid Ben. Though Robin had been a little quiet today, first because the flip-flops she'd worn hadn't protected her toes from the deck hardware, so she'd taken one of the padded seats and stayed there. Then the swells had turned her a little green. But now it seemed she'd recovered. "What I'm really interested in," she said, "is catching some rays out here."

With that, she stood up and peeled off the long T-shirt

she'd been wearing, to reveal a tiny bikini and a lot of Robin.

Will took one brief, appreciative look, but shot a glance at Ben when Robin began fiddling with her top.

"Hey, Robin," Ben said, glancing back at her, "I think we'd better cool it. Will's running for office, and a lot of voters are on the conservative side."

"Who's gonna see?" Robin squinted around at the waters surrounding them.

"All it takes is one boat—and somebody on board with a telescopic lens." Will spoke with the authority of someone who'd spent time on stakeouts. "And the next thing you know, a blurry photo is showing up on someplace online." He looked over at Sunny. "And they're claiming it's you."

Sunny glanced down at what she called her seagoing Daisy Duke outfit—cutoffs and a shirt tied above her waist, with deck-shoe-soled tennies and no socks. "Hey, I don't think an A-line dress and a pillbox hat are going to work out here."

"Besides," Robin scoffed, "I'd be surprised if that Nesbit guy even heard of the Internet."

Will frowned. "Frank Nesbit got to be sheriff by being a damned good politician—and a bare-knuckles one at that."

Will ought to know, Sunny thought. Nesbit once bounced his father out of the job. Not even Will could tell whether the car crash that killed his dad shortly after losing the election had been an accident or something else. Either way, Frank Nesbit had remained sheriff ever since, and whenever the election cycle came up, billboards sporting portraits of an ever-graying Frank Nesbit appeared beside main roads, touting his record of keeping Elmet County safe.

But not everyone bought that line, arguing that Nesbit massaged crime statistics, artificially downgrading more dangerous offenses in order to make his numbers look good. Sunny's dad was one of those dissenting voices, and he and several other Kittery Harbor politicos had helped install Will as a town constable, grooming him for a race against Nesbit.

As Sunny had seen in recent weeks, though, this insurgent campaign wasn't easy. Like a lot of places, Elmet County politics wasn't exactly a two-party system—more like one-and-a-half parties. Folks had to get pretty fed up with the people in office before they'd vote for the opposition. That meant the party primaries were the only voting that really counted. And for Will, it meant a lot of speeches to homeowners' associations—and no topless boat rides to the Isles of Shoals.

Robin pouted, but she kept her bikini top on, arranging herself as best she could on the padded seat in the stern of the boat for maximum sun. Sunny fiddled with the ends of the blouse she'd knotted along the line of her ribcage. "You think I'm underdressed for this boat ride? I thought we were taking it easy."

"I think you look fine." Will himself was wearing an open short-sleeved button-down shirt over a tight tee that made the most of his rangy build, with a pair of cutoffs and boat shoes. "We just have to be aware that other people will be looking—and yeah, judging."

The boat trip lived up to every promise, offering up glimpses of seals, lighthouses, scenic rocky shores, and sea breezes. But for Sunny, the sudden intrusion of politics had taken something away from the outing—the fun. She felt distracted all through the journey around the islands.

As Ben steered about, heading for home, a large sailing yacht cruised past in the distance, its distinctive red, white and blue canvas billowing on the breeze.

Robin immediately perked up. "Oh, wow, that's Caleb Kingsbury's yacht!"

Ben glanced back from his post at the wheel. "How do you know?"

"From TV, silly. It was on *Eagle Eye*. They did a whole piece on the announcement of his niece Priscilla's wedding and about the whole family," Robin said. "The Senator, the governors, and Caleb. The best part was that yacht, I think it's called the *Merlin*. It's named after a pirate ship or something one of his ancestors sent out during the War of 1812."

"Do you mean a privateer?" Sunny asked. "They were sort of early defense contractors. The government gave them the legal go-ahead to raid and seize cargos from enemy merchant ships."

"Like pirates." Robin shrugged. "Whatever you want to call it, that *Merlin* came home with a hundred thousand dollars."

"Before inflation," Will joked, but his eyes grew serious as they followed the vessel, almost three times the size of Ben's boat. "Kingsbury's got a lot of nerve, sailing in these waters after what happened."

"I know, right?" Robin said. "They mentioned that on the show, too, about the girl who drowned under his boat."

"That cost him his seat in Congress." Sunny remembered the scandal, which had happened during the summer of her junior year in college. Caleb Kingsbury had been found on top of his overturned boat—the dead girl had been beneath it. "He was just getting ready to run again, but after that, none of his father's political friends wanted anything to do with him."

"Well, it couldn't have hurt him much if he's out there sailing a fifty-foot schooner." Ben adjusted their course slightly.

"So what's the scoop on this celebrity wedding?" Sunny asked.

"You don't know?" Robin sounded incredulous. "Priscilla Kingsbury is marrying Carson de Kruk in a couple of months. It'll be the biggest thing to happen around here this fall. *Eagle Eye* said the families will be spending some time at the Kingsbury estate, getting to know one another."

Sunny might not be up on the local wedding gossip, but even she knew the name Carson de Kruk—son of multimillionaire Augustus de Kruk. "If Caleb Kingsbury is sailing in for this get-together, I wonder how the de Kruks will make their entrance," Sunny said. "They've got more money than God."

"Maybe they'll pile it all up and come parasailing down from the summit," Will suggested.

"One thing's for sure," Ben said, going from sea captain to traffic cop. "Driving anywhere near Wilawiport is going to be a real mess—especially round the Kingsbury compound. They may not be Kennedys or Bushes, but they're sure to have TV crews and lots of gawkers around. Now I know why I'm being posted up there. I was supposed to keep quiet about it. But if it's on TV . . ." He shrugged.

They reached the dock where Ben was renting space without spotting any other mysterious schooners, and the two couples parted ways. Will gave Sunny a lift home.

"Do you want to come in?" she asked as they turned onto Wild Goose Drive.

When she saw Will hesitate, Sunny said, "I promise there are no paparazzi hanging around."

"It's not that—or you." Will fumbled for words. "It's your dad. Whenever he gets hold of me now, he's full of advice."

"Well, he kind of considers himself your unofficial campaign manager." Sunny pointed out.

"Emphasis on the unofficial," Will said.

"Hey, he and Zach Judson and the other members of the Kittery Harbor political faction got you back here in the first place."

"I know. It's just that it's gotten so complicated." Will ran a hand through his hair, and made a face as his fingers got stuck.

Sunny grinned. "Yeah, salt water will do that. You know, some folks intentionally spray the stuff onto their hair to get more volume."

"Well, all it does for me is to make everything clump together."

She laughed. "Better than the frizz of death, which is what I get. Come and have a quick drink, then you can plead the need to take a shower and escape if Dad gets to be too much for you."

Will agreed, and together they walked to the front door, then headed into the living room to find Sunny's dad, Mike Coolidge, sitting on the couch with their neighbor Helena Martinson.

"Well, you two look dry, so I guess Ben Semple didn't sink the boat on you," Sunny's father greeted them.

"No, we had a nice little jaunt," Sunny assured him, glad to see her Dad looking so well and relaxed. When she'd come home from New York City to tend him after his heart attack, it had been touch and go for a while. But now he was eating healthily and getting in a three-mile walk every day, though his unruly white curls needed a trim, as usual. His piercing blue eyes were fondly aimed at Mrs. Martinson, whom Sunny suspected was the other reason for Mike's improvement. There were plenty of widows available in town, but her dad had gravitated to Helena, and Sunny could see why. Mrs. Martinson was everything Sunny wanted to be when she grew up—or at least grew older. Petite, graceful, with a figure that Sunny could only envy and blond hair that had somehow gone platinum with age, Mrs. M. was definitely a catch . . . and Sunny was glad that Mike had caught her.

"Kinda nice, being able to sit around without worrying about furry critters underfoot," Mike said.

Helena nodded. "We had a pet-free day. Your Shadow was out visiting, and I left my Toby playing in my back-yard." She shuddered slightly. "I just hope he hasn't gnawed his way through the fence or knocked a tree down."

The ungainly pup Mrs. M. had adopted had grown considerably . . . and didn't show any signs of stopping yet. Combined with a bumptious puppy-dog personality, Toby's awkward stage wasn't always charming.

"I didn't think they could breed golden retrievers with Godzilla." Mike shook his head.

"So, did you enjoy your day off?" Mike turned round to include Will in the conversation. "Lord knows you won't get many until after the primary."

"Too true. In fact, I was reminded of what can go wrong

in a political career," Will said, "when Caleb Kingsbury went sailing past us."

"The Kingsburys? They're definitely out of my league. Now there was a political dynasty still looking for a crown." Mike shook his head. "Although at least his father, Thomas Kingsbury, reached out to folks in Kittery Harbor the last time he ran. Tom was 'the Senator' to everybody, even his kids. He was kind of a stiff old coot, which worked against him in the end. The party, even long-time supporters, dumped him for a younger, more with-it candidate."

"From what I hear, the kids didn't turn out too happily," Will added.

"The eldest, Nate, came out of West Point as a newly minted second lieutenant, and his dad sent him off to Vietnam to become a war hero. Apparently the Senator forgot that people could become casualties, which is what happened to Nate. Lem, the second son, was campaigning for the old man's seat and got killed in an accident up in the mountains." Mike paused for a moment. "You know, that's why the term 'landslide' became a taboo political term among the Kingsburys." He went on, "The Senator's grandsons haven't done too shabbily, though. Lem Junior is a governor down south, and his kid brother Tom is one of the youngest governors in the country out west. You can't exactly call the Kingsburys kingmakers, though. Even with both of their states together, the best they can deliver is seven electoral votes."

"And Lem Junior got pretty well trounced in the last round of presidential primaries," Sunny recalled. "He was out before South Carolina."

Mrs. M. spoke up. "Nate, Lem, Caleb . . . putting the

names all together like that, it begins to sound like the cast from *Hee Haw*."

That got a shrug out of Mike. "The Senator was very big on early American names. It's not uncommon in these parts. Although maybe not in such volume."

"And he seemed to do well enough as Thomas Kingsbury," Helena Martinson added.

"Thomas Neal Kingsbury," Mike corrected. "His Neal relations were the really rich ones. They've got an old family mansion up in Wilawiport, on Neal's Neck, their private peninsula."

"If the house is up in Wilawiport, the Neals probably were robber barons," Mrs. M. said. "You had to make your money before 1929 to build an estate up there." She confided to Sunny, "Just like the Piney Brook people look down their noses at what they call the 'new money' putting up McMansions in the new developments, the Wilawiport crowd looks down on the Piney Brook mansion set because they made their money around World War II."

"As I said, out of my league." Mike turned back to Will. "We've got a sheriff's primary to win. Are you all set for your next speech?"

"The 99 Elmet Ladies." Will glanced at Helena. "At least I can depend on one friendly face in attendance tomorrow evening." Mrs. Martinson was a leading light in that county-wide civic group.

"I'll be there, too," Sunny loyally promised, wondering where she could find a sufficiently conservative outfit on short notice. Maybe something with a bustle.

"Not every face will be friendly, though," Mrs. M. warned. "Lenore Nesbit is a founding member."

"The sheriff's wife?" Sunny thought hard, but she couldn't remember ever meeting the woman. "Do you think she'll be a problem?" She tried to lighten the mood. "From your tone of voice, I'd be expecting the Wicked Witch of the West."

"Oh, no, Lenore is quite charming," Mrs. Martinson said mildly. "So charming, you'll hardly feel the knife as it goes in."

2

Sunny didn't know how to answer that, so she was glad when the doorbell rang and gave her an excuse to escape. It was Rafe Warner, delivering Shadow home.

"He was pretty much a gentleman," Rafe reported as he put down the cat carrier, "except for a little roughhousing with Portia." He grinned. "She egged him on."

An imperious "Meow" came from the grilled front of the carrier. Shadow didn't mind being transported in the carrier . . . but he didn't like being cooped up in his own house. Sunny undid the latch and the big gray tomcat stepped out, immediately twining his way around her bare ankles. He paid special attention to her shoes, making Sunny wonder if she'd stepped into some trace of Ben's last fishing expedition.

Rafe's grin grew wider as he watched. "That Shadow is a smooth one. Moving from one girlfriend to another."

"I'm just glad you're okay with having Shadow over to visit Portia." Sunny bent and picked up Shadow, then waved good-bye to Rafe as he headed back to his car.

Shadow wormed his way out of her arms and onto her shoulders, draping himself around her neck like a large and internally warmed fur collar. Sunny wore him like that back into the living room, but he quickly abandoned her once she sat down, climbing to the top of the chair, then jumping down to the floor and investigating the other people in the room.

Mike and Mrs. Martinson got a fairly cursory examination, although Shadow made a sort of sneezing noise around Mrs. M. *Probably catching a whiff of Toby,* Sunny thought.

Shadow was more circumspect as he approached Will. While it didn't reach the level of cold war, there was definitely a respectful antagonism between the two. Will and Shadow were both pretty stubborn and didn't find much to agree on— except, maybe, for Sunny. And Will had yet to forgive Shadow for the time that the cat had literally crashed a romantic moment, falling from the roof of the house just as he was making a move. Even so, Shadow was enough of a snoop that he couldn't help checking Will out for any interesting smells—especially Will's Top-Siders.

"Whatcha catching there, little guy?" Will asked with a smile. "A whiff of fish head or fish guts? I keep telling Ben he's got to clean the decks more often."

"Of course, that's why any man buys a boat," Mrs. Martinson said in a tart voice. "The chance to do marine house-keeping."

Sunny remembered that as a kid, she'd often seen Mrs. M.'s late husband coming home from fishing expeditions. He'd had a boat, too. Whenever Mr. Martinson enjoyed a good catch, he'd share it with the neighborhood. Nice, but Sunny remembered her mother's delight at getting stuck with the job of gutting and scaling a fresh fish dinner.

Whatever it was Shadow had been smelling, he finally finished his rounds, walked back in front of Sunny, sat back on his hindquarters, and stared up at her.

"I know that look," Mike said, "and I never go to sleep if I see it in the furball's eyes." He deepened his voice. "Feeeeed meeeeee."

Sunny rose. "Well, we'll see if he wants dry food or something to drink."

"Speaking of feeding . . ." Mrs. M. got up from her chair, too. "I'd better get home to see what damage Toby has done to my backyard."

"I should be heading home, too." Will joined Helena as she went for the door.

After they said their good-byes, Sunny headed down the hall to the kitchen, with Shadow leading the way and Mike trailing after.

"Do you think it was something we said?" Mike asked as Sunny laid out some food for the cat. Mike stepped over to where Shadow leaned into his bowl, delicately crunching away on dry food. "Or was it something the furball did?"

*

Shadow was just as glad to see the visitors leave. He'd put in a hard day, chasing and playing with Portia, the calico cat with the irresistible scent. Now he was ready for a nice nap. Besides, you never knew what two-legs would get up to when you put them in large groups. Sometimes they'd sit around talking loudly, setting little things on fire to breathe the smoke, turn on the picture box or the box that made noise, drink that stuff that made them act silly . . . and then they'd forget that there was someone to watch out for on the floor. Shadow had lived in houses like that, and it could get dangerous.

Luckily, Sunny and the Old One weren't that way. They didn't make the picture box too loud, Sunny liked to play, and the Old One left Shadow alone for the most part. Even their visitors weren't too bad. The She who visited with the Old One wasn't grabby, and she knew the good places to scratch. If it weren't for the fact that she smelled so much of dog, Shadow wouldn't mind having her around.

Sunny's He was another story. Shadow remembered how that one had held him helpless, keeping him from meeting Portia for a long, long time. Shadow wasn't about to forget that. If it happened once, it could happen again. So Shadow kept a wary eye on that one, even when he came in with strange and interesting aromas.

That reminded him. Shadow turned back to Sunny, inhaling deeply, trying to identify the elements of the bouquet wafting from her. Some were familiar, like Sunny's own scent. And there was the faintest smell of fish coming from the things on her feet. Others he couldn't identify, like the sharp tangy odor from back around her heel. Most of all, he caught an odd fragrance still enveloping her, one he sometimes sensed in town when the wind came blowing across the big water.

It was a scent to stir the blood, wild and salty.

Shadow turned from his bowl and ran his tongue along Sunny's bare leg until she jumped away with a surprised noise.

Yes, definitely salty. It went well with the crunchy food he was eating.

*

The next evening, Sunny looked critically at her reflection in the bedroom mirror. Was she ready to deal with the 99 Elmet Ladies and Will? Spending time outdoors on the boat yesterday had strengthened her tan—and left a spray of freckles across the bridge of her nose and her cheeks. Her outfit involved neither a pillbox hat nor a pantsuit. Sunny wore a simple belted dress in muted green, something nice but a tad fuddy-duddy that had sat in her closet for a long, long time.

I guess I should be glad it still fits, she thought. *It's one of the first things I bought when I moved to New York.*

Sunny had a nice figure, but spending most of her day sitting in front of a computer was enough to shift the sand in even the daintiest hourglass. She'd upped the exercise quota this summer, and now she was glad of it as she checked the fit of the dress.

She'd managed to wash the salt out of her hair, but her auburn curls were as unmanageable as ever, a genetic bullet from her father and his own mass of curls. She really needed a cut and styling, especially if she was going to have to attend more of these dressy events with Will. But the one beauty parlor in the area that could control her mop was pricey.

She'd actually gotten a raise for her job as webmistress

and general office worker monkey at the Maine Adventure X-perience, MAX for short. Sunny would've thought her boss, Ollie Barnstable, more likely to donate a kidney than fork over a little more in her paycheck but he'd actually come across pretty generously. Still, it seemed really ridiculous, spending it all on her hair. *Had Jackie Kennedy dealt with problems like this?* That irreverent corner of her mind was having a field day. *Did Hillary Clinton?*

Catching movement in the mirror, she turned to find Shadow sitting in the doorway, watching her.

"Don't tell me you're smelling mothballs," Sunny told him.

She headed downstairs to the living room, where her father had installed himself with the Sunday papers on his lap and the TV remote in his hand.

"You look nice," Mike said. He seemed in a mellow mood after a lazy day and a salad supper.

"Sure you don't want to come, Dad?" Sunny teased. "You could have a front-row seat to watch politics in action."

Mike shook his head. "Not after I got a pass from Helena. There's a very smart woman. She told me, 'Togetherness is fine, but there's nothing like the meeting of a ladies club to put a strain on it.'" He grinned. "Besides, I think she's afraid one of the ninety-eight other ladies might try to poach me."

The mention of the other women reminded Sunny of something. "Do you think the sheriff's wife is going to make trouble?" That thought had been nagging at her ever since Helena had mentioned Mrs. Nesbit.

"I've met Lenore a couple of times, usually when I was up at the county seat for some political confab or other,"

Mike said. "For the most part she kept to herself. But when she opens her mouth, watch out."

"Thanks," Sunny told him. "That makes me feel a whole lot better."

Mike spread his hands. "What is she going to say? Will doesn't have any interns to fool around with—" He abandoned that line of thought when he caught the look she sent him. "He has a good reputation as a solid cop. One you've helped him achieve. Whatever she says, if she says anything at all, it can't be too bad."

Even so, Sunny felt uneasy as she walked the few blocks over to pick up Mrs. Martinson at her place. Helena was out on her porch. "I thought I'd spare you a greeting from Toby."

From the level of excited barking inside the house, Sunny was just as glad.

Mrs. M. held out a set of car keys. "Would you mind driving the Buick? The evenings are still long, but it will be dark by the time we're heading back."

It wasn't the first time Sunny had done the driving, so she led the way to the car, opening the passenger-side door for Helena. The car started up without a problem, and Sunny noticed the gas gauge read "full."

All prepared for the journey, she thought. *I hope.*

She took local roads over to the interstate and headed north. The Elmet Ladies usually met in the county seat of Levett, which was sort of enemy territory for Will. Most of his support came from people like Sunny's dad, down in the southern end of the county, folks around Kittery Harbor who felt they were getting shortchanged by the movers and shakers up in Levett.

This could be a chance for Will to make some inroads in Frank Nesbit country.

As long as Mrs. Nesbit doesn't overturn the applecart. Sunny pushed that thought away.

Sunny got off at the exit for Levett, and Mrs. M. directed her to a lodge hall that the Elmet Ladies had rented for the evening. There were definitely more than ninety-nine people inside, and some of them weren't even ladies. Sunny hadn't expected to find so many political junkies in this neck of the woods. Maybe this was a good thing for Will.

Helena took her around the room, introducing Sunny to people, and in some cases, reintroducing her to the mothers of old classmates or people who'd been ahead of her at school.

Then her eyes lit up. "Here's someone you really should meet." The someone was a young woman, younger than Sunny, and she was surrounded by a buzzing cluster of ladies. Helena deftly inserted them into the crowd, moving forward until she could make the introductions. "Sunny Coolidge, this is Priscilla Kingsbury. Priscilla, Sunny."

So this is the bride-to-be, one of the fabled Kingsburys, Sunny thought. Priscilla had sandy blond hair, cut short in a fairly utilitarian style, and wore a plain khaki dress not that dissimilar from the one Sunny had on. *Hmmmm. Maybe I have a future as a political helpmate, at least in the wardrobe department.*

As Priscilla turned to them, Sunny was struck by the girl's eyes, large, dark, and intelligent, the best feature in an otherwise pleasantly pretty face. She also displayed a killer smile and a sharp memory. "Nice to meet you, Sunny. And good to see you, Helena."

"Priscilla is helping with our food pantry," Mrs. M. explained. That explained a lot. Helena had made keeping the local food pantry stocked her personal mission. Jobs were still scarce around the county, and a lot of families needed help in stretching their food budgets.

"We just provided some seed money and discussed best practices." Priscilla smiled. "It's passionate folks like Helena who really got it off the ground. If we can find more people like that in neighboring counties, we can try setting up a regional pilot program and even wind up with a model that we can use nationally."

Sunny nodded, impressed. "Sounds pretty serious."

Priscilla laughed, flashing that smile again. "It makes a nice change from forever talking about wedding plans."

"Speaking of which . . ." A lady off to Priscilla's left cut in. "Have you considered using local goods and services for the wedding? That could be a real economic boost."

Priscilla turned to her, looking a bit harassed. But the woman on Priscilla's right stepped forward with an answer. "I'm Fiona Ormond, Ms. Kingsbury's wedding planner. Some elements of the wedding— the gown, for instance— will of necessity come from New York. But there are many other supplies and services, of course, we're looking to source locally."

The planner had a handsome, slightly square face, and blond hair with dark roots showing at the part. *Proof that she's a busy woman who doesn't get distracted by mere vanity,* Sunny's irreverent alter ego suggested. With her crisp business suit and a smile that could cut paper, Fiona was the classic stereotype of the go-getting New York career woman.

Is that what Will thought he was seeing when he first met me? Sunny wondered. She looked over to the stage, where he stood looking out at the crowd. Will smiled when he spotted her. *At least he's changed his mind now.*

"I guess this isn't the time or place to discuss life on the campaign trail," Helena whispered with a smile as she moved away from Priscilla and deftly snagged them a pair of aisle seats. As usual, Mrs. M.'s timing was impeccable. No sooner had they sat down than the chairwoman called the meeting to order.

Once everyone was seated, Will set off on his stump speech. It wasn't an attack speech. Will was respectful of Frank Nesbit, praising him as a good administrator who worked well within the county government. Will had practiced and refined his words, working with Mike and other members of his "Kittery Harbor Kitchen Cabinet." As Will concluded, he said, "Just as his billboards say, Frank Nesbit has done a good job of keeping Elmet County safe. But now the job is changing. We've had drug labs appear, even dealt with a serial killer. What you don't know *can* hurt you. So you have to ask yourselves: are you safer not knowing what's out there or being aware of the potential crime situation?"

Sunny tried to listen like the reporter she used to be, rather than a girlfriend. She thought Will sounded pretty good, and judging by the applause, a lot of other people in the audience did, too. Then the chairwoman opened the floor for questions.

A voice came from the rear of the hall, pitched so everyone could hear. "But how do you become aware of the potential crime situation? Would you be sending officers out looking for trouble?"

Sunny twisted in her seat to get a glimpse of the questioner, a handsome woman with a frosting of gray in her short, dark hair.

"Lenore Nesbit," Helena Martinson whispered in Sunny's ear.

Did Will recognize his antagonist? Whether he did or not, he responded to Lenore with a smile. "For most cops, it's the other way around. Every time a law enforcement officer goes out, there's the possibility of trouble finding him—or her. That's a difference between the sheriff and myself—I've pounded a beat in several different locations."

"So is that your policing policy, that our officers should be 'pounding a beat' rather than, for instance, driving on traffic patrol?" Lenore asked.

Will refused to be drawn into that trap. "I think we know what the situation is on the interstate through outlet-land," he said. "There's a lot of traffic, and people get a little crazy when it comes to bargains. Plus, I'm aware of the revenue generated from giving tickets to folks from outside the state. It's a fiscal enhancement for the sheriff's department and for the county, as well as a valid safety issue."

So Ben Semple will keep his job, Sunny thought.

Lenore thanked Will and disappeared while others in the hall asked questions or expressed concerns. The chairwoman was just beginning to wrap things up when a surprise visitor arrived.

Frank Nesbit walked into the hall, wearing his usual green sheriff's department Windbreaker, his trademark silver mustache as carefully groomed as ever. He might as well have stepped down off one of his campaign billboards.

He made his way to the front of the hall, shaking a lot

of hands on the way. "I'm not here to steal my opponent's thunder," Nesbit said as he faced the crowd. "The past few years have shown that Will Price is a very talented, experienced officer. Right now we have a situation that calls for both of those qualities: the Kingsbury-de Kruk wedding. So I'm appointing Constable Price as my liaison officer for the duration, effective immediately, so he can help us work with all the other law enforcement agencies providing security for the celebration."

While everyone applauded the sheriff's generous response, Nesbit shook hands with Will, who did a good job of looking pleased. But Sunny could tell otherwise, and so could Mrs. Martinson. "What's that old rascal up to now?" she asked in a low voice.

They didn't get an answer until Will finished pressing the flesh and almost everyone had left the hall. "That's one I didn't expect," Will growled as he escorted Sunny and Helena to the Buick. "If the wedding goes off without a hitch, Nesbit cements his reputation as a great administrator, appointing the right man for the job. And if anything goes wrong, it will all be my fault."

"That is clever, in a twisted kind of way," Sunny had to admit.

"But here's the kicker," Will said. "It also means that I'll have to spend a lot of time up in Wilawiport, giving me even less of a chance to campaign."

"And there you have it in a nutshell," Helena Martinson said. "The difference between a cop and a politician as sheriff."

3

Since it was a work night, Sunny couldn't stay out late to help Will figure out how to deal with this latest political curveball. By the time she got Mrs. Martinson home, it was just about time for bed. Sunny arrived at her house to see her father watching the late news.

"Somehow, Will's speech didn't make it into the national newscast." Mike grinned at her. "How did it go?"

"As far as the speech went, that was pretty good. But afterward . . ." She recounted what happened with Frank Nesbit's surprise visit.

"Not wanting to steal Will's thunder? Of course he did." Mike frowned. "And Nesbit's shoveled enough happy horseflop with the Kingsburys to know damn well this isn't the plum job he's making it out to be."

Sunny nodded. "Will already figured out it's a

heads-Nesbit-wins, tails-Will-loses situation. And it will keep him stuck in Wilawiport instead of campaigning."

That got a deeper scowl out of Mike. "Just means we'll have to pull up our socks and work all the harder to get the word out. Is Will taking it okay?"

"He knew from the start what he was getting into," Sunny said. "And we all knew the sheriff wasn't going to make it any easier." She looked down. "I'd better get out of this outfit and into bed."

She'd already spotted Shadow making a slow circle around her, watching intently. It wasn't often that Sunny wore nylons, and she wanted to get safely out of reach before Shadow's nosiness overcame his usual caution. Cat claws and pantyhose did not make a good combination.

Up in her room, she quickly changed into pjs. Shadow shouldered the door open and came in, looking relieved to find her back to normal.

Sunny sat on the floor, and Shadow crawled into her lap, arranging himself for a good petting.

"Yeah," Sunny told him, "life would be so much easier if all any of us needed was a good belly scratch."

*

The next morning Sunny breakfasted with her dad, who was already dressed for his daily hike. "Going up to outlet-land to walk in the air conditioning," he said. "The weather guy last night said to expect some more hot air," Mike winked. "He didn't say whether to expect it from Will, Frank Nesbit, or any of the Kingsburys."

Whatever the cause, the prediction was right. The air

felt unseasonably warm as Sunny walked out to her Wrangler for the ride into town.

Monday-morning traffic flowed more freely than it had on the weekend. At least all the people visiting on Saturday and Sunday excursions had gone home. But Sunny saw plenty of vehicles with out-of-state plates, lazing along, enjoying the scenery—and clogging the roads. Considering her line of work, boosting tourism and booking accommodations at the Maine Adventure X-perience, Sunny realized that the waves of tourists were partly her doing. Obviously, not all—there were things like great scenery, discount goods in the outlets, and a state tourism bureau involved. But her promotional copy and the time and effort she put into the website made a contribution, too. So in a way, one could argue that the traffic-laden roads were a testament to her success.

Be interesting to use that as an excuse if I'm late, Sunny thought.

Either way, she beat the clock into the office, fired up the computer, and started checking e-mail. A few minutes later, Nancy the summer intern arrived and started a pot of coffee. Nancy was supposed to have been working on the local paper but had found publicity and promotional work more interesting than the nuts and bolts of journalism. Sunny didn't necessarily agree with that herself, but having an assistant web lackey around had made life a lot easier—she'd miss Nancy when the girl returned to school in a few weeks. For now, though, they divvied up the morning's tasks and set to work.

Around eleven o'clock, they had a real surprise when their boss, Oliver Barnstable, also showed up. Ollie was a local boy who'd left town to make good, then came back to spread his money around his old hometown. The MAX office wasn't just about tourism, it also served as home base for a variety of his mysterious enterprises. The whole back wall of the office was lined with locked file cabinets containing all the dealings of Ollie's mini-empire.

"Looking good, Ollie." Sunny's compliment was genuine as Ollie maneuvered inside with his walker. Although he was still undergoing in-patient rehab for his broken leg at a facility up near Levett, Ollie had wangled taking a few hours a week off-site, to take care of business. The rehab was doing him a world of good—he was svelter, his eyes were clearer, and his temper was much more peaceful.

Just then, Ollie bumped his walker into the edge of a visitor's chair and let rip with an expletive.

Well, comparatively more peaceful, Sunny amended. But really, altogether, her boss was much improved from the irascible guy who'd hired her, the one who'd earned himself the nickname of "Ollie the Barnacle." Sunny suspected that was due to Elsa Hogue, an occupational therapist who had taken more than a professional interest in her patient.

Ollie gave Nancy a key and instructions to open one of the back file cabinets, and he soon had the contents of a folder spread out on a desk, reading them over.

They all worked in silence until an actual visitor arrived in the form of Will Price.

"How goes the campaign?" Ollie asked in the tone of someone with a vested interest. He'd surprised Sunny—and Will, too—by offering to switch his support from sheriff Nesbit to Will's insurgent candidacy.

"Just dandy." Will didn't even try to keep the disgust out of his voice. "I just wasted my whole morning on what looks to be an enormous time-suck." As Will explained the assignment Nesbit had stuck him with, Ollie's eyebrows drew together.

"Clever, pushing you off to the sidelines," Ollie said.

"No kidding!" Will burst out. "I was just up on Neal's Neck, talking with the head of Kingsbury's private security, a guy named Lee Trehearne. To put it as nicely as possible, the guy was patronizing. Besides his own guys, he has a detachment of Maine state troopers—the Senator still has pull—plus executive protection details from two other state police forces covering governors Lem and Tom. The way they see it, the contribution of local law enforcement lies in traffic control. I might as well have been assigned to be a school crossing guard."

"Got to hand it to old Frank." Ollie shook his head, still admiring. "He's good at this stuff."

Under the circumstances, Sunny felt it was only fair of her to take Will out to lunch to lick his wounds. But then another visitor arrived—Ken Howell, the editor, publisher, printer, and pretty much everything else on the local paper, the *Harbor Courier*.

Sunny assumed he was there for intern Nancy, but instead Ken came straight to Sunny's desk. "Back when you first came back to town and talked to me about a newspaper job, didn't you mention you could handle a camera?"

Sunny wondered where he was going with this, but nodded. "I was always pretty good, and after some papers began firing their whole photographic departments and expecting the reporters to shoot pictures, I figured it wouldn't hurt to look ahead. So I took classes in photography and media—not that it saved my job." Even though it happened more than a year ago, it still irked Sunny that she'd gotten laid off while on leave taking care of her dad.

"Here's the situation," Ken said. "My regular photographer is away on vacation, and his backup managed to break an arm using a hand winch to pull a boat onto its trailer. There's a press conference this afternoon on Neal's Neck about the Kingsbury-de Kruk wedding."

"Yeah, we've been hearing a lot about that." Will still looked disgusted.

"I heard about what Nesbit pulled, and I'm sorry." Ken's long, bony face was serious. He was another member of the Kittery Harbor group backing Will. "But we knew he wasn't just going to hand the keys over to you. You'll have to pick your appearances for maximum effect—"

"And hope a picture of me directing traffic doesn't turn up on TV or in a paper," Will finished for him.

"Not in my paper," Ken assured him. "At this point, I'm wondering if I'll get any pictures at all. It's one thing to cover an event with pictures and interview people later. But this is supposed to be a Q and A, and it's kind of hard to ask questions while staring through a viewfinder. Can you help me out, Sunny?"

Sunny glanced over at Ollie, and so did Ken. "Can you spare her for a while?" he asked Ollie.

"I can handle things," Nancy eagerly volunteered.

"You weren't planning to strip down the computers and polish the insides—anything like that, were you?" Ollie asked Sunny.

Smiling, she shook her head. "Not for another couple of weeks at least. Besides, I won't be that far away, and Nancy can always call my cell if there are any problems."

Sunny was trying to play it cool, but she could feel her pulse starting to race. Much as she tried to convince herself that she'd closed the book on her journalism career, she was a reporter at heart. If she had a chance of making a living as a journalist, even on a tiny local operation like the *Courier*, she'd bag her job at MAX in a heartbeat.

But as Ken had explained, the job just wasn't there. She'd thought at first he'd just been threatened by the idea of having a big-city reporter trying to horn in on his baby, but the honest fact was he was using print jobs on his presses, doing circulars for local stores and such, to keep the newspaper afloat.

Sometimes Sunny wondered if she'd made a mistake, seeking a career in a dying field. Then someone offered her a chance to go to a press conference, and she was immediately all fired up.

"Did I ever mention that I met Augustus de Kruk once?" she said.

Ollie asked what everyone else was thinking. "How did you get through to a big-bucks guy like de Kruk?"

"Well, maybe 'met' is pushing it a little," Sunny admitted. "I was in the same room with him and about ninety other journalists once, when he talked about his latest building project."

"Did anyone call him Emperor Augustus?" Ken was in full interview mode now.

"Not to his face. But from what I saw, the nickname suits him. He was pretty darn autocratic. No questions. It was a case of get into the room, take down what he had to say, and get out. I got the impression he wouldn't bother even having a conversation with anyone who has less than a nine-figure fortune."

That widened Nancy's eyes. Ollie cleared his throat. "He's a touchy old goat."

Sunny laughed. "Like with his name. He tells everybody 'de Kruk' rhymes with 'truck.' It drives him crazy if anyone pronounces it 'crook.' I worked on a story about when Augustus tried to sue a little bar in Brooklyn out of existence, claiming they were using his name—and the wrong pronunciation. Turns out the place had been founded more than a century and a half ago by a distant ancestor who *did* pronounce his name 'de Crook.'" Sunny grinned. "Augustus lost that one. The place wound up with landmark status because Walt Whitman used to drink there."

"That's great stuff," Ken said enthusiastically, then paused. "Not that we could use it in this story."

"Hey, I'd be happy just doing the pictures." Sunny turned to look at Ollie. "If it's okay with you."

"Who am I to stand in the way of American journalism?" Ollie sighed and leaned back in his chair. Then he came forward again. "And if you get any more de Kruk stories, I'd love to hear them."

"You'll probably see more of the Kingsbury compound than I'll ever get to," Will complained.

*

So, not too much later that day, Sunny sat in the backseat of Ken's old Dodge, fiddling with a freshly minted press pass and making adjustments to a camera that was probably even older than the car.

"They probably aren't going to announce anything very important," Ken said, loading an extra supply of batteries from a box on the car seat into his jacket pocket. Sunny knew about that from the older reporters she'd worked with, batteries had been the life's blood for the all-important recorder. She'd used a rechargeable minidisk recorder herself, but Ken was more old school. "Probably they want to establish some ground rules, keep us at arm's length while they relax before the wedding. I'm told everybody in the family has turned up already."

"Will mentioned the Senator and both governors would be there," Sunny told him. "And we saw Caleb Kingsbury's yacht sailing by on Saturday."

"There you go." Ken had to pay a little attention to his driving. They'd taken the coast road, which made for a very scenic—albeit sometimes demanding—drive, as the highway hugged the rocky shores. In any event, Sunny wasn't in a position to enjoy the scenery as she tried to familiarize herself with the equipment.

By the time she finally looked up, they had reached the outskirts of Wilawiport, a prosperous town, and found themselves at the end of a long parade of various news vehicles.

"Looks like the whole gang is here," Sunny said when she spotted microwave masts on several of the vans ahead of them. "The networks, as well as the local affiliates, are getting into the act."

"That's what happens on a slow news day," Ken said. "But I don't intend to let them slow *me* down." The public road ended at a sawhorse barrier with the notice, NO TRAFFIC BEYOND THIS POINT, and a couple of Maine state troopers nearby to back up the message. Their blue gray uniforms with the black pocket flaps were unmistakable—not to mention the black Mountie hats they wore. Ken made a turn onto a side street. "Figured this would happen. That's why I called ahead to a pal in the area."

He pulled into a driveway and parked his car a few blocks away from the beginning of the private road that led onto Neal's Neck. Lugging their equipment, Sunny and Ken approached the official roadblock on foot. As they came to the last intersection, Sunny spotted a very harassed-looking Ben Semple trying without much success to unsnarl the traffic.

A beefy-looking trooper waved them down, checked their credentials, and even took a cursory glance inside Sunny's camera bag. Finding nothing more lethal than a couple of extra lenses, he let them in.

"Pushing things a little, aren't they?" Sunny looked from the barrier to the last two houses facing the public road. "They've cut off access to both of their neighbors here."

"Those aren't neighbors. The Kingsburys bought both those places in order to keep prying eyes at bay. They also serve as extra guest quarters when a lot of people are visiting the property," Ken explained, politely stepping aside as a pair of young women dressed in about as little as Robin Lory had worn on Ben Semple's boat emerged from one of the houses and strolled ahead of them. "From what I hear, today's get-together is supposed to introduce the families and the members of the wedding party to one another."

"How nice for them." Sunny watched the girls go off to the left while a guy in a dark Windbreaker with "Security" in large white letters on the back turned to watch them. As Ken and Sunny approached, however, the security guy directed them down a path to the right.

Sunny glanced over her shoulder as she followed Ken. Mr. Security was still checking the girls out.

They joined a growing crowd of newspeople facing an

improvised outdoor stage, and Sunny began worming her way through the assembled camera people and press photographers to find a decent vantage point.

As it turned out, she really didn't have to kill herself. There wasn't much worth photographing. Ken had predicted correctly, this was just a preliminary press conference, conducted by Fiona Ormond. No famous—or even semi-famous—Kingsbury faces were in attendance. Fiona repeated several times in different ways that this was just a social gathering, a chance for the families to spend time together well in advance of the wedding itself. In spite of her attempt to downplay the visit, she also tried to lay down some press ground rules, stressing the security arrangements around the nuptials both now and months in the future.

Either they're afraid of party crashers or paparazzi, Sunny thought as she nevertheless dutifully shot various angles of Fiona as she spoke on the stage, turning a bit to catch some of the cameras and press people as well. For Ken's purposes, just having all these media people converging on the county would make for a good story. Asking a question would just be icing on the cake.

But Ken did speak up, making a rather pointed inquiry about how many local businesses would be contributing to the upcoming nuptials. *Good one,* Sunny thought, fighting her way around to get a picture of Ken as Fiona launched into a speech similar to the one Sunny had already heard her give at the 99 Elmet Ladies event about looking into local sources for services like catering, transportation, flowers, and so forth. "We're even inviting local bakers to submit designs for the wedding cake," she finished.

"Are the de Kruks staying here for the wedding

preparations? Have they arrived yet?" a new voice cut in, brashly asking what everyone really wanted to know. The Kingsburys were big fish, especially in Wilawiport, but there was no doubt that it was the nationally prominent de Kruks who had drawn all this attention.

The questioner's voice sounded familiar, and it seemed to be coming from over near Ken. But when Sunny spotted the speaker through her viewfinder, she nearly dropped her camera. It was Randall MacDermott, her old boss from the *New York Standard*. He looked the same as ever, still tall and slim, with a ruddy face—"like a map of Ireland," as the saying went. His generous jaw held a trace of dimple, his expressive lips set in an impish half smile. *Oh crap,* Sunny thought, quickly turning away. The fact of the matter was that they had once become something more than editor and reporter. Randall and his wife had separated, their marriage was finished, all that was left was signing the divorce papers, he'd told her. So she'd dated him. But while she'd been away taking care of her father, things had changed. The paper got a new owner, heads were rolling, and the next thing Sunny knew, Randall was back with his family—and she was out of a job.

As the press conference ground to an end, Sunny tried to blend in with the crowd, slouching a little so her distinctive mane of red hair wouldn't be as visible. She risked a glance over at Ken. *If I go over there to join him, we'll be right under Randall's nose,* she thought, frantically looking for someplace to take cover as the crowd began to disperse.

The only spot she could see was a clump of decorative bushes. Moving crabwise with her head down, she darted behind the foliage—and collided with someone who was already there. A strong arm caught her as she bounced back and nearly fell. Sunny looked up to see another face she recognized—from photos, at least.

It was Caleb Kingsbury, uncle of the bride.

His hair was longer and shaggier than it had been in his Congress days. Grayer, too. But even with lines grooved in around his eyes and mouth, he still looked like a mischievous kid. Maybe it was those bright blue, innocent-seeming eyes.

"I'm so sorry!" Sunny said, checking that she hadn't dropped her camera or any of the other equipment.

"No harm done." Kingsbury cocked an inquiring eyebrow. "You know, when this hoedown is done, the security people will want you to go thataway." He gestured toward the crowd of media types and the road off the peninsula which lay beyond them.

"I know," Sunny said, "but if I go thataway, I'm going to bump into someone I really don't want to meet. An old colleague—"

"More than that, judging from the look on your face." Kingsbury laughed. "Or that look either. Hey, I used to be a politician. I learned something about reading people." His impudent blue eyes twinkled. "I could help, you know. What say I give you the nickel tour of this place?" Kingsbury looked a little embarrassed as he added, "But you'd have to put your camera away."

He offered his arm, and Sunny shrugged, putting her camera in its case. *Why not?* The alternative was facing Randall, and besides, this way she'd get a story she could dine out on with Ollie, at least.

As they stepped out from behind the shrubbery, Sunny spotted Ken Howell looking for her. But when he recognized Caleb Kingsbury beside her, he gave her a quick thumbs-up and walked away. Not that either of them could have foreseen this, but like all good newspeople, they both understood you had to follow the story. Even before they'd set off for Neal's Neck, Ken had made sure she had cab fare to get back home if necessary.

"I don't need to tell you," he'd said. "You've got to be ready for any eventuality. Who knows? You might wind up in conversation with somebody and get some useful background." Sunny couldn't help cynically wondering if this had been Ken's plan all along, though how could he have known?

Still, Caleb Kingsbury was pleasant as he led her around to the rear of the stage. A guy in the usual black security Windbreaker moved to stop Sunny, but Caleb waved him off. "It's okay, George. She's with me."

They came upon a miniature parking lot with several golf carts lined up. Kingsbury brought Sunny to the second in line. "It's a little easier to get around in these. They're free for anyone in the compound, except for that one." He pointed to the cart he'd bypassed. "See the U.S. Senate seal on the windshield? That one's just for my dad."

"The Senator," Sunny said.

Caleb shrugged. "Yep, that's even what I call him. Families have their ways—odd names and such. For instance, I'm Cale." He gave a little laugh. "And it's not because some folks think I'm just a bitter vegetable. My brother Lem started calling me that when we were little kids. And my niece Priscilla christened herself 'Silly,' although we spell it *C-I-L-L-I-E*. It could have been worse. You should have heard what she came up with before that, when we tried to call her Prissy."

"Been there," Sunny told him. "My mom was a music lover who named me Sonata, but I go by Sunny. Last name Coolidge, no relation to the president, sorry."

Cale nodded. "There you go, then." He followed a path that took them past a large, professional-looking tennis court. "Do you play? Between us, I think my family's real religion is tennis. God help anyone who picks up a racquet against us." Farther along, they came to the big house Sunny had heard about, a large, rambling shingle structure that looked as if it had thrown out several wings in the course of its existence.

"Grandfather Neal built the place more than a century ago. He was a real pistol—and I mean that literally. There are a couple of bullet holes in the dining room ceiling where he tried to shoot a wasp that had stung him. Those must have been the days. During Prohibition, the story is that he had his own private rumrunner delivering right to the wharf. Not that he sold the stuff. It was all consumed on the premises, in parties that I hear would've put Great Gatsby to shame." Cale paused for a second. "After my father inherited the place, there was a lot more decorum than rum."

Sunny got the feeling Cale wasn't a hundred percent behind that notion.

He drove on in a large loop that took them to the point of the peninsula where carefully tended green lawns abruptly ended in a rocky drop to the sea. "You have to admit, it's a hell of a view," Cale said. "On days when the water gets really rough, you can catch spray from the rocks even up here. When I was a kid, this was my favorite place. I used to sit here and imagine I was steering straight out to sea."

"And now you get to do that for real. Your yacht came past us on Saturday by the Isles of Shoals."

"You saw the *Merlin*?" Cale asked in surprise.

"A beautiful boat. And an interesting name—for a privateer," Sunny said.

Cale laughed again. "You know that story, too, eh? It's just a reminder. The Kingsburys started out as preachers. Sometimes I think that politics is just another form of preaching for them. The Neals, though, they were always pirates in one way or another, whether on the sea or on Wall Street."

He leaned back in the golf cart's seat. "People always tell me I've got a little too much Neal and not enough Kingsbury." He grinned. "Works out fine if you're going to be the family's eccentric uncle." Then he started up the golf cart again. "So now you've seen the famous compound. Hope it wasn't a big disappointment."

They rounded a curve, and all of a sudden a swimming pool appeared ahead of them, where a party was apparently underway. Sunny spotted the two girls she'd seen on her way to the press conference. One of them, a tall brunette who seemed in danger of falling out of her violet bikini, was dancing with a glass in her hand.

"The young people," Cale pointed out. Sunny recognized the sandy-haired girl, in a much more sensible bathing suit, before Cale nodded toward her. "That's Cillie over by the springboard. Carson's the blond guy beside her."

Carson de Kruk was tall and slim, throwing his head back to laugh at something Cillie was saying. With her fair coloring and more refined features, Priscilla didn't look much like her uncle Caleb; maybe, like Carson de Kruk, she took after her mother's side. Or maybe she represented another genetic string. It had to be more than twenty years since Priscilla's father had died in that accident while campaigning. Sunny only had blurry memories of a guy with Kennedyesque hair on political posters. She couldn't remember Mrs. Lem Kingsbury at all, except that the woman had suffered a breakdown and later died.

Cale waved, and Priscilla waved back. "Put on a suit and join us, Uncle Cale!" she called.

"No way," he replied. "The last thing your party needs is an old fogey hanging around."

He drove past the pool, shaking his head reminiscently. "Used to have a lot of fun there, back in the day."

Soon enough, they arrived back at the little parking area. "Your inconvenient fella should be long gone by now," Cale said.

He was right. As they came back up to the makeshift stage, the area was empty except for a few Kingsbury security staffers who gave Sunny surprised looks as Cale escorted her past them. "The troopers take their job really seriously," he said, as they reached the roadblock. "No cars allowed to stop. I hope they didn't scare off your ride."

"I'll be fine," Sunny replied. "I'm a local, from down in Kittery Harbor."

"Well, then, good luck, neighbor." Cale smiled. "It was nice to meet you, Sunny."

Sunny smiled back. "Thank you for being so gallant—and gracious."

She waved good-bye and passed the troopers . . . then saw Will Price, fuming, in a Kittery Harbor patrol car.

4

Sunny walked over to the open driver's-side window. "I hope Ken Howell didn't ask you to come up here and get me," she said.

But as it turned out, Will hadn't even known Sunny was still around, nor did he now think to ask why she'd been there so late after the press conference. "I just had another wonderful meeting with the head of security around here, Lee Trehearne," he vented. "Some security. I got to hear all his complaints about what a traffic jam the news trucks caused, and how we'll need more officers to handle crowd control on the day of the big event."

Will shook his head in frustration, but he did agree to give her a lift back to Kittery Harbor, where Sunny dropped off the camera with Ken Howell, who immediately had one of his interns working to download the photos. "That I can trust them to do," he muttered to Sunny. "They still have a lot to learn before I can let them actually take the pictures."

"All I've got are shots from the press statement," she said apologetically. "When Caleb Kingsbury took me around the compound, it was on the condition that I didn't take any pictures."

Ken shrugged philosophically. "Not surprising. That's pretty much what always happens. The only pictures that come out of there nowadays are official photos. Even the stuff on Facebook looks professionally staged and vetted. Anything else to report?"

"I got a lot of old family stories—interesting, but I don't think there's any way to tie them in with the statement by the wedding planner. Oh, and one piece of hard news, if you can really call it that: Carson de Kruk is already in the compound. Cale pointed him and the bride-to-be out to me as we passed by a pool party."

"Cale, eh?" Ken cocked his head. "How was Mister Kingsbury?"

"Very nice," Sunny replied. "But whether it was politician nice or pickup-artist nice, I couldn't tell." She grinned. "Or maybe he had nothing better to do, and helping me out of an embarrassing situation appealed to him. I spotted someone in the crowd, my former editor." She paused for a second. "We were an item, once. Seeing him sort of threw me off."

Trust Ken to be all business at such a revelation. "You don't usually see an editor out in the field, unless it's for a small operation like mine," he said. "Why do you think a New York paper like the *Standard* would send him all the way up here?"

"I don't know, and I'm sorry, Ken, but I don't want to find out," Sunny told him. "If I talk to anyone who's still on the paper, it's sure to get back to Randall, and I'm in no mood to deal with him."

Outwardly, Ken accepted that, but Sunny could sense the wheels turning in his head. "I wonder where he's staying," the editor said.

"Well, I can assure you he didn't get a bed and breakfast reservation through the MAX site," Sunny replied. "In the old days, especially for an editor, the *Standard* would have sprung for the best hotel or motel nearby. But working on a tighter budget, I don't know how that affects the old expense account." She headed for the door but then stopped and glanced over her shoulder. "And let me repeat, I don't care."

Sunny returned to the MAX office to find everything going smoothly. No smoke was pouring from the back of the computer, Nancy sat at the keyboard posting information to one of the databases. "Ollie tried to hang around until you came back, but he got a call from the rehab center. I heard Elsa's voice on the line, so he didn't put up a fight." Nancy leaned forward eagerly. "So how'd it go? Give me all the details, I'm living vicariously through you."

"The press conference wasn't very exciting," Sunny told her. "They had the wedding planner telling the newspeople how to behave. Not exactly riveting stuff—especially since any reporter worth his or her salt would happily break any of those rules for a good story. But," she added as Nancy's face fell, "Caleb Kingsbury did take me on a personal tour of the compound."

Nancy obviously recognized the name—and judging by her expression, she hadn't heard good things about its owner. "Isn't he kind of a skeevy guy?"

Sunny had to laugh. "That's something you learn in the

journalism business, Nancy. It's the skeevy guys who usually give you the best stories."

Nancy looked unconvinced. "Did you see anyone else?"

"I saw Priscilla Kingsbury and Carson de Kruk, but at a distance," Sunny said.

Nancy leaned forward, all eagerness again. "What did they look like? Is Carson as good-looking in person as he seems in the papers?" Nancy asked. "He doesn't look at all like his dad."

"No, Carson was lucky enough to get his mother's genes," Sunny agreed, though she wasn't sure which one of Augustus de Kruk's ex-wives was Carson's mother. His father had gone through a string of spouses, mostly blond, all beautiful. Which had certainly helped to balance out the genetic books, since Augustus himself looked like a bald eagle suffering from some kind of digestive upset.

"So . . . what are they like?"

"You mean, are the rich really different, the way people say?" Sunny shrugged. "I've met a couple of rich people, and they certainly have concerns and a view of the world I can scarcely guess about. The house there was probably bigger than this whole block, and I've never had servants jumping to take care of me."

"Neither have I," Nancy sighed.

"On the other hand, the pool partly looked like a pool party. Nobody seemed to be wearing a solid gold bathing suit. I bet there were expensive designers involved, but I couldn't really tell that from a distance. It was just people drinking and dancing. So I'd say not all that different, really."

Not that I'm likely to find out for sure, Sunny thought. *Neither MAX nor a journalism job would put a place like*

Neal's Neck in my future. Not unless I married someone like Augustus de Kruk. Sunny shuddered a little. *Or maybe Cale Kingsbury. Wonder what it would be like to live on a yacht?*

They finished out the day's work, and Sunny headed home, where Shadow met her at the door and gave her a brief once-over. But Sunny didn't hear the usual background noise of the TV as she walked down the hall to the arched entrance for the living room. "Dad? You home?" she called.

Mike sat stiffly on the couch, his arms crossed and a stern expression on his face. "I called Ken Howell, trying to see if there was some way to get extra coverage about Will since he'll be tied up in Wilawiport. Imagine my surprise when I heard where you'd been. What was he thinking, letting you go off on your own with someone like Caleb Kingsbury?"

Sunny had faced this kind of inquisition before, whenever she got involved with guys whom Mike considered inappropriate boyfriends. But the last time this had happened had to be during her freshman year in college.

She fought down the urge to laugh. That would only make things worse. "Well, Dad, I didn't go out sailing with him," she said. "And since the place was crawling with press and security people, I figured he'd probably control himself."

"I'm sure that poor girl who drowned didn't think anything bad was going to happen to her, either." Mike harrumphed, but Sunny could see in his eyes that he'd begun to realize how ridiculous this conversation was.

She gave him a smile. "I wouldn't worry, Dad. He didn't ask for a date."

"Yeah. Well. You know how these rich people can be."

Mike unbent a little. "And rich and famous, that can be a really nasty combination."

"I know, Dad. I'll tell you all about it over supper." Sunny headed for the kitchen with Shadow at her heels. Mike already had the table set, so Sunny just had to get the cold dishes out under Shadow's supervision. It was lucky that they still had leftover salad stuff for supper. A bottle of flavored seltzer, and they were all set.

Mike enjoyed the story of her jaunt to Neal's Neck. He'd heard the stories about the rum-running and the attempt to shoot the offending wasp but was interested in the details that Sunny gave. Maybe too interested, when Sunny mentioned Randall MacDermott.

"I never met that Randall fella, did I?" Mike said when she finished. "He was one of your New York beaus."

"Like I had so many of them." Sunny tried to dismiss the subject.

"And you say he's up around here somewhere?" Mike went on innocently.

"Dad, he's ancient history now. A mistake I made." Sunny put her fork down and gave Mike a look. "One I don't want to revisit."

"Of course not," Mike hastily agreed with her. "Did you tell Will about him?"

"Dad!" Her tone of voice was enough to bring Shadow over, rising to put his forefeet up on the chair seat to see what had upset her.

They finished the meal in silence and went to the living room to watch TV. Sunny sat on the floor, distracting herself by playing with Shadow. As he crawled over her lap, he often stopped to sniff at the side of her leg—the left side, which had faced Caleb Kingsbury as they'd buzzed around the family compound in the golf cart.

Don't tell me he keeps a captivating cat aboard that yacht of his, Sunny thought as she gave Shadow a good scratch between the ears. *I don't think you'll be heading over to Neal's Neck for any play dates, kiddo.*

*

Shadow closed his eyes. Playing with Sunny was always fun. But the best part of all was being able to lie in her lap, boneless, his paws splayed out, his belly up and unprotected. For most of his life and in most of the world, that would be suicide. He knew he could do it here, though, because he was safe with Sunny. She was gentle and would never let anything bad happen to him. He could utterly relax around her.

And, of course, he might also get a tummy rub.

As he stretched out, his paws just kneading the air, Shadow let his head fall back on Sunny's left thigh. Then he turned round, sniffing. There was that fragrance again, very faint. He could just detect it . . . a combination of several scents that mixed together into something wonderful to inhale.

It wasn't like what had happened when he came across Portia's scent. That had just about driven him crazy. And it wasn't like his response to Sunny's natural scent. That made him want to be close to her, enjoy her warmth and her breathing, the feel of her hands caressing him. No, this was a made smell, like some of the things Sunny sometimes put on. Frankly, Shadow didn't like most of those. Why mess up a perfectly good scent with some odd, made-up smell that usually made Shadow want to sneeze? But this one was surprising, a good smell he'd like to investigate.

He shifted around in Sunny's lap, thinking. This was another one of those weird two-leg things. They were never content to let things be. They had to make things to go fast, to make hot air cold and cold air hot. Of course, they *did* do some pretty amazing things with food. In his travels Shadow had sometimes had to hunt for himself, and he knew how difficult that could be. But Sunny often went out and a little while later would come back with all kinds of food. When he was a kit, Shadow thought the two-legs had to be the greatest hunters ever.

Now, of course, he knew about the big houses where humans went for food. When he was on the street, he'd sometimes gone behind those places and found food for himself—some of it going bad, some of it running and squeaking when he came along.

Shadow shook that memory away. Those had definitely not been good times. Why should he even think of them, when he was having a wonderful time with Sunny?

She leaned over him, whispering, and laid a hand on his belly fur. He brought both forepaws down to trap it in place, wriggling with delight. The faint trace of scent from her leg only heightened his pleasure.

He closed his eyes, trying to memorize the combination. Whenever she came back from whatever strange two-leg places she visited, he'd check for this scent again. . . .

*

Sunny found herself yawning before the detective show her dad liked was underway. She wasn't even paying attention when they brought out the big plot twist before the ads for the halfway point. It was hard enough just to keep her eyes open.

"I guess I did too much today," she said, yawning and stretching. Shadow jumped out of her lap, ready for some other game. But Sunny just wished her dad a good evening and padded her way up the stairs and to her room.

By the time she had her pajamas on, Shadow had come upstairs and joined her. She'd gambled that the warm weather wouldn't hold up after the sun went down, so she'd opened the window before sitting down to dinner. Good bet. The temperature in the room was just right. With a sheet and light blanket, she'd be fine.

She'd just turned off the light and arranged herself comfortably when a small head butted her just above the elbow. Shadow was demanding that she open the circle of her arms and let him in. Sunny obliged, and they lay together in the dimness. She closed her eyes and listened to the sounds of their breathing, hers growing longer and longer until she was asleep. She dreamed that Shadow was howling in her ear: "Get up! Get up! The phone!"

Sunny opened her eyes. No sign of Shadow, but the phone *was* bleating away. She fumbled for it in the blue green light from her clock radio and finally got the handset to her ear. "H'lo?"

"Sunny? Ken Howell here."

Does he ever sleep? Sunny wondered blearily, trying to make out what time it was. *Two a.m. Wonderful.*

"Sorry to call so late, but—Look, I just got a tip that something happened out on Neal's Neck. I'm heading out there, and frankly I could use a photographer."

"What happened?" Sunny's reporter side was instantly awake and coherent.

"I'm not sure. Somebody spotted lights on the shore. Not party lights, searchlights, up on top of the cliff. That's never happened before. There may be an accident or some other kind of trouble."

Sunny found herself sitting up. "I'll be there—"

"Hello? Hello? What's wrong?" Mike's voice came over the line, sounding old and frightened. He always equated late-night calls with bad news.

"It's Ken Howell, Mike," Ken said. "Sorry to wake you, but I need to borrow Sunny's services."

"She's got work in the morning," Mike protested. "Of all the damn fool—"

"Dad, I'm going to go," Sunny told him. "Ken, I'll meet you at the paper in twenty minutes." Yes, she might be stumbling around like a zombie tomorrow—or rather, later this morning. But her taste of the reporting life the previous afternoon had been like a long-withheld dose of a forbidden drug. She had to have another fix.

Sunny started getting dressed under the disapproving eye of Shadow, who'd appeared in the doorway. He didn't like changes in schedule, especially when those changes involved people getting up and going places in the middle of the night.

"Sorry, fella," Sunny told the cat. "I should be home before sunup. And if not, Dad will feed you."

She drove to downtown Kittery Harbor, where the town still had its original crooked cobblestone streets cramped close to the harbor. Ken Howell ran the *Courier* from an ancient structure that had probably started off life as a waterfront storehouse. Now it was home to a virtual museum of printing presses from more than 150 years of putting out the paper. Plus, of course, the equipment to produce today's editions.

Sunny suspected that there was also a bed hidden somewhere on the premises. Although he supposedly owned a house, Ken seemed to live at the *Courier* offices.

He greeted her at the door, carrying the camera case. "Ready to go?"

"Are you driving, or am I?" Sunny asked.

"Neither." Ken led the way onto a dock where a man waved to them from beside a cabin cruiser. As she got closer, Sunny recognized him as Ike Elkins, an occasional fishing buddy of her dad's. Ike had cleverly figured out a way to subsidize his hobby by offering coastline tours, a service he advertised on the MAX website. If Sunny had any more doubts about how they were getting up to Wilawiport, Ike offered the clincher by handing her and Ken life jackets. "Get those on, and we're set to go."

Sunny buckled herself into the vest and clambered aboard, taking the camera case from Ken. Then he donned the safety gear and joined her on the deck. Ike boarded as well and led the way to the bridge, indicating a couple of comfortable-looking built-in chairs. "Have a seat. And do me a favor: stay there. It's going to be interesting enough heading up the coast in the dark without any distractions."

With that, he turned off the cabin light and dimmed the displays on the instruments. Sailing in darkness required excellent night vision for the person steering, so—lights out. Sunny had gone on fishing expeditions with her dad before the crack of dawn, so she understood. From her seat, she saw that Ike had more than the average amount of high-tech sailing equipment; besides the GPS display by the wheel, she also saw what looked like a radar screen.

Ike returned from casting off the lines that held them to the pier and followed her eyes. "Yeah, sometimes I like to take the old girl out at night. When I do, I try to make as certain as possible that we'll come back."

Sunny couldn't fault that. No sense in becoming a statistic.

Ike started up the boat, and off they went. Sunny listened to the throbbing of the engine and the occasional burst of radio chatter as they moved away from the lights of town into seeming emptiness. She was thankful the sea was relatively calm, because they were sailing blind. The usual landmarks and points of reference were gone. They might as well have been sailing on another planet.

Cruising up the rocky shores of Maine was a heck of a lot less scenic in pitch darkness, and a little unnerving, too. What if one of those rocks turned up in front of them?

Ike certainly worked hard to avoid that scenario. Besides his high-tech gadgets, he sometimes consulted a chart, using a flashlight with a red lens. "Doesn't affect the night vision," he explained when Sunny asked about the red light.

Ike stood behind the wheel, glancing at the GPS and checking the radar screen, but also constantly turning his head, scanning conditions not just ahead of them, but to the sides and even behind. Sunny had no idea what, if anything, he was seeing out there; the only things she could see were bright stars up above—lots of them—if she craned her neck.

Ken sat in a very stiff pose, leaning forward as if he were propelling the boat onward by sheer force of will. In the dimness, Sunny could see his expression grow more and more frustrated. "Can't we go faster?" he finally asked Ike.

"Sure, if you don't mind running into someone—or something," Ike replied, changing course slightly. In the distance, Sunny now made out little green and white flashes—the running lights of another vessel. "This speed gives us enough leeway to react if something turns up on our path."

"If we'd driven, we'd be up there in half an hour," Ken grumbled.

"And you'd be stuck at the roadblock closing off Neal's Neck." Ike turned his head, keeping an eye on the other boat, then glanced back at Ken. "If you're in such a hurry, too bad you didn't have a friend with a helicopter instead of a boat."

From time to time, they passed areas of gauzy brightness, street-lit downtown areas of various ports. For the most part, they might as well have been traveling in outer space.

Another bright spot appeared ahead. Ike checked his navigational aids. "Okay. This is Wilawiport." He sent the boat in a wide curve to avoid crashing into Neal's Neck.

Was this what it would have been like ninety years ago, when fast-moving motor launches delivered crates of contraband booze to the Neal mansion? Sunny wondered. *Aside from the lights,* she thought as she suddenly found herself squinting against a blinding blast of light. After some blinking, the glare resolved itself into a trio of floodlights, arranged on top of a small cliff, focused down onto the rocks and the water.

"This is it!" Ken grabbed the camera case, taking out

one for himself and one for Sunny. It felt awkward in her hands, unbalanced, most of the weight ahead of her hands.

A telescopic lens, she thought.

Ken was already snapping off pictures, and she joined him. But as the lens brought what was going on in the distance into focus, she almost dropped the camera into the drink.

Men in the black Windbreakers of the Kingsbury security team and a guy in state trooper gray were down on the tide-tossed rocks, hanging from ropes, trying to get some sort of a harness onto a pale white form . . . a dark-haired woman in a bikini, who lolled lifelessly in the would-be rescuers' arms.

5

"Oh, my god!" Sunny blurted out. That was as far as she got before one of the lights atop the rocky height suddenly shifted to pin them in a shaft of radiance sixty feet long.

"Stop that boat!" an amplified voice boomed across the water. Somebody up there must have a bullhorn.

"Damn! They caught us!" Even as he spoke, Ken kept feverishly taking pictures.

"They probably heard the engine," Ike told him. "This isn't exactly a stealth boat, you know."

"We're sending a launch out," the amplified voice announced. "Prepare to be boarded."

"They have no legal right to do that," Ken burst out, his camera still to his eye, snapping away.

Ken may have a point, Sunny thought, *but it could take months in court to establish the fact, our word against theirs. Here and now, we're facing a bunch of Kingsbury security guys who won't be pleased to find us photographing the scene. If they grab our cameras, what are we going to do?*

She put her camera on the deck at her feet, digging out her cell phone. This wasn't going to be easy. Sunny knelt, resting her elbows on the gunwale of the boat, creating the closest thing she could to a tripod. She engaged the camera in the phone, aiming for the scene on the rocks while using all the tricks she'd learned in her photography classes. The results of a nighttime distance shot from a rocking boat wouldn't be crystal-clear—probably too fuzzy for publishing—but she could hope that it would be legible enough to show what was going on. She kept clicking as fast as she could focus while the people on the top of the rocky prominence hauled the body up from the rocks.

As she worked, another floodlight sent a dazzling beam onto Ike's boat. Sunny blinked her eyes, finally locating flashes against the glare. They were pretty well spaced apart.

Caleb Kingsbury's yacht, I bet, Sunny thought, while continuing to take more pictures.

Apparently the new lighting revealed what she and Ken were doing, because the voice on the loudspeaker became more urgent. "Put those cameras down! This is invasion of privacy!"

Ken put his camera down and turned to Ike. "Can we outrun them?"

Ike shook his head.

I was afraid of that. Sunny returned to her phone, quickly scrolling through the images she'd shot. She silently blessed Ike for having a marine signal booster with all his electronics, because she saw bars on her screen. Frantically choosing the best of the harshly lit pictures, she directed them to Ken's e-mail. "Are your interns awake?"

Ken glanced from the oncoming powerboat to Sunny. "Sure. I wanted everything ready in case we had to go to press."

"Then call them and tell them to download these pictures," Sunny told him. "The security guys may get us, but they won't get them."

They had a couple of touchy minutes as a Kingsbury powerboat approached, a black-jacketed security guy with an assault rifle in the bow, and all the other guys on the boat keeping one hand on their holstered pistols. The cameras went into their bags and onto the security launch before Sunny and Ken did. Sunny felt a little better for that, actually, realizing how easily the bag could have plopped beneath the surface of the water, an unfortunate "accident."

Both boats headed for a small wharf on the far side of Neal's Neck. Sunny, Ken, and Ike were ushered off their boat and up a set of rickety steps, where an additional welcoming committee of Kingsbury security people waited, surrounding the guy with the bullhorn.

Sunny wondered if he'd even needed the bullhorn in the first place—his voice was almost as loud as its amplified version when he shouted at them, "What were you doing, interfering with our operation? Mr. Quimby here says I could have you arrested for trespassing!" He gestured to a gray-haired man wearing a perfectly crisp suit and tie, notwithstanding the hour, but with deep frown lines in his face. Quimby might as well have worn a neon sign saying, "Lawyer."

"Trespassing? Are you and Vince Quimby claiming a twelve-mile limit around Neal's Neck these days, Trehearne?" Ken inquired. Sunny noticed he'd eased his cell phone out of his pocket, and was fiddling with the controls.

Lee Trehearne, the head of security for the Kingsbury family, choked back what he wanted to say in answer to that. Despite currently looking as though he were on the verge of a stroke, he seemed like the capable, man-in-charge type: tall, and with a commanding presence. There was maybe a little flesh softening the line of his determined chin, but no way did Trehearne give the impression of being soft.

His eyes were like chips of flint as he glared at Ken. "Mr. Howell. What did you think you were doing, lurking off private property at this time of night?"

"I had a tip," Ken replied. "Someone saw lights on the point and gave me a call. I came to see if it was news." He paused for a second as the local paramedics came by, trundling a gurney with an ungainly shape strapped in place and covered by a black plastic zip-up bag.

A body bag, Sunny thought.

Ken lowered his head for a moment. "Looks like sad news, I'm sorry to say."

That didn't cut any ice with Trehearne. "I won't have you turning a tragic incident into some sort of vulgar media circus." He leaned toward Ken. "The Kingsburys won't have it."

He broke off as a couple of state troopers approached from the edge of the cliff. Sunny recognized both of them, she'd seen them on duty at the roadblock. She also recognized the man in the rumpled suit whom they accompanied.

Lieutenant Wainwright was shorter than Trehearne, his hair was thinner, and he had actual jowls rather than a mere softening of the chin. But he had sharp eyes, and Sunny knew from experience that the investigator had a sharp mind.

Wainwright's not a guy to come out for just anything, even if it happens on the Kingsbury estate, she thought, suddenly flashing on how Trehearne had used the word "incident" rather than "accident."

"Well, folks, let's see if we can clear this up." Wainwright was obviously going for the "good cop" role in this little drama. His pleasant expression congealed a little when he recognized Sunny. "You," he said. "Miss . . ." He drew out the title, trying to recall Sunny's name. "Miss Coolidge. I certainly didn't expect to run into you out here."

"This is Ken Howell, who runs the *Harbor Courier,*" Sunny deflected. "Ken, this is Lieutenant Ellis Wainwright of the state police, criminal investigation division."

Ken's nose twitched. He might not have recognized the homicide investigator by face, but he'd certainly heard the name. "How do you do?" he said.

"Mr. Howell asked me to accompany him to follow a lead about curious activity here in this compound," Sunny said to Wainwright. "Since he didn't think our press credentials would get us in, Mr. Howell decided on a more indirect approach."

Wainwright gave a sour nod, all trace of Mr. Good Cop gone. "And you couldn't have come along at a worse moment. That poor girl deserves more dignity than you're about to give her."

"I think she deserves the truth." Ken glanced over at

Trehearne, who'd just been handed their camera bag by one of his flunkeys. "Instead of being swept under the rug in the name of public relations."

Trehearne hefted the bag. "You have no proof."

Wainwright tapped the binoculars that hung around his neck. "If you spent a little more time looking than shouting, Trehearne, you might have noticed that Miss Coolidge also used her cell phone."

"And e-mailed the pictures on already," Sunny added.

Ken held up his phone, too. "And I've been streaming everything going on here directly to my office."

Trehearne looked like Dracula discovering he'd just taken a big bite from a loaf of garlic bread.

"So why don't you return their property, Mr. Trehearne," Wainwright said tiredly. "If they're going to run a picture, it might as well be a decent one."

Lawyer Quimby silently nodded, his frown lines even deeper.

With his jaw clenched, Lee Trehearne handed the camera bag over to Ken, who immediately slipped it over his shoulder. "So we're free to go?"

"Yes, sir," Wainwright responded. "I'm sure you're eager to get back to Kittery Harbor as quickly as possible, so you'll stay on land." He turned to Ike. "You don't mind sailing back alone, do you?"

"Fewer distractions," Ike said.

A trooper escorted Sunny and Ken to the roadblock, where Sunny expected Ken would either call a cab or one of his local contacts. Instead . . .

"Will?" Sunny burst out in disbelief

Will Price stood leaning against his black pickup, his

Kittery Harbor Police Force badge prominently displayed from his jacket pocket. "You weren't the only one Ken called tonight," he said as he opened the door. "And since I could take the land route, I was here a while ago. As the local liaison officer, I was able to breeze right in, although when Trehearne finally saw me, he exiled me back here."

"Did you see or hear anything?" Ken let Sunny in first and then climbed aboard with the camera bag cradled in his lap like a baby.

"Nothing I can say on the record," Will replied, starting the truck's engine. "So whatever I mention has to be strictly unofficial, with no attribution." He shuddered briefly. "That's all I'd need."

"But with Wainwright here . . ." Ken shook his head. "It doesn't look good."

"The girl who died," Sunny suddenly asked Will. "Did you get a look at her?"

"Only from the top of that cliff," Will said.

"Could you make out the color of her bathing suit? Was it black?"

Will shook his head. "Purple."

"Ken, one of the girls we saw here earlier was wearing a purple bikini," Sunny frowned. "She came out of that house by the roadblock and walked in ahead of us."

Ken's thin face creased as he worked his memory, then he nodded. "You think it's the same one, Sunny?"

"I'm not sure, but I saw that girl again later, at the pool party," Sunny said, "with a drink in her hand and dancing. She looked pretty . . . uninhibited. Could it be a case of having more to drink than she could handle and wandering a little too close to the edge?"

"That's the story Trehearne was trying to sell from the moment I got there." Will looked disgusted. "And he was pretty heavy-handed about it. But one of the troopers—Hank Riker, a buddy of mine, we were in the same troop—left the roadblock and went down on the rocks for a look. He said there were bruises on her throat, the kind left by human fingers. He's the one who called Wainwright and made Trehearne's guys leave things as they were down there until the lieutenant arrived."

"Good man," Ken said. "It can't have been easy standing up to the Kingsburys on their home ground."

"I'll tell you, I didn't see any actual Kingsburys while I was in the compound." Will shook his head as he drove. "All I saw was Trehearne and that Quimby guy—the lawyer. Maybe they're all lying low."

"Possibly it's crisis management," Sunny suggested. "No one around to say anything stupid."

"Maybe," Ken said, "but it looks guilty." He leaned across Sunny to talk to Will. "Have you got a name for this girl?"

"Eliza Stoughton," Will replied. "She apparently came as the date of the best man, Beau Bellingham. A couple of the young people turned up when the body was first found, and I spoke to a few of them before Trehearne shooed them all away from me. For a group that was supposed to be bonding, they broke pretty quickly into bride's faction and groom's faction."

He glanced over at Sunny. "Several of the groomsmen mentioned that Eliza had been drinking pretty heavily and had gotten 'kinda nasty' as one of them put it, though Beau Bellingham dismissed it as the mojitos talking. Frankly, I wondered if he'd been hitting the mojitos, too. He couldn't seem to take in the fact that Eliza was dead—kept talking about her in the present tense. He let slip, though, that Eliza'd also gotten into it with Tommy—that's Thomas Langford Neal, the matron of honor's husband."

"Interesting situation there," Ken said. "At one point, the Kingsbury watchers actually thought that the Neal boy and Priscilla Kingsbury might get married."

"Ew, aren't the two of them cousins?" Sunny said.

"Second cousins, same great-grandparents."

"Still seems a little too close for comfort." Sunny frowned, looking out the windshield at dense forest around them. Except for Will's high beams, it was almost as dark on the road as it had been out on the water.

"Was Carson de Kruk there?" she asked Will.

Will shook his head. "Neither he nor Priscilla turned up. I'm guessing somebody probably convinced them not to."

"Somebody named Trehearne?" Ken said.

"Could be," Will agreed. "When he saw me talking with the wedding party, Trehearne nearly killed himself getting them away from me and getting me off to the roadblock."

"That guy definitely wanted to control the story," Sunny said. "His people looked ready to shoot us when they came out to Ike's boat. And then they grabbed our cameras."

"And now you say he was maybe trying to hide witnesses," Ken added.

"So what do you think?" Sunny asked. "Is he just being fanatical about not letting the Kingsburys get any dirt on their shoes, or something else? The way you're saying he tried to downplay the whole situation reminds me of how Sheriff Nesbit—"

She broke off with a gasp, turning to Will. "You said you were in a no-win situation. If everything went okay, Nesbit would come out smelling like a rose. But if anything went wrong, you'd get blamed. And now something has *really* gone wrong."

Will sighed. "It's not as if either of us could have predicted this. But yeah, I'm sure that after Nesbit and his cronies get done with it, the story will sound a lot worse. 'How could a seasoned police officer let something so terrible happen at the pre-wedding meet and greet?' "

"So, after spending years pretending that Elmet County has never had a crime problem, now all of a sudden Nesbit will think it's a big deal." Sunny looked over at Will, who was busy keeping his eyes on the road. "You know what I think?"

"What?" he asked.

"I'm beginning to think that politics really stinks."

That got a chuckle from Ken Howell. "I've been following politics for more than fifty years now, and it seems the field never gets much cleaner—or the participants any smarter."

"Yeah, well, I'd rather deal with Frank Nesbit than the problem Lee Trehearne and Ellis Wainwright have on their hands."

"You mean the publicity?" Ken asked.

Will shook his head. "They've got an apparent murder on a peninsula cut off from the mainland by a checkpoint and guards. It's the equivalent of a very large locked room."

"That's right," Sunny said. "Trehearne won't be able to claim that some hobo or transient did it."

"Not unless the guy turns out to be a former Navy SEAL," Will laughed, and then went quiet. "So the suspects come down to staff, security, guests, or the family."

"Who just happen to be super-influential. You're right," Ken admitted. "It's going to be a real mess."

"Well, if anybody can straighten it out, I'd bet on Wainwright," Will said. "The guy is a pro. And who knows? In the end, the story may turn out to be sadly simple—people drinking too much, an argument that goes too far, and then it's too late."

"Real open-and-shut stuff." Ken's voice sounded sour. "Until the expensive lawyers get involved."

*

Will wanted to drop Sunny off at her house, but she insisted on going in to the *Courier* office with Ken. This was a real news scoop, the kind that required a special edition, and Ken would be killing himself to get one out. The least she could do was help.

They arrived at the old warehouse to find the interns already at work . . . in a poisonous atmosphere. It seemed that someone among the summer helpers had leaked one of Sunny's cell phone pictures. They'd called Ken with the news while he was still in the car, but the horse was already out of the barn by then. The picture by itself was too indistinct for anyone to run, but the phones in the *Courier* office were ringing off their hooks as various news organizations called for confirmation of the story. Ken let his troops admit that there had been a death on Neal's Neck—so long as the *Courier* got the credit. *That probably means a whole caravan of media people will be converging on Neal's Neck to get more of the story,* Sunny thought. The job facing Wainwright and Trehearne wouldn't be getting any easier, nor would they be grateful to her or Ken for precipitating that.

She pushed the thought away to concentrate on the job at hand, working with Ken on a front-page story while the interns manned the photos. Sunny wasn't happy that their reportage depended so heavily on unnamed sources; sources whom Trehearne and Wainwright, not to mention the Kingsburys, would easily identify as Will Price. The sensational aspects—a party in an exclusive compound, a victim who'd been drinking—didn't put Eliza Stoughton in the best light, either. Sunny couldn't forget the state police lieutenant's comment: "That poor girl deserves more dignity than you're about to give her."

At least they'd found a photo to run that didn't make Sunny feel as though they were working on one of those awful old-time tabloids that had featured pictures of dead babies found in garbage cans. It showed one of the Kingsbury security guys with his back to the camera, holding Eliza Stoughton in his arms as his colleagues prepared to haul her body up the cliff. His broad back with SECURITY in large letters blocked the view of Eliza's face and torso, leaving only her legs and one arm showing.

It was a shot Sunny had gotten, and Ken insisted on giving her a photo credit. By that time, sunlight was beginning to filter through the windows, and Sunny was too tired to argue. They put the paper to bed, and Sunny sat numbly at a desk, not even noticing the noise of the press in action. She finally roused herself and called home so Dad wouldn't worry. "And don't forget to feed Shadow," she finished.

"You're sure you're okay?" Mike repeated for about the tenth time. "I was up early and heard stuff on the radio."

Sunny assured her father that she and Ken were perfectly fine, that Will had taken care of them, and that Mike would be able to read the whole story in the *Courier.* By then it was late enough in the morning that Sunny staggered over to the MAX office just in time to open up.

Nancy came dashing in moments later and stared at Sunny. "You look like you slept in those clothes," was the first thing that popped out of her mouth.

Sunny looked down at the sweatshirt and jeans she'd worn for the journey to Neal's Neck. Probably not the most professional-looking office wear.

"No, I definitely did not get *any* sleep in these clothes," Sunny replied.

Nancy goggled at her. "You were at Neal's Neck again, weren't you? They said on the news that a local paper had broken the story."

As she spoke, one of Ken's interns, looking bright and energetic, came into the MAX office with a pile of special edition copies, which he placed on Sunny's desk.

He must be on something to be so cheerful after the night we had, Sunny silently groused, and then had the unworthy wish that the guy would share whatever it was.

Nancy pounced on the paper. She'd read a paragraph, stop to stare at Sunny, read another one, stare again, and kept it up until Sunny finally said, "If it sounds exciting, well, then we did our jobs. But really, it wasn't. A lot of it was boring, sitting in the dark wondering if we were there yet. Then there were a couple of minutes of craziness, spiced with a bit of terror. At one point I was afraid we were going to get shot as trespassers—"

Sunny broke off when she realized Nancy was just eating this up.

"Anyway, what I need now is coffee." Her stomach protested at the thought. "Maybe coffee and a muffin," Sunny amended. "And eggs. Maybe tea instead of coffee. I don't want to burn a hole in my stomach." She fished in her pocket and found a couple of bucks, which she held out to Nancy. "Would you mind going over to Judson's Market and seeing what you could get in the way of breakfast? I'd go, but . . ." After sinking into her desk chair, Sunny wasn't sure she had the energy to get out again.

Nancy took the money and came back a few minutes later with a scrambled egg on a roll and a large cup of tea. Sunny dug in gratefully, but forced herself to ration her bites. She didn't want to scarf the whole thing down while Nancy was still giving her the hero-worship stare.

They settled back into work—at least Nancy did. She even got the coffeemaker going. The phone rang, and Sunny picked it up to hear Ollie Barnstable's voice. "Well, the local news shows are all talking about your midnight ride," he said.

"It was more like two a.m." Sunny broke off to yawn.

"Was Will Price there, too? It seems a dead body can't turn up in this neck of the woods without the two of you being in on it up to your necks."

Sunny sighed. "Yes, Will was there. And he's sure that Nesbit's people will try to make the most of it."

"Well, I'm sure your dad and his cronies will work on damage control." Ollie paused for a second. "Speaking of damage control, do me a favor, Sunny. Stay away from the office equipment. Judging by the way you sound, you're liable to break something."

Sunny took his advice, sitting at her desk and confining herself to simple tasks done slowly. She left answering the phones to Nancy, who spent a lot of the time saying brightly, "I'm sorry, she's not here."

That was how Sunny knew some other newspaper person or TV reporter was trying to find her to ask idiotic questions.

Nancy lies pretty well, she thought, listening to the girl deal with another member of the slavering press pack. *Maybe she* could *have a future in journalism—or PR.*

Still, round about the point of lunchtime, Sunny had pretty much stopped working at all, afraid she might make Ollie's prediction come true.

She was fighting to keep her eyes open, debating whether she could safely drive home, when the office door opened and Randall MacDermott walked in.

"I need your help," he said.

6

Sunny had to admit that Randall MacDermott was still an attractive man, though up close she could see that a slight dusting of gray had appeared at the temples of his luxuriant head of brown hair, and there was no mischief in his face today. He looked worn, even worried, as he stared down at Sunny.

Now he shook his head. "I'm sorry. I realized that sounded silly the moment the words were out of my mouth," he said. "Let me try again." He forced a smile and a brighter tone of voice. "Hey, Sunny. I saw your name in the photo credit on the front page of the local paper. Somebody at the newspaper office told me I could find you here. Are you free for lunch?"

When Sunny hesitated, trying to find a way out of it, Nancy said, "Go on. I'll cover for you."

Traitor, Sunny thought unkindly. It wasn't as if Nancy had any reason to know that the very last thing Sunny wanted to do was go spend time one-on-one with Randall. *Well, why not?* the scornful voice inside Sunny's head chimed in. *Just get it over with now while you're too tired to care.*

"Okay," she said, getting up from the desk. Sunny suggested the Redbrick Tavern, where the food was good and reasonably priced. The waitress seated them in captain's chairs and began reciting the day's specials. Sunny didn't even hear her. She was too tired, and too busy wondering what Randall thought they had to talk about.

His blue eyes peered anxiously at Sunny as the waitress finished her spiel, then he thanked her in a preoccupied voice. Sunny ordered a hamburger and fries, comfort food. Maybe the protein in the burger would fuel a comeback. Randall went for the same with a pint of beer.

One sip, and I'd be out, Sunny thought. She ordered an iced tea.

They sat in silence as they waited for their drinks to arrive, the noise of the lunch crowd, mainly tourists at this time of year, clattering around them.

Randall finally spoke up. "It's been a while. Good to see you, Sunny. You look as great as ever."

One, maybe two lies out of three sentences. Nothing about this was how Sunny had envisioned seeing Randall again. Admittedly, those visions had had a lot of revenge fantasy involved, with Sunny receiving a Pulitzer Prize and Randall admitting how wrong he'd been. Sunny had imagined herself in a designer gown, looking perfectly made-up and classy. *Instead, I probably look like I've just been dug out of a pit,* she thought. Well, Sunny could be a journalist, too. *Just stick to the basic questions, find out what he wants,* she told herself. *Who, what, when, why.*

"How are you doing, Randall?" That was still an acceptable journalistic question.

Randall responded with a *what*. "Nowadays they call me editor-at-large."

That didn't strike Sunny as a good thing, not for a guy working at a paper ruthlessly trying to cut expenses. It sounded as though his next promotion would be editor-out-the-door.

"So, what brings you up to this neck of the woods? The Kingsbury-de Kruk wedding seems an odd kind of assignment, even for an editor-at-large."

"I'm up here on my own, Sunny. The paper thinks I'm taking some vacation time. What they don't know about me using my press card won't hurt them."

Sunny knew the next reportorial question to ask. "Why?"

"I'm following a story." Randall leaned across the table. "Do you remember the Taxman?"

"I remember him every April," Sunny replied. "And I often say unkind things about him."

Randall shook his head. "Not that taxman. Don't you remember sitting in bars after we put the paper to bed, with the old hands telling stories—ones that they couldn't print?"

Sunny dredged up a memory. "A society blackmailer, some sort of cross between Robin Hood and the Godfather— is that the one you mean? I remember one of the older crime reporters loved to talk about that. What was that guy's name? Izzie—Izzie Kritzik! Whatever happened to him?"

"He retired," Randall said, not meeting Sunny's eyes.

Sounds as though he went into retirement about as

willingly as I went into the larger job market, she thought. *At least I hope Izzie got a pension out of the deal. All I got was the Maine Adventure X-perience.*

Randall was about to say more, but the waitress arrived with their order. There was a brief moment of silence as they both attacked their burgers. When Randall finished chewing, he sighed. "Izzie didn't know what to do with himself in retirement. He died recently, and in his will, he left me several boxes of notes. One file held everything he'd found out about the Taxman."

Sunny frowned, trying to remember more about the older man's war stories. "What was the deal with this Taxman? He was supposed to be a merciful blackmailer? After getting the goods on people, he'd be satisfied with a one-time payment. But God help them if they didn't make it, right?"

Randall nodded. "Unlike most blackmailers, who keep demanding money until they drain the victim dry, the Taxman was fairly reasonable—as long as you paid. Izzie talked to one fellow who was in line to become the president of a major corporation. The guy didn't believe the Taxman actually had the goods on him and refused to cough up. Turned out there was plenty of proof—documentation that the man was conducting several affairs with company funds. He wound up out of a job, divorced, and in prison . . . the poster child for what happened if you ignored the Taxman. What really rubbed salt in the wound was that the cash demand wouldn't have broken the bank."

"So he's not a pig, but there's still a *Godfather* aspect." Sunny lowered her voice in a bad Marlon Brando impersonation. " 'Some day, and that day may never come, I'll call upon you to do a service for me.' "

"Right. The money was part of it, but the favors he was able to extract were more important. Izzie talked to one woman who expected to move from her seat in Congress into an ambassadorship. She had paid off the initial demand, but the Taxman later asked her to shepherd a bill through her House committee. Instead, she let several colleagues pressure her into backing off—and suddenly some embarrassing photos surfaced to sink her diplomatic career before it even got launched."

"The favor bit probably explains why the Taxman can be content with a relatively small bite when it comes to money," Sunny said. "Even after the payoff, he holds onto the incriminating information, giving him leverage with former victims to rope in new ones. That could be a favor, too."

Randall nodded encouragingly.

Sunny stared at her former editor. "Come on, you can't take this sort of thing seriously. It's like an urban legend for reporters. You'd probably do better going after D. B. Cooper. Nobody knows who he really was, but at least there's verifiable evidence that he hijacked an airliner and parachuted away with the ransom payment."

"I was just as doubtful as you are when I used to hear Izzie in the bars," Randall said. "But he had a banker's box full of notes. He'd talked to people who'd had some spectacular downfalls after not paying, and who were now kicking themselves that they hadn't just paid up or done what they were asked to do. Izzie knew how to get things out of people, and they probably wanted to vent, but even though he managed to get that far, none of them would ever say anything on the record. They were too scared of the Taxman. Once burned, twice shy."

"Why would they talk at all?" Sunny ate some fries as she listened to Randall's answer.

"They didn't—not officially. The victims were specifically warned off from talking to the police or the media, but the stories about blackmail and one-time payments still spread around as rumor and gossip. Izzie thought it was some perverted form of advertising. It made the Taxman's job easier with the next victim."

"Sounds like Izzie had an answer for everything." *So what do you expect me to do to help you, and why should I?* Sunny added silently. *Unless you intend to take a page out of the Taxman's book and blackmail me into doing a favor.* She considered that for a second. *Nah. He's got nothing anymore.* So she didn't bother to keep the skepticism out of her voice as she asked, "Are you really telling me that you're taking the old guy's pet theory seriously?"

Randall's reply was a vigorous head bob in the affirmative as he took another bite of his burger. Once he'd swallowed, he said, "I got interested and did a little checking. Some of the people Izzie talked to have died by now."

Sunny rolled her eyes. "That's convenient."

"And some of them wouldn't talk to me." Randall had a sip of beer before he went on. "But a couple did, and they told me the same stories they'd told him. I kept my ear to the ground, and I heard more."

"Really?" Even as Sunny scoffed at this story, she had to admit that Randall had piqued her interest. He wasn't some cub reporter out on his first rodeo. He was a professional.

"And all this brought you up here? Why—" She broke off. The answer was obvious: the big wedding prep. Big enough to be wedding of the year, if not the decade, around here, for sure. Two famous families about to face a media blitz. A very unfortunate time for some past indiscretion to surface. Perhaps a very profitable time for a blackmailer.

"So who's got the dirty linen?" Sunny asked. "The Kingsburys or the de Kruks?"

"That's the thing. The person I wanted to talk with was Eliza Stoughton," Randall replied, almost causing Sunny to send a mouthful of iced tea out her nose. As she recovered, Randall went on. "Some of the people I'd talked with about the Taxman mentioned that she'd been poking around, too."

Sunny coughed and took another sip of her tea. "You think she was being extorted?"

He shook his head. "About a year ago, she took a big financial hit. I think that was her making the payment. But she was trying to figure a way out of owing the favor. I think the Taxman made a demand she couldn't or wouldn't meet, and Eliza lost her life over it."

Having someone threatening to ruin your life unless you did as they commanded—that might be a reason to drink too much and lash out. Sunny shook her head, trying to stir up some activity from her brain cells. She must be pretty tired to be taking any of this seriously. And instead of waking her up, the food was only making her feel more sluggish. Too much blood heading down to the stomach, not enough getting up past her neck.

She pushed her plate away. "Randall, this makes a pretty interesting story. But I'm really too tired to be having this conversation. Besides, I think it's fiction, not journalism. After all, why would this shadowy blackmailer, who had the atomic option of ruining Eliza Stoughton's life, kill her instead?"

"I think maybe she recognized him," Randall said. "Or her. If so, that person may still be out on Neal's Neck."

Will's locked-room mystery again, Sunny thought.

Randall pushed his plate away, too. "I know I'm rolling the dice, following up on this," he said. "But what else can I do? I need a big story, Sunny. Something that can save my job—or make me more attractive to other news organizations. It was a real shock to see your name in print this morning. Where did you learn to take pictures like that? And when I went to their office and the kids there told me what you'd done to get the story—whoa!" He shook his head in wonder. "If this Taxman thing pans out, it could be a career changer. For both of us. That is, if we worked together on it. You've got all the local knowledge, and I've got all the background that Izzie collected. If we teamed up, it would be just like the old days."

"Not exactly like the old days. How's the family, Randall?" Sunny ruthlessly poured cold water over his enthusiasm. "Speaking of family," she went on without waiting for a reply, "I'm in this small town to be closer to my dad. Maybe you remember I came back here to take care of him after his heart attack. He's much better now, thanks for asking, but he still needs someone around. As for that photo you praised, I took classes to make myself a more valuable employee for the *Standard.* Funny how that worked out. At least some of the media stuff I learned helps me run a tourism website. That's how I earn a living around here, along with doing the occasional piece for that little paper you mentioned."

She paused, partly to draw breath but mainly because of the pained look on Randall's face. *Maybe it would have been better if I'd gone with my first plan and just smacked him,* she thought. Instead, she stood up. "You stay and finish your food. I'm going home to sleep."

Sunny got up and left the Redbrick, her steps a little wobbly, both from exhaustion and a little leftover adrenaline from what she'd just said to Randall. That made her laugh a little. *Folks will think I had a liquid lunch.*

She walked back to the MAX office, but no way was she going to try and drive the Wrangler home. Sunny made up her mind. "You've been covering for me all day as it is," she said to Nancy. "I'm going to make it official and head home to bed."

Then she called the number she'd known since childhood. Mike answered the phone.

"Hi, Dad," Sunny said. "I need some help. Do you think you could drive me home?"

Mike came to pick her up on the double, his eyes anxious as he came through the office door.

"Don't worry," Sunny told him. "I'm just tired." She yawned. "Really tired."

Sunny kept yawning the whole way home, bigger and bigger until she was afraid she'd dislocate her jaw. "Maybe that hamburger for lunch wasn't a good idea."

"Not when you've got a drive ahead of you," Mike agreed. He ought to know, having been a trucker who'd delivered road salt to over half of New England.

He escorted her into the house and up the stairs. "Do you want to take a shower?"

"After I wake up," she replied. "Maybe in a day or two."

Sunny kicked off her shoes and sat on the bed fully clothed. The sheet and light blanket lay in disarray. She hadn't had time to make the bed after Ken had called. Swinging her legs up, Sunny pulled the sheet over herself. Her dad's face loomed over her and he bent down to give her a kiss on the forehead. "I'll take care of supper. You just rest."

He left, and for a moment Sunny seemed to float on her mattress. *Yes, eyes closing, just sink into the darkness . . .*

All of a sudden, she felt a weight on her chest. Sunny's eyes popped open, and she found herself nose to nose with Shadow, who sniffed very determinedly at her.

"If you start talking again," Sunny murmured, but she didn't finish the sentence. Her eyes closed again, and she was asleep.

*

From his vantage point over Sunny, Shadow tried to inhale every nuance of scent off of her. One of the things he liked about living with Sunny and the Old One was how orderly things usually were, with few surprises. Oh, sometime the Old One's She would come over with that foolish, yellow-colored Biscuit Eater who'd woof and knock things over, but Shadow could deal with him.

But when people started leaving the house in the middle of the night and not coming back even after the sun had been up for a long time, that was not a good thing.

At least he didn't smell smoke on her breath, or that pungent stuff the two-legs drank to act silly. He got a whiff of meat and some other kinds of food, and rising from her clothes was that salty aroma she'd come home with the other day. There were a couple of other scents Shadow couldn't identify, but they didn't smell like trouble to him.

It had taken him a while to remember it, but he'd finally realized that the fragrance he'd noticed on Sunny when she came home yesterday could mean difficulty ahead.

He'd stayed with several sets of two-legs, couples that he'd thought of as mated pairs. Then one of the humans began coming home at odd times, or leaving during the night. And when they came home, Shadow would find traces of made smells on them, sometimes odd, sometimes nice. Then, sooner or later, the humans would end up making loud noises at one another.

Shadow never understood that. Between cats, a hiss, maybe a cuff or a show of claws, would settle the question of who was boss. But the two-legs would go in for loud noises and sad noises, wet faces and throwing things. It could get on a peaceful cat's nerves.

Then, all too often, one of the humans would leave. And the next thing that happened was that Shadow would find himself back on the street.

He really, really didn't want that to happen here. Sunny lived with the Old One, but Shadow thought she might end up mating with the He that kept coming around. Shadow had his problems with that one, but he didn't seem too bad for a human male.

And he didn't wear made smells.

But Shadow had detected another smell on Sunny. Maybe it was nothing, but it made him nervous, just like Sunny coming home to sleep while the sun was out made him nervous.

He skulked around on her bed, his tail lashing to show his displeasure. Usually he'd at least consider snuggling with Sunny, to enjoy an occasional drowsy pet from her.

But she was fast asleep already, her mouth open and making that odd *skrawwwk* noise that humans sometimes made when they slept.

No, Shadow wouldn't nap with her.

She'd probably turn over on me right when I got comfortable, he thought.

*

Sunny woke up feeling a bit more human, if not fully rested. The shadows were growing long in her room, so it must be almost evening. She must have zonked off for three or four hours. Sighing, she stretched, sitting up in bed. Her blinking eyes caught a flash of movement down at the bottom of her ajar bedroom door. A small, gray striped face peered suspiciously in at her, then disappeared.

"What's the matter, fella? Did Dad forget to feed you?" Sunny got up and went to the door, but the hall was empty. Shadow had already darted off somewhere after letting his displeasure be known.

Heaving a deeper sigh, Sunny went to get her bathrobe and then headed for the shower. She wasn't about to give Shadow another show.

After a long session under the rushing warm water, Sunny felt cleaner on the outside but definitely empty on the inside. She put on shorts and a T-shirt and headed downstairs. Mike was already at the table, arranging rolls and cold cuts. "It's all 'food police' approved," he told her. "Low fat, low sodium, low taste."

"It's not that bad," she protested, and Mike shrugged.

Sunny noticed that her father had put out a bowl of salad. He'd also cored and sliced several McIntosh apples. "Figure we could do like you see in restaurants, and use them on the sandwiches with a little mayonnaise, or whatever they call that healthy stuff in that jar you bought." He smiled. "I figured you must be up when the mange-ball came down and got something to eat." Mike nodded at Shadow, who was crunching away at his dry food, apparently unaware of their presence until Sunny went over to pet him. Somehow he managed to avoid her hands while still keeping his head in the food dish.

Sunny gave up and returned to her father, who laughed. "He's miffed with you for creating a stir when he's the only one who's supposed to be up and patrolling the house."

"How did you feel about the stir?" Sunny asked.

Mike's smile slipped a little. "It worried me, not knowing what you were going off to do. After reading the *Courier*, though, I don't think I'd have felt any better if I *had* known what you were letting yourself in for." He sighed. "At least Ike Elkins was about the safest guy you could have picked for a midnight boat ride."

"I'll give you the whole story while we eat," Sunny promised. "If you don't think it'll ruin your appetite."

"Just try," Mike said stoutly, plunking a bottle of seltzer water on the table.

They made healthy inroads into the food, though Mike shook his head in dismay at Sunny's description of spotting Eliza Stoughton. "She sounds like just a kid."

"Definitely younger than I am," Sunny said.

"And you saw her when you were there before?"

"Parading through the compound in her purple bikini and dancing by the pool as if she didn't have a care in the world." Sunny frowned, snagging a slice of apple and chewing on it. If Randall's story was right, Eliza had had a lot of cares. Enough, maybe, to prove fatal.

Mike rose from the table and began setting up the coffeemaker, something he never did after supper.

"Are we expecting company?" Sunny asked. If it turned out to be Mrs. Martinson, there was a good chance of scoring a piece of her famous coffee cake.

"Will Price said he'd drop by," Mike replied. "I spoke with him on the phone while you were in the shower." He seemed very interested in his coffee preparations. "I'm afraid it's going to be tiresome politics. You may find yourself dropping off again."

"We'll see." After helping her dad with the dishes, Sunny zipped around the living room, piling up the newspapers and collecting some of Shadow's cat toys from the floor.

Will arrived late and still in uniform, the expression on his face warning of a foul mood. "Well, even though I was short on sleep, I liaised brilliantly with the other crime busters out on Neal's Neck," he announced. "Kept traffic moving smoothly in spite of all the news trucks stopping in front of the compound to do remote shots. Not to mention all the idiots rubbernecking to see the crime scene." He shook his head sourly. "At least all the evening newscasts are done for the time being. I'll probably have to get back there for the ten and eleven o'clock broadcasts."

"It's going no better with the people out there?" Mike said.

"Trehearne considers me *persona non grata*," Will replied. "He doesn't even want to let me past the troopers' roadblock. Says I'll pass along everything I see to the *Courier*."

"We kept your name out of the story," Sunny said

defensively. "Mainly, we discussed things we'd seen while we were there ourselves, either for the press conference . . . or later."

"You did mention the arguments Eliza got into," Will pointed out. "I was the one who told you that."

"We kept it vague, only mentioning that there were reports of arguments, not going into specifics, and not naming a source." She remembered how heated her discussion with Ken had gotten over how they should treat some of the stuff that Will had mentioned on the ride back to Kittery Harbor. Ken had wanted to go whole hog, but Sunny had wanted to soft-pedal Will's revelations, arguing that they'd ruin him as a source. Journalistic sugarcoating. She hadn't wanted the story to blow back on Will, but from the look of him, her attempts at concealment hadn't worked.

Will shrugged. "Trehearne's still blaming me." He looked over to Mike. "So, how much hay has Nesbit been making, while I was away on glorified traffic duty?"

"It's more of a whispering campaign," Mike reported. "Frank's not coming out and actually saying anything, but after the big show of turning the responsibility to you, a lot of his online supporters are suggesting you weren't up to the job, letting a murder happen on your watch."

"What a crock!" Will burst out, following up with some choice epithets about the Internet, then apologized to Sunny.

"You won't get an argument from me," she said. "I probably say the same thing about ten times a day."

"Considering the scope of my authority there, the only way anyone could hold me responsible for someone getting killed would be if they got run over by an out-of-control dump truck." He finally sat down, and Sunny gave him a cup of coffee. "So what does the rest of the kitchen cabinet say?" he asked Mike.

"That it hits at what should be your strongest point, your experience and competence." Mike frowned. "Now, we can't afford to run any sort of a poll. But Zach Judson's been sounding out people in his market, and some of the fellows with connections up near Levett have been asking around, and I won't sugarcoat it, it looks as if this has hurt you."

"So what should I say?" Will asked.

Mike dithered for a moment. "The boys think it's not so much what you should say as what you'll have to do. They think you'll have to find whoever killed that girl."

Sunny kept her hand firmly on her cup. At least she hadn't had a mouthful of coffee for this latest news flash from crazy-town.

Will sat in silence for a moment. Then he turned to Sunny with an inquiring expression.

"Don't look at me," she told him. "I was asleep while Dad and his cronies hatched this nutty idea."

"What's so nutty about it?" Mike argued. "You and Will have investigated mysterious deaths before."

"But in those cases, someone we knew was involved first," Sunny said. "We never butted into a case."

"That goes double for me. I'm a cop. I can't just go off investigating cases I haven't been assigned to," Will said. "Besides, I wouldn't say that Kingsbury compound is impregnable, but it's darn close. It's almost impossible to get into Neal's Neck right now. And Lee Trehearne, the head of security out there, doesn't even want me inside his perimeter," Will added. "So how could I even talk to any of the witnesses?"

The doorbell rang, and Sunny excused herself to go and answer it. *Probably another of Dad's political buddies, come to offer Will more useless advice,* she thought.

But when she opened the door, she didn't find one of Kittery Harbor's geezer politicians. Sunny didn't even find a man.

It was Priscilla Kingsbury. The bride-to-be wasn't wearing as much makeup as she had when visiting the 99 Elmet Ladies, and her outfit was less formal—though not swimsuit casual. "Hello, Sunny," she said with a nervous smile. "We didn't get a chance to talk much the other evening, which is really a shame. Wilawiport isn't next door, but I've read some of your articles in the *Courier*—and some of the articles about you and Constable Price. I've spent more time up at the compound than anyone else in the family, so I'm a little more tuned in to local news. Oh, I'm doing this all wrong." Priscilla seized Sunny's hand. "I think you're the only person I can trust, and I hope you can help me."

7

"Wha-wha-why?" Sunny asked, staring at the young-est member of the Kingsbury dynasty. "Why do you think I'm the only one who can help you?"

Now Priscilla looked embarrassed. "Sounds a little over the top, doesn't it? But I've heard good things about you from Helena Martinson and other women in the 99 Elmet Ladies. And I have read your stuff." She bit her lip. "All the other people writing and talking about Eliza make her sound so horrible. They slant things to make it seem as though she brought trouble on herself. Yours was the only story that didn't pile a lot of innuendo on top of the facts."

The girl still clung to Sunny's hand as if she were afraid to let her go. "Eliza was a mess yesterday, and I tried to find out why, but she wouldn't tell me. She'd always been on the fringes of our crowd, only here because she was Beau's date.

Frankly, I didn't know her well enough." Priscilla blinked away tears. "Maybe if I had gotten her to talk—"

She broke off, clamping her lips together for a moment. "I wasn't a good friend. But I'm hoping you and Constable Price can get to the bottom of this, the way you did that time when everyone else was busy pretending that nothing had happened."

Whoopee, Sunny thought, *we're a famous crime-fighting duo—sort of.*

Priscilla was already rushing on. "I'm beginning to find out what that feels like—the everyone pretending everything is fine part. Mr. Trehearne is trying to keep the whole compound nailed down, and Uncle Cale thinks that's because he's afraid that one of the reinforcements he brought in for wedding security may have killed Eliza."

The girl paused for a moment, looking at Sunny. "Uncle Cale says hello, by the way. He thought you were pretty smart."

I guess the question is whether he stressed the pretty or the smart part. Sunny took advantage of the brief interruption in Priscilla's flow of words to get her own thoughts in order. The girl might be petite, but she was like a force of nature once she got going. Sunny led Priscilla into the house. "As it happens, Will Price is visiting right now," she told the girl. "Why don't you come in, and we'll all talk?"

Mike was surprised to see their visitor, but he immediately offered her a cup of coffee. Hospitality was part of the Kittery Harbor Way, the ethos that Sunny had grown up in. So had Will, although he kept a cop's wariness behind his good manners as Priscilla accepted and joined them at the kitchen table. Even sitting down, she seemed to give off an aura of "full speed ahead."

"I'm glad to catch you both," she said to Will and Sunny. "You have to understand that our family is all over the country these days. My big brothers Lem and Tom are responsible for their states, and although I grew up with my grandparents after my folks died, they live mostly at their place on the Connecticut shore. The winters are usually milder there. I'm the one who stays here in Maine, working with Uncle Cale—or rather, for the Act Two Foundation. He travels thousands of miles a year, visiting our local offices and fund-raising. We help programs all over the country, from food insecurity to prisoner rehabilitation. I work closer to home, in Boston, Providence, and of course here in Elmet."

Mike nodded. "Helena mentioned you helping out the food pantry."

"Since I'm more local, I'm aware of your . . . reputation," Priscilla said to Will.

He frowned, considering something. "I wonder if Trehearne is, too. Maybe that's why he's trying to keep me out of the compound. I'm supposed to be the local law enforcement liaison for your wedding," he explained to Priscilla. "But your security guy only wants me outside directing traffic."

"Mr. Trehearne doesn't like *any* outsiders getting past his perimeter," Priscilla said. "That even includes the state police." She made a face. "I can understand his attitude a little better now. It feels like our place is under siege. The security people have caught photographers creeping around in the neighbors' yards, trying to get pictures of us. I had to sneak out with the cleaning staff to come here."

"That's our problem, Ms. Kingsbury," Will said. "Your home is pretty much sealed off. Makes it difficult to talk with witnesses and so on."

"Oh, call me Cillie," Priscilla told him. "That's the nickname I grew up with, and the one my friends use." She took a sip of the coffee Mike had handed her. "I think Uncle Cale and I may have a way around the locked-in problem. We're going to suggest embedding a reporter in the wedding party get-together. A local reporter. You, Sunny."

Sunny stared at Priscilla, speechless. But her inside reporter was jubilant . . . and a little impressed. *Quite the bold move, there. I guess Uncle Cale is more than just a pretty face.* "You do realize that I'm not a full-time reporter," she finally said. "I do have a day job. And I'll have to talk to the publisher of the *Courier.*" Although she suspected that Ken Howell would jump at the opportunity.

"Well, we haven't sprung our idea on the rest of the family yet," Cillie told her. "But if you could get things ready on your side, I think we can push this through on ours."

Family politics, Sunny thought. *And this is a political family.*

The bride-to-be sipped her coffee. "I thought we should postpone the marriage," she said abruptly. "Even though the wedding is a couple of months away, it still seems too soon, you know? I didn't feel right talking about wedding plans while people were discussing when to release Eliza's body." She had trouble saying the last word. "I called her family to ask about memorial services, and they asked us— no, *told* us—not to come. They want to keep things private, and they figure we'll draw reporters like you-know-what draws flies. We'd turn it into a circus, and they d-don't want that." Tears appeared at the corners of her eyes, and she blinked furiously to get them under control.

"How can I go ahead as though nothing happened?" Priscilla took a deep breath. "But it's like politics. I got outvoted. Carson's dad, Mr. de Kruk, was insistent about staying the course." Her voice sounded a little empty now. "Something to do with his schedule. He'd cleared the week around the wedding date and didn't want to rearrange things."

Sunny didn't think that sounded like a good beginning for a marriage, but she didn't reply. What, really, could she say?

Cillie changed the subject slightly, showing a little more spirit. "We've had enough trouble with the Emperor Augustus. At first he wanted the wedding to be some sort of reality TV spectacular, broadcast from the top of one of his construction projects with a congregation of thousands, the New York Philharmonic playing the wedding march, and Cirque de Soleil doing aerial acts while we came down the aisle."

Sunny had to laugh. "Who would he get to officiate? The Pope?"

Priscilla laughed, too. "Probably someone more fundamentalist, with his own TV church and lots of audience appeal." Then she got serious again. "But Carson put his foot down, thank goodness. He said it was bad enough being an extra when his dad did the TV thing. And he ought to know—he'd done it since he was a kid." She sighed. "It was a struggle, but Carson got Augustus to go along with a small wedding, with our local pastor, just the family, and a few close friends."

She went silent, but Sunny could finish it up. *And now one of those friends is dead.*

Priscilla tried to change the tone again, this time going cynical. "So we don't think Old Augustus will mind you covering things, except he'll probably crab that you're too local. But he's already gotten enough mileage—and footage—out of the preliminaries. The engagement bash he threw was quite a show. Plenty of friends and acquaintances got lots of free champagne, and of course all the celebrity reporters were there."

Sunny looked over at Will, trying to get a cue from him. "I'll be honest," he said. "We've been talking over the . . . circumstances of Ms. Stoughton's death. I've got certain reasons to be interested in how the case is handled."

"Because of the primary campaign against Sheriff Nesbit," Priscilla said promptly. When Will looked surprised, she reminded him, "I was at your last campaign stop with the 99 Ladies."

Will nodded, then turned to Sunny. "What do you think of this proposition?"

"I'll have to clear things at work," she said. But there was nothing crucial going on in the next week. Besides, Ollie wanted Will to win the primary—and he wouldn't be averse to hearing a little insider gossip, either. "And get Ken Howell on board." Though that shouldn't be too difficult either.

"Then we've got a plan," Cillie Kingsbury said briskly. "Here's a number where you can get in touch with me. It's a no-name cell phone."

A burner phone, Sunny thought as she jotted the number down. *I suppose you need one—or maybe a dozen—if you're in the public eye.*

Cillie's manners were as good as Mike's. She thanked him for the coffee, then said, "I've got to go. There are a couple of other errands I need to take care of while I'm out of jail."

They saw her to the door. That's when Sunny noticed the car and driver pulled up in the driveway behind Will's pickup. It wasn't a local cab. Cillie must have some friends in the vicinity willing to help out. Patient friends, to sit and wait while she had coffee. Sunny squinted and made out a head of blond hair . . . and a set of fingers restlessly tapping at the wheel. It was Fiona Ormond, Priscilla's wedding planner.

Guess she's got to be professionally patient, Sunny thought.

"Let me know if you can make things work on your end." Cillie shook hands all around. "And thank you again."

"Well, that was interesting," Mike said after they closed the door.

"Kind of like having a whirlwind invade your life," Will said. "I mean, she was pleasant and polite, but she seemed awfully damn confident that we'd just line up and go along with her plan."

"The rich really are different," Sunny said. "And despite the nicknames, not silly at all."

She headed to the kitchen and called Ken, who nearly jumped through the phone in his eagerness to agree. "We can do a special section in our weekly edition, and you'll write a daily blog on our website." Ken's laugh came out suspiciously close to the "MMMwahahaha!" of mad scientists in the movies. "Let the other outlets scavenge off us for a change."

Having gotten Ken's okay, Sunny dialed the number for

Ollie's room at the rehab center. It was getting late, and she knew they turned the phones off there in the evenings.

Ollie picked up on the second ring, sounding reasonably mellow. "What's up, Sunny?" he asked after she said hello.

Sunny reported Priscilla's visit, explaining the embedding idea and why they thought it was necessary to go along. "It's beginning to look as though Will won't win unless he can do something about this case," she told him. "And that means we have to get someone into that compound. This seems the best way to accomplish both things."

Ollie was silent for a moment. "If you think Nancy can handle things at the office, I'll say okay. Just remember, you'll have to wrap this up pretty quickly. You won't have Nancy forever. Labor Day is coming, and she'll be heading back to school."

"I know." Sunny sighed. "And thanks, Ollie."

She hung up. "Well, that's all set. He's giving me the time."

"The least he can do," Mike harrumphed. "How long have you been working there without a vacation?"

"Some vacation this is," Sunny scoffed. "Snooping among the rich and famous." Then she got more serious. "I suppose I'll have to do some homework on who's who in the compound. The only ones I've met are Trehearne and Caleb."

"And Cillie," Will pointed out.

"But there are a whole lot of other people out there. The other Kingsburys, the de Kruks, not to mention the wedding party." Sunny had seen them all on her tour, but not up close and personal.

"I know someone who might be able to help." Will

grinned as he reached for the phone. Half an hour later, they were drinking more coffee with Ben Semple and his girlfriend Robin Lory—the secret resource Will had thought of, a walking who's who of local celebrities.

"Oh, wow," Robin said when they told her that Sunny might actually be going out to Neal's Neck. She happily offered up her full store of gossip to help Sunny prepare.

"So, there's the Senator and his wife. They're getting kinda old, but he's definitely the head of the family, the whatchamacallit."

"Patriarch?" Ben suggested.

"Right. That," Robin agreed. "Then there's his grandsons, Governor Lem and Governor Tom, and their wives. You don't hear much about the ladies, and as for the guys, that's all political stuff." Obviously Robin found the "political stuff" less gripping than the news of who was sleeping with whom.

"Who else?" She thought for a moment and then answered herself. "Caleb Kingsbury, the Senator's son, of course."

"I met him," Sunny said.

For the first time, Robin looked impressed with Sunny. "Really? Is he as nice as he looks on TV? He's always joking with the reporters and the photographers. You know, he's kinda old but he's single—divorced since the scandal."

"The scandal nearly crucified him," Will pointed out. "I guess Caleb decided it was better to befriend the media than to fight them."

Maybe that explains why he was nice to me, Sunny thought. "How about the wedding party?" she asked aloud.

"I don't know for sure," Robin replied. "But I read a

whole thing in the *National Inquisitor* the other day about who's supposed to be coming up. Beau Bellingham is the best man. He's really good-looking, like a model, and he's in med school. He was Carson's best friend in college. Eliza Stoughton came along as Beau's date—I don't know if she was hoping to make it as a bridesmaid. She worked for an advertising agency in New York City." Robin went on, "She'd been engaged to someone else but broke it off. Oh, and Priscilla's matron of honor, Yardley Neal, who has been her best friend since they were kids. Her husband is Thomas Something Neal."

"Langford." Will supplied the name.

"Right. For a while people thought the Neal guy and Priscilla were going to get married. They've known each other forever, and they're some kind of cousins. Ick."

"Yeah, I heard that, too." Sunny made a face. "He couldn't have Priscilla, so he married her best friend? Something icky about that, too."

"He works on Wall Street, his dad is a big shot there." Robin frowned. "I'm trying to remember. Something happened with the father. Did he get sick?"

"No, he got scared," Mike piped up. "Retired abruptly after there was some talk about investigating insider trading. He was a name partner in the firm, though, so the kid will probably wind up as one, too. Just a matter of time."

He stopped when he realized everyone else in the room was staring at him. "Hey, I'm retired. I like to read the paper every day. Even the business pages. It's not like I have some big-shot stock portfolio, but I like to keep an eye on things."

Sunny brought them back to the topic at hand. "So that's

the best man and matron of honor. Who else? There was another guy there," Sunny said, remembering the group by the pool.

Robin nodded. "Right, he's got a funny name. Van Tweezers?"

"No, Van Twissel," Will said. "Peter Van Twissel."

"I think his family and the de Kruks go way back." Robin shrugged. "Otherwise, I don't know much about him."

Sunny thought that over. *So, either he doesn't do anything to interest the gossip community, or maybe he doesn't do anything, period.* "He's a rich kid," she said. "Does he really need a job?"

Ben looked as if the concept of not needing a job was completely foreign to him. "Nowadays, they usually do something."

"Even if it's only counting the family money," Mike added.

"Is that what Carson de Kruk does?" Sunny asked.

"More or less. He works as a junior executive in his dad's company," Robin answered. "That's what they call it—junior executive. And I heard that Augustus de Kruk has him on a short leash, financially. Carson racked up a ton of credit card bills in college, and his dad's been making him pay them off from his salary. But when he gets married, Carson is supposed to get a big raise so he can afford to start a family."

So there's money involved if the wedding goes through, Sunny thought. In fact, the whole Kingsbury-de Kruk union seemed like some massive financial merger. Eliza Stoughton had been seen arguing with Carson, and she was also being blackmailed, at least according to Randall MacDermott. Did that tie in? Was that even real?

All this seemed more than she could hold in her head.

Maybe you won't have to, an unworthy thought wormed its way up. *Maybe the Kingsburys won't even allow you into their precious compound.* Priscilla had seemed pretty confident that she could swing the job of getting Sunny onto Neal's Neck, essentially as an undercover agent. But she and Uncle Cale didn't strike Sunny as the power brokers in the Kingsbury family.

Will glanced at his watch. "Well, I'd better get back up there. The damned newspeople are going to start showing up at the roadblock again—live feeds on the scene for the late newscasts."

"I'll lend a hand," Ben volunteered. "Let me just take Robin home and get into my uniform."

They said their good-byes and headed to their respective vehicles. Sunny waved good-bye, then headed to the kitchen, the piece of paper with Priscilla's number clutched in her hand. She hadn't wanted to make the call with everyone watching. A lot rode on this, and Sunny didn't want the extra pressure.

Mike seemed to understand. He went into the living room and clicked on the TV.

Shadow turned up, as he often did after company had left. He seemed to pick up on Sunny's nervous mood, rubbing against her legs as she walked down the hallway to the rear of the house.

With a half smile, she dropped to one knee and scratched him behind the ears. He kept pushing his head into her hand.

"Thanks, guy, but I can't keep putting this off." She went to the kitchen, got the phone and dialed.

Priscilla Kingsbury answered after the first ring. Had she been sitting with her cell phone in hand, waiting for this call?

"Hi, it's Sunny. I got the okay from my boss."

"Great!" Cillie broke in. "Everything's set on this end. We can put you up in one of the guesthouses if you need to stay." She paused for a second. "You should probably bring a couple of changes of clothing and a bathing suit. Do you think you could be here tomorrow morning by eleven?"

Now it was Sunny's turn to pause. "Um. I guess so."

"Fine. I'll send a car for you. Parking's kind of limited out here on the neck."

And I guess my old Wrangler isn't the kind of car that would get compound room, Sunny silently finished. Still, she'd already agreed to this. Too late to back out now. She chatted for a moment more with Priscilla, said good-bye, and hung up.

She sighed. *Now all I have to do is find a couple of outfits that will look casual but elegant beside a pack of super-rich kids.*

She started for the stairs, then stopped.

And a bathing suit.

The next morning, Sunny had breakfast with her father and tried not to trip over her cat, who was keeping himself underfoot. Shadow had not responded well to the travel bag she'd placed in the front hall. He'd sniffed it, butted it with his head until it fell over, and then trotted over to Sunny, his expression demanding, *What do you think you're doing?*

"You'll do fine," Mike assured her over his bowl of cereal. "The reporting you can do standing on your head. As for the other part—well, you've shown you can handle that, too."

"I'm so glad you're pleased." But then Sunny apologized for her sarcasm. "Sorry, Dad. I feel like I'm going away to camp—and I'm afraid the other kids won't like me."

"Want me to stick around until you go?"

She shook her head. "No, you should probably get your exercise in before it starts to get too hot."

They washed the dishes, and then Mike surprised Sunny by giving her a kiss on the forehead. "Those other kids will love you. I do. Good luck, and have a good time."

When Mike left to go on his daily three-mile walk, Shadow accompanied him to the door, apparently hoping he'd take the offending suitcase away.

When Dad didn't, Shadow turned to Sunny with a dark look.

*

Shadow did not like this at all. This was definitely not a good thing. When two-legs brought out those square-things, it meant they were going away for a long time—or maybe forever.

He didn't understand it. There hadn't been any noise, any shouting at all. In fact, the Old One had been especially nice to Sunny, bringing her food. They'd sat down as if this were the beginning of any other day.

Except it wasn't. That thing was by the door.

Finally, the Old One got up and started down the hall. Shadow followed him, hoping he would pick up the bag.

Oh, he'd miss the Old One a little. In spite of their differences, they'd managed to get along all right. But Shadow could live without him.

The Old One did not pick it up.

Shadow turned to Sunny. This was very, very bad.

*

Sunny was getting annoyed. In the time between Mike's departure and the Kingsbury car's arrival, Shadow had turned into the Incredible Clinging Cat. If he got any more claws into her new top, she'd have to tell people it was eyelet lace.

She had thought she'd feel pretty bad about saying good-bye, even if it was only for a week or so, but Shadow had gotten almost frantic, pushing himself into her petting hands, trying to hook onto her again.

Maybe I'd better wait for the car outside, Sunny decided.

She headed down the hall—and into the Battle of the Bag. Shadow had knocked it down and draped himself over it. Trying to get his not-inconsiderable weight off it wasn't easy, especially when he dug his claws into the fabric, refusing to let go. Every time she got one paw loose, he'd hook in the other.

In the end, she was hot and sweaty, holding him out in one hand at arm's length by the scruff of his neck, the bag held in her other.

The toot of a horn came from outside.

"This is not the good-bye I had in mind," Sunny told the cat, puffing a little. "But I guess it's the best I can manage."

She hefted Shadow down the hall in the direction of

the kitchen, opened the front door, and quickly slammed it behind her. Even through the solid door, she could hear his howling wail from inside.

Sunny hurried toward the black town car that had pulled into her driveway. A thickset man in a dark Windbreaker and a baseball cap sat behind the wheel. Probably one of Lee Trehearne's security guys.

He stared at her for a moment, then averted his eyes. *Yeah, I know I look like I just ran the hundred-yard dash to get out here, but he's not supposed to notice things like that with a client.* She shook her head, straightened her clothes, and continued toward the car.

The driver got out to open the door and take her bag. He was staring again, but this time behind her.

Sunny turned. They'd recently installed a new front door. This one had a decorative mail slot. Now the brass flap that covered the slot was pushed out, and a gray-furred paw lashed frantically around in the opening to the accompaniment of horrible, mournful noises.

Sunny shrugged at the driver as she took her seat, not sure whether to laugh or cry.

8

It took most of the half-hour ride to Neal's Neck for Sunny to calm down after that scene with Shadow, requiring plenty of deep breathing and a lot of taking in of the beautiful, serene scenery.

Concentrate, Sunny urged herself. *You can't arrive looking like a wrung-out dishrag. Priscilla is depending on you. And so is Will.*

She had control of herself by the time the town car arrived at the roadblock at the entrance to the compound and parked just inside. As she waited for the security guy to get her bag, Sunny checked out the state troopers. Each wore a badge over the left breast pocket of his uniform, a name tag over the right, which made it slightly easier as Sunny tried to spot the name of Will's pal, Hank Riker.

"We were assigned together up near the Canadian border and were pretty tight," Will had told her. "If you need help, he'll probably come through for friendship's sake. But if it's anything serious, Hank's a trooper first. He'll go to Wainwright. Hell, he's the one who called Wainwright here in the first place." *Even so, Riker may be the only halfway friendly face in this place,* Sunny thought as she scanned another name tag. She realized the owner was giving her a sort of weird look of his own.

That irreverent alter ego in the back of her head quickly responded. *Well, would I like some stranger looking at my chest?*

"Sorry, Trooper Smithwick," she said taking in the printed name. "Just trying to get myself acclimated."

Before Sunny could embarrass herself any further, Priscilla Kingsbury came walking up, wearing a bathing suit under a terrycloth wrap. "No problems getting up here?"

"Just a few getting out the door," Sunny said without elaborating. The driver brought over her bag. Sunny gave it a quick check to make sure Shadow hadn't torn the side open with his claws, then arranged the strap over her shoulder. "As you suggested, I brought a few things."

From the look Cillie was giving her, apparently she should have brought a lot more.

"I can always go home and get something else if I need it." Sunny pasted a synthetic smile on her face. "Maybe I should have asked. Do you dress for dinner?"

"The Neals did when they lived in the big house," Priscilla's smile was more genuine—and a little wicked. "But that was because Great-Grandfather Neal liked to watch people sweat. It's a lot more free and easy nowadays. After all, this is supposed to be a summer place, where people can relax."

Still, Priscilla didn't look very relaxed as she led the way to the house on the right-hand side of the street, the same one Sunny had seen Eliza Stoughton coming out of two days earlier.

"We girls—and Yardley's husband Thomas—have been bunking in here." She pushed the door open, catching Sunny's glance. "Nothing much gets locked around here, unless you want privacy," Cillie said. "The perk of having all this security around. Anyway, this is the ground floor." The house was larger than Sunny's but built along the same lines. A center hall with a stairway leading upward. Living room on the right, and a smaller parlor on the left. The furnishings were clean and serviceable, but on the plain side of luxurious. The living room held a lot of Early American furniture, but Sunny didn't think any of it was antique. Just old.

This was one of the houses that the Kingsburys had bought basically as cover, a means to shelter their inner compound. Sunny suspected that they'd purchased it furnished as is, and suddenly found herself wondering where the previous occupant had gone—and if they'd done so willingly. *Oh well,* she thought, *at least the Kingsburys probably paid over market value for it.*

Priscilla led the way through the living room to a dining room with a good-sized table surrounded by bentwood chairs, each with its own little tufted seat cushion. Then she turned, headed for a pair of swinging double doors, and revealed the kitchen, with an enormous old-fashioned gas range, a refrigerator probably as old as Sunny, and a huge, ancient sink.

Priscilla watched Sunny take it all in. "Yankee thrift," she said, confirming Sunny's impressions. "A lot of this stuff came with the house when the Senator bought it."

Sunny nodded. "Good enough for a summer vacation home." She knew the drill. That was part of the Kittery Harbor Way, too.

"If you're looking for marble step-down bathtubs with whirlpool attachments, try my Cousin Tommy's place in Palm Beach." Priscilla laughed. "Or one of Augustus's palaces. When you're invited out here, you're expected to 'rough it.' " She went through the kitchen out into the center hallway and back to the stairs. "Mainly that room is being used as wedding central. Another is being used by Tommy and Yardley." Priscilla paused for a moment. "I had the spare room set up for you. Didn't think you'd want to sleep where Eliza had."

"Um, no. Thanks," Sunny said.

Her hostess led the way up the stairs, then shot another quizzical look at Sunny. "Do I need to tell you 'off the record' all the time?"

"Certainly for stuff you want to keep private," Sunny replied. "I don't think the sleeping arrangements need to be publicized."

Cillie nodded. "So let's get you settled, and then I'll introduce you to people."

Sunny stashed her bag beside a pile of white towels on a comfortable enough looking bed with a chenille spread. Nothing ostentatious, and nothing very personal.

"You may want to change into a bathing suit." Priscilla

opened her terrycloth wrap to reveal a bikini. "We've been hanging around at the pool." She made a helpless sort of shrugging motion, just as she'd done when she'd mentioned being outvoted. "I can't say I'm wild about it."

It might not make a good impression after someone died under suspicious circumstances, Sunny thought. *And, of course, that's where Eliza got into all the fights the other day.*

"Problem is, there aren't that many places to go in the compound. My grandparents are in the big house, and nobody disturbs the Senator. My brothers and their wives took over the tennis court. We'd either be sitting in here getting on one another's nerves, or out on the lawn somewhere, doing the same."

Sunny nodded. The seaside view with the rocks below would bring up unpleasant associations, too. Aloud, she said, "Okay. Just give me a minute."

She quickly changed into the navy blue one-piece she'd brought, snagging a towel and wrapping it around her hips. Then she rejoined Cillie, and they went downstairs and out the door. It was a weird sort of déjà vu for Sunny, walking along the path to the pool, especially when they passed a security guard and she glanced back over her shoulder and saw him looking after them. But he was wearing sunglasses, so Sunny couldn't figure which of them he was checking out.

Before they even reached the tennis court, Sunny heard a series of rapid-fire noises: *Thwock! Thwock! Thwock!*

Then, as she got closer, she saw two guys who looked to be in their mid-thirties, complete physical opposites. One was short, compact, and agile, racing all over the court to make shots. His opponent was tall and rangy, all arms and legs in his tennis whites, galumphing around—but still arriving in time to drill shots back. From the looks on their faces, the men were conducting a war rather than playing a game. Cillie smothered a laugh as they came closer. "Now you've really learned something about my family. Tennis is our religion, and the court is our altar of sacrifice."

Almost exactly what Cale told me, Sunny thought. "And what are you offering up?" she asked. "Sweat?"

"Not to mention a little blood," Priscilla told her. "The tall one is my older brother Lem. The shrimp is Tom. He and I both take after the Neal side of the family."

"Nothing wrong with being petite," Sunny said. "At least for women. Short guys like them, tall guys like them, and designers love them—or so says my dad's friend Mrs. Martinson." She readjusted the towel around her hips. "Me, I wouldn't know."

"Oh, come on, you've got a great figure," Priscilla protested.

"And a job that tends to put more on it," Sunny replied gloomily. "Sometimes I wish I could just fit into a little black dress and be elegant. Or maybe be a tall blond drink of water in an ice blue gown."

"Lem married one of those." Priscilla nodded beyond the court to where a small group of people sat on lawn chairs arranged under the shade of colorful umbrellas. A tall, Nordic-looking woman took a sip of iced tea from a long glass, her face expressionless under a large pair of sunglasses. "Deborah's a perfect political wife—or a born press manager. Whenever she opens her mouth, the perfect phrase emerges."

Priscilla waved to the onlookers, and one of them, an

energetic-looking brunette, waved back. "Tom's wife, Genevieve, is livelier, but she shoots from the hip."

"So she'll give me better quotes," Sunny quipped, then stopped at the look of chagrin on Cillie's face. "Look, I'm supposed to be doing a color piece on your family getting ready for a wedding, not a political hatchet job. For the rest, well, we'll have to talk about that."

A white-haired woman wearing a broad-brimmed straw hat suddenly burst into laughter at something that had happened on the court. The man beside her leaned forward in his chair, scowling.

"That's Grandmother Kingsbury," Priscilla said. "And the Senator, of course. He's always the referee for these bloodbaths. What do they say on that TV show? All of his judgments are final."

"They look pretty busy with the game." Sunny turned again to watch Priscilla's brothers sweating on the court. "Maybe you can introduce me later. Right now I'd like to meet your friends." *AKA the people who argued with Eliza Stoughton,* she added silently.

The atmosphere around the pool was much more subdued today compared to what Sunny had seen on her tour with Caleb. The music wasn't as loud as it had been, and the people seemed a bit quieter, too. Carson de Kruk was the first to notice them and came over immediately, greeting Cillie with a kiss, and then shaking hands with Sunny.

With his blond hair and slim figure, he was the picture of a conventionally handsome young man. When the nuptials had been announced, Mrs. Martinson had said Carson de Kruk was perfectly cast—he already looked like the figure of the groom on a wedding cake.

Close up, however, Sunny noticed the thinning of the hair at his temples and the dark patches under his eyes. "Thank you for agreeing to do this," Carson said in a low voice as he shook hands. "The situation has been so awful, with those people outside swarming to get at us."

Sunny responded with a sympathetic smile, wondering what exactly Priscilla had told her prospective husband— or the others—about what she was really doing there. Was he only in on the embedded reporter idea? Or did he know that Priscilla also hoped that Sunny could shed some light on what had happened to Eliza?

Something to ask Cillie—when I get her alone again, Sunny thought. Not as though that seemed likely to happen anytime soon. As soon as they realized Priscilla was there, the rest of the wedding party clustered around her. When Cillie introduced Sunny as a local reporter who was going to spend some time with them, Sunny watched for the reactions. No one seemed overjoyed. They all seemed, unconsciously or not, to move a little closer to one another.

No matter what's going on between them, they want to present a united front to the outsider. When she considered it, Sunny couldn't really blame them.

Carson's best man, Beau Bellingham, looked as if he'd just been roused from a deep sleep, and his reaction was about as polite as might be expected from a hibernating bear. In fact, with his thickening middle and tousled, shaggy hair, he had a bit of a bearlike quality that was only strengthened when he blinked, nodded, and headed back to the shade of a beach umbrella.

"Beau's always on call at the hospital," Carson said, trying to smooth over his friend's brusque response. "This is his first chance for some solid rest in years, really. Not to mention his first visit in these parts."

The Neals, Tommy and Yardley, were more polite but still vaguely dismissive, in the same way that Sunny had seen rich people treat servants. They followed the proper forms, but seemed to look right through her.

Only Carson's other groomsman, Peter Van Twissel, met Sunny's eyes as they shook hands, and he greeted her with a skeptical smile. "I hope they didn't tempt you into this job with a promise of fun-filled days." He gestured around the pool. "This is about as close as it gets to a resort around here."

"I'm a local girl," Sunny told him. "A pool beats most of the swimming around here." With that, she removed the towel she was wearing and slipped into the water, letting out her breath in a big puff at the shock of the cool water.

But despite the water's low temperature, she had told the truth. Compared to the local lakes and the ocean, even in summertime, the pool's water was sun warmed and a lot more comfortable. She swam a few laps just to give her muscles a stretch, keeping a covert eye on the wedding party. Beau had apparently gone back to sleep, sprawled on a scatter of pillows and towels. He'd pulled a green cotton surgical shirt over his baggy surfer-style swim trunks. Carson and Priscilla moved to the far side of the pool, their heads together in conversation.

Tommy and Yardley Neal were in the same pose as the betrotheds, but they sat by the entry gate of the pool, out of effective earshot from anyone. Peter took his ease in a long beach chair, slathering lotion all over himself in preparation to take some sun. With the dark glasses he had on, Sunny couldn't tell whether his eyes were following her or not.

She continued swimming until her arms began to feel pleasantly tired, and she figured she should have settled into the background a bit. Then she pulled herself out of the pool, toweled off, and draped the terrycloth around her neck like a stole. The afternoon sun felt pleasantly warm after her dip.

Sunny took a seat in the deck chair next to Peter. "Could I steal some of your sunblock?" she asked. "I didn't think to bring any with me."

He reached down and passed over the bottle. "Hope you're not disappointed it's not some hand-compounded rich man's potion," he said. "I picked it up at Target before all the excitement hit."

"Target, huh?" Sunny looked him over. Peter seemed an odd friend for Carson. He was tall, skinny, and naturally pale, with wispy hair that couldn't make up its mind to be brown or blond. Not a frat-boy type like Carson or Beau. Sunny noticed that Peter's bony fingers had dozens, maybe hundreds, of tiny scars.

He gave her a self-deprecating smile. "Unlike some people in this compound, I've been known to patronize discount stores," he said. "I may be hanging out with the de Kruks, but it's more because of my potential rather than what I'm worth right now. You see, my dad is in computers—special orders—and I've been messing in them since I was a kid, working my fingers to the bone coding on the keyboard when I wasn't burning them with solder or acid or some other nonsense. Now Carson and his dad are bankrolling me, hoping I'll be the next Steve Jobs or Bill Gates." He gave a very boyish grin. "Or both rolled together. Augustus made his fortune from construction projects, honest-to-Pete bricks and mortar. Carson is betting on information being the next frontier for his family to conquer."

"And you're going to help?" Sunny asked.

"He has faith in me. When we got stuck together in the same room as freshmen in college, I figured 'here's the rich kid who'll expect me to do his homework.' As it turned out, he tutored me in French. And yeah, I built him a computer. It didn't hurt that we both had Old Dutch names. There aren't many New Yorkers like that anymore. But it's more about the future than the past. I'll spare you the nerd-speak, but with de Kruk backing, my company is poised to do big things."

It sounded like the American Dream, twenty-first century style. But Sunny wondered how Peter felt being included in such an intimate party. Was it a sign of Carson's friendship? Or was it a business decision, a mark of de Kruk favor for someone they hoped would be a moneymaking asset?

The problem is, once you start thinking that way, the whole Kingsbury-de Kruk affair starts looking more like a business merger. Sunny frowned at the thought, glancing over toward Carson and Priscilla. They seemed happy enough together, but not the stuff of a heart-flopper romance. Had they naturally gravitated to one another in the rarefied social orbits they occupied, or were they making the best of a deal between their families?

Maybe I'll get a better idea when I meet the rest of the family at dinner, she thought, but it was not to be. Dinner was an excruciating meal, like dining at the grown-ups' table times ten. Instead of lowered guards, Sunny got a lot of not-in-front-of-the-servants civility from Priscilla's older brothers. Meeting the Senator was another kind of trip. It wasn't just that the man acted as if she should kiss his ring. He conducted himself as if he were always on camera, as if every word and action were being recorded. Sunny had covered enough political races to know that nowadays candidates labored to come across as just plain folks. Not Thomas Neal Kingsbury. He was of another generation, giving off a feeling of *noblesse oblige* and rose-garden campaigning.

No wonder he never made president, Sunny thought.

As for the de Kruks, Carson's parents had yet to arrive. Some sort of business hitch was keeping Augustus in New York.

The meal itself was a lavish buffet arranged on sideboards—no staff visible—in the dining room of the main house. After serving themselves, the diners then sat at a table that could accommodate all the guests plus another half dozen or so.

Caleb Kingsbury arrived late, still drying his hands on a paper towel. He gave Sunny a conspiratorial wink, then got a lot more formal as he approached. "I apologize, sir," he said to the Senator, who of course had taken a seat at the head of the table. "I was getting my hands dirty aboard the *Merlin*. By way of apology, I'd like to invite anyone who wishes to join me for an after-dinner sail." He grinned at the group. "A shakedown cruise, to make sure the new fittings work as they ought."

"I like the sound of that." Priscilla took Carson's hand.

"Anything that's a little different," Beau Bellingham agreed, still looking half-asleep. At least he'd combed his hair for dinner.

"You're sure it will be safe?" The Senator's wife didn't sound like a grande dame, more like the anxious mother she was.

"Everyone will wear life vests, and we'll be back before nightfall, mother," Cale soothed. At the table, Sunny found herself seated between Deborah Kingsbury, Governor Lem's wife, and Fiona Ormond, the wedding planner. The cool blonde asked a couple of questions to determine just how big a media deal Sunny was, but after hearing that Sunny would just be blogging for a local paper with zero help for her husband Lem's political aspirations, Deborah pretty much left her alone. Fiona, on the other hand, had lots of questions about local businesses.

"Currently, my big interest is transportation," she said, displaying perfect manners and taking small bites. "The people coming to this event will have certain expectations. After arriving in a private plane, they won't want to be ferried here by the Podunk car service." Fiona asked about several livery car companies, but Sunny had to admit complete ignorance. Kittery Harbor was a pretty blue-collar town. Except for weddings and funerals, there wasn't much call for limousines.

Fiona frowned. "I don't want to go completely out of the area and have to source things in Portsmouth or Kennebunkport."

"You may want to look in Saxon, that's a pretty up-market town," Sunny suggested. "Otherwise, I'll check my local sources."

AKA, ask Mrs. Martinson, she silently admitted. Who else could she turn to when it was a question of class? The food was delicious, but dealing with Fiona was a chore. Oh, she was polite, but determinedly on target. *Maybe I'm just not used to dealing with that New York vibe anymore,* Sunny thought. *If this was how I acted, no wonder I had a hard time when I first came back home.*

When the meal finally ended, only the young people took up Cale's offer of a sail. Yachts weren't on Fiona's transport list. The governors were just as happy to rest after their grueling day of tennis, and the Senator and his wife were disinclined.

Beau pleaded fatigue, in spite of his daytime hibernation, and headed off to bed. Peter begged off, too. "I'm not a good sailor," he said, putting a hand over his stomach.

"Are you a sailor, Sunny?" Priscilla asked.

"Of course she is," Cale answered before Sunny could. "She mentioned she'd seen me sailing in while she was out on the water the other day."

Sunny nodded. *At least he didn't mention the boat I was on the other night.*

They left the house, cut across the lawn, and went down the old set of steps to the wharf jutting out from Neal's Neck. This must have been where the fabled rumrunners would've made their deliveries. The modern-day picture was a lot quieter. A humble rowboat bobbed in the water at the end of the pier. Along the side, though, a glitzy motor launch—the same one that had launched the pre-emptive strike on Ike Elkins's boat, and what they'd use as transport over to the yacht—was tied up to the pilings. A couple of security men stood by with a supply of life vests.

Sunny was a little surprised to see Lee Trehearne there, and apparently Cale was, too.

"Everything all right?" Cale asked as he stepped past to check the launch.

"Yes, sir," the security chief replied. Then he turned to Sunny. "I hope you're enjoying your stay, Ms. Coolidge." If his voice got any colder, icebergs would be appearing on the horizon. "It's a very busy and difficult time for the family, we want everything to go as well as possible."

Translation, Sunny thought, *don't go making things worse.*

Aloud she said, "Everyone has been very kind." She slipped her arms into a vest, clipped and buckled herself in, and stepped into the launch. At least she had enough experience on boats, mostly courtesy of her dad's fishing buddies, that she didn't end up sprawling. As soon as everyone was aboard, the security guys undid the lines. Cale started the engine, and they headed out for the *Merlin.* The double-masted boat seemed to grow ever larger as they got closer.

The transfer from the launch to the low-slung deck of the schooner was a bit trickier, but Sunny managed it. Priscilla stepped aboard easily, but Carson made a misstep that required a quick grab from Tommy.

Sunny drank in the quiet elegance of the *Merlin*'s fittings, all polished wood and brass hardware, not a scrap of fiberglass that she could spot. She'd been on larger vessels before, but nothing like this. "This is quite the boat," she told Cale, who gave her an almost boyish grin.

"Shame it can't keep a straight course," Tommy Neal whispered to his wife in a voice loud enough for Sunny to hear. "It always falls off to port."

Cale gave no sign of having overheard. But a few minutes later, he said casually, "You're a sailor, aren't you, Tommy? Maybe you can give the old man a hand, getting the sails up."

Somehow, Sunny noticed, that meant Tommy taking on all the dog labor. A short while later, he was drenched in sweat and staring daggers, as Cale sat behind the wheel in the stern of the schooner. The ride itself was amazing, scudding along with the wind, the red, white, and blue sails billowing against a glorious sunset. Sunny had been on sailboats before, but this was the closest she'd ever come to flying.

Cale obviously caught her enjoyment. He patted the deck beside his chair, and Sunny joined him.

"Did you understand what that jackass said about my boat?" he asked.

"That it has a tendency to head off to the left from the wind," Sunny replied.

Cale nodded. "A miserable thing to say. Even if it's true."

"I think you've made him regret it." Tommy sat on the narrow deck, arm wrapped around a mast, his free hand mopping his face.

"Maybe a little more." Cale raised his voice. "Hard a-starboard."

He turned the wheel, and the *Merlin* went into a right turn, the wind puffing out the sails, the boom on the mainsail swinging so that Tommy Neal had to duck. So did Sunny, but she was farther away from the mast and had more time. "You're bad," she told Cale.

"I prefer to consider it fun-loving, and I suspect you've got a streak of that yourself, surprising a newspaper person," Cale responded with that bad-boy grin. "Maybe that's how the Kennedys managed to make friends with so many press people. Kindred spirits."

"So you're giving it a try?" Sunny asked. "Are you considering another crack at politics?"

Caleb Kingsbury made a face and shook his head. "That's way behind me. You ever heard of John Profumo?"

"Give me a minute." The name sounded vaguely familiar, but Sunny had to search her memory. *Sounded Italian. Something gangster related?* She shook her head. *No. Bad stereotype. Something political? Bribery? No. Something foreign. Well, Italian politics had lots of scandals. Wait, that was it. Scandal. But not in Italy . . .*

"A British scandal?" Sunny said out loud. "Maybe fifty years ago?"

"Close enough," Cale told her. "He was a bigwig in the British Ministry of Defense fooling around with a call girl who was also sleeping with a Soviet agent. By the time it all shook out, it brought down the Conservative government. That's all anybody remembers."

Sunny nodded. That was all she remembered, too.

"What impressed me, though, was what Profumo did afterward. He went to work cleaning toilets for a charitable foundation and in the end wound up running it, even receiving royal honors before he died. I'd call that a hell of a second act for his life."

Cale was silent for a moment concentrating on his steering. "That's why I set up the Act Two Foundation."

"The one Priscilla works for," Sunny said.

Cale nodded. "I may not be a politician anymore, but I've got the gift of gab. That, plus the family name, helped open a few wallets. And I think we do some real good, helping people get through changes in their lives." He grinned. "One of my favorites is a program we run teaching computer skills to folks who lost manufacturing jobs . . . where the instructors are people just out of prison for hacking. Two rehabilitations for the price of one." He grinned again.

"Sounds as though you're accomplishing some good with your second act," Sunny said.

Cale's face softened a little. "I think even the Senator has gotten behind it now. He deeded this place over to the foundation." His expansive gesture took in all of Neal's Neck.

"And the Senator probably also beats out the estate tax on the land." Sunny's voice sharpened as she slowly realized the implications. "And since the compound belongs to a nonprofit, does that mean there are no property taxes to pay for all the state and local cops involved in the wedding and the Stoughton case?"

"There are certain considerations when a family has more than two nickels to rub together." Cale's hands grew white on the ship's wheel. "Have you ever heard the saying, 'shirtsleeves to shirtsleeves in three generations'?"

"Ancient WASP wisdom," Sunny replied.

"I've collected proverbs like that from all over the world," Cale told her. "The Japanese say rice paddy to rice paddy. In Italian, it's 'Dalle stalle alle stelle alle stalle'— from the stable to the stars to the stable. The Scots put it another way: 'The father buys, the son builds, the grand child sells, and his son begs.'"

It's the nagging worry of all the haves, Sunny thought.

That somehow they or their descendants will end up as have-nots. She said nothing, but she suspected that her disapproval leaked out somehow.

Cale's face looked grim as his eyes scanned the horizon. "My grandfather was the first Kingsbury to make any money, by getting involved with the Neals. Before then, we were mainly country preachers. Sometimes I think the family only went into politics for a bigger congregation. The thing is, my grandfather didn't make all that much, and my father has spent a lot of it. I'm not going to be the one who blows what little family fortune we've got left."

Says the man with the fifty-foot yacht and a private peninsula, Sunny thought. She sighed, and decided she'd better change the subject. "So tell me more about the work your foundation does?" she asked, and predictably he puffed with pride, launching into a long spiel of success stories.

Sunny nodded and smiled at the right places, massaging Cale's ego. Just getting onto Neal's Neck had left her dangling in a strange position. She couldn't afford to lose a potential ally before she even began investigating.

9

As soon as the Old One returned home and opened the door after Sunny left, Shadow had darted between his legs to run outside. He'd crisscrossed the lawn and the driveway, frantically casting about for a scent and fighting back the mournful howl that threatened to erupt and tear out his insides.

Sunny was gone, gone, gone. She'd thrown him away and left, maybe forever. Shadow's nose couldn't even find a trace of her. This was very bad indeed. He wanted to cut loose with his loudest battle-yowl and claw everything to ribbons—houses, grass, people, he didn't care. At the same time, he wanted to lay down and be sick. He didn't seem to have any strength at all.

Shadow leaned against a tire, panting after his race

around the front of the house. At least here he was in the shade, out of the sunshine. The heat would have been stifling–

Wait a minute, Shadow thought.

He took a couple of steps along the big pile of metal that blocked out the sun. Then he reared up, stretching his forepaws against the door, bringing his nose to the seam in the metal, breathing in deeply. Yes, that was a trace of Sunny's scent. This was *her* go-fast thing.

Shadow felt a little quiver of hope. The two-legs loved their go-fast things. At least, all the humans he'd seen seemed to. When they went away, they usually hollered, climbed into these big, wheeled things, and roared off. Shadow had never seen a human just leave a go-fast thing behind.

He dropped back onto four feet, thinking hard. *Maybe Sunny wasn't gone forever—at least, not yet,* he thought. *What should I do?*

It was difficult to decide, because he was being distracted. The Old One had appeared in the doorway of the house, clunking a spoon against a can of food. Shadow sniffed the air. The good kind of fish.

He abandoned the go-fast thing, heading quickly across the grass and up the steps. He had a plan now.

First, he would eat the good fish.

Then he would keep an eye out for Sunny. She wasn't going to leave him behind that easily.

*

Sunny finished her first day on Neal's Neck with mixed feelings. She felt that at least she was fitting in, or at least moving to the background where she could observe people without having them stare at her. On the other hand, doing that meant keeping quiet, so she hadn't really gotten her investigation off the ground.

She sent Ken her first blog post (she'd written about the sunset boat ride, which made for some good copy . . . better than how charitable foundations could be used for tax avoidance, the subject she'd initially been tempted to write about), and she figured that should help nail down her cover as a frothy celebrity reporter. She worried about the image she'd used—leaving the land and all its troubles behind— might seem a little callous, considering that one of those troubles was a dead girl. But the feeling of freedom, having the wind at your back, that was pretty good. So were the details about the amount of effort a sailboat required. Tommy Neal's work and sweat was properly recorded.

The folks in the guesthouses kept pretty early hours. Maybe that was because the only TV was an ancient portable—no flat screen taking up half a wall. The couples started disappearing first, and no one stayed up to watch the news, either by habit or because they were sick of the media by now. Sunny was alone by the weather report and turned off the tube. She went up to her room to call her dad and wish him good night. She'd just hung up with him when her cell phone rang again.

"Just thought you should know the website has lit up like a Christmas tree in the hours since you posted," Ken Howell reported happily. "People from everywhere are reading and leaving comments. Boston, New York, even some guy in Hawaii, *Hawaii*, I'm happy if we get someone from Portsmouth or Augusta!"

"Well, it should certainly get the *Courier*'s name around," Sunny said.

"Yup," Ken hesitated. "I guess I should thank you and the interns again for setting up the online site."

"Nancy suggested it after working on the MAX site for a while," Sunny told him. "You should thank her. I just gave advice." She hoped Nancy wouldn't regret her bright idea. Ollie had insisted on them putting a link from the *Courier* site to MAX. Nancy might now find herself dealing with a deluge of accommodation requests from would-be celebrity gawkers.

Maybe I should temper people's expectations, Sunny thought. *That would make a good topic for tomorrow's blog, how totally secure and inaccessible Neal's Neck really is.*

She suggested as much to Ken, who immediately gave his assent. "Let 'em follow all the excitement on our site via your blog."

Laughing, Sunny glanced at the time and said, "Okay, Ken. We'll see how tomorrow goes." She clicked her phone shut and sat on the bed to put her shoes back on. It was shift change on the roadblock—time to talk with Will.

She went down the stairs and out the door, spotting Will's friend Hank Riker taking over one of the positions at the roadblock. He gave her the barest of nods as he adjusted his Mountie hat. Sunny's response was equally guarded. They'd both silently decided it was better not to let on about their connection.

Out in the street past the sawhorse, Ben Semple sat in a Kittery Harbor patrol car. He also pretended not to know Sunny as she passed and took a left at the next intersection.

A block later, she spotted another patrol car, this time with Will behind the wheel.

Sunny opened the passenger side door and slid in. A moment later, Will started the engine, and they moved quietly through the shaded, shadowy streets.

"So how's it going?" he greeted her. "Did any of the folks in the fortress up there let slip a crucial clue?"

"Not hardly," Sunny admitted. "Has any of your professional police work uncovered anything?"

"It's mainly state police work," Will admitted with a sigh, "passed along by Hank."

"Did you get anything from MOM?"

Will shrugged. "My mom usually told me to shut up and do my homework."

Sunny rolled her eyes at Will's sense of humor. "I meant Motive, Opportunity, and Means."

"Yeah, yeah. Motive still looks pretty short. Eliza Stoughton came to Neal's Neck because she was dating Beau but didn't have much to do with the Kingsburys. She was also friends with Priscilla and her matron of honor, Yardley, but it doesn't seem like she knew the husband, Tommy, that well."

"Well enough to get into an argument with him," Sunny pointed out, "as well as with Carson de Kruk."

"True, at least according to the rumors. And if we accept manual strangulation as the means of death, it would indicate that a male did the deed," Will said. "Which leads to opportunity. Priscilla gives Carson an alibi."

"Apparently, they were together, but not exactly sleeping." Will waggled his eyebrows, though his voice grew more serious as he went on. "Lieutenant Wainwright estimates the time of death as between shortly before midnight, when Eliza was last seen alive, and one-thirty, when her body was discovered. The Neals also have a joint alibi, having tucked themselves in together."

"How about the guy who brought her here—Beau Bellingham?"

"He says he was asleep, alone," Will replied.

"That doesn't look good for Beau," Sunny said. "He's a big guy. He wouldn't have had a problem strangling Eliza, or lugging her body around to dispose of it."

"Yeah, he'd be suspect number one, except the security footage doesn't show anyone leaving the guesthouses."

That got Sunny sitting up straight. "You mean they've got surveillance cameras set up inside the compound?"

"Not as fancy as that ring of steel thingy you had in New York City," Will said. "What is it, more than four thousand cameras, I read somewhere."

"That wasn't *my* ring of steel," Sunny told him. "That was in lower Manhattan, and I lived in Queens."

"Well, this is Wilawiport, and it comes down to the same old question—security versus privacy." Will shrugged. "This is supposed to be the family hideaway, and they don't want to be on candid camera all the time. So the surveillance is set to protect the perimeter, not monitor the occupants."

"Which means the private road, the checkpoint, and what else–the guesthouses?"

Will nodded. "The front and back yards. Anybody sneaking around there should have been recorded, but when Wainwright and Trehearne checked the hard drives, they only saw Eliza leave a dark house, and then—nothing. Nobody in or out, not even a squirrel."

Sunny frowned in thought. "But as you say, the security is facing outward, to keep intruders away. If you were inside the perimeter . . . The cameras around the guest-houses cover the front and back."

"As I said," Will frowned, too, trying to follow her logic.

"And I suppose there must have been coverage along the side of each house where they faced the neighbors," Sunny went on.

"There's a tall board fence, no greenery to hide in, and cameras along the whole thing," Will assured her.

"How about the opposite side of the house, behind all these lines of defense?" Sunny asked.

Will opened his mouth to answer and then stopped. "I don't know," he admitted. "There's no side door."

"But there are windows," Sunny pointed out.

"And it wouldn't hurt to ask if they were covered." Will considered the situation for a minute. "I'll bring it up with Wainwright. At this point, Bellingham has to be the prime suspect, with Peter Van Twissel as the dark horse. He's the only member of the wedding party Eliza didn't tangle with. If she wasn't with Bellingham, maybe she made a rendez-vous with Van Twissel, who also has no alibi."

He shook his head. "It all probably boils down to who was sleeping with whom, and when. This case is turning into the kind of thing you might expect from a dive bar like O'Dowd's, not in the run-up to a millionaire wedding. Arguments plus alcohol, things go too far, and a girl winds up dead."

"What was the argument about?" Sunny asked.

"Not sure," Will replied. "Apparently from the moment they arrived, Eliza kept sniping at Beau until he finally told her to shut up, and then the war began."

Sunny shifted uneasily on her seat. "That's not much of a motive."

"As I said, it's more like something out of O'Dowd's." Will shrugged. "Except there, it probably would've been settled with broken beer bottles. Not every murder involves a criminal genius. Sometimes it's just an angry drunk."

"Unless there is another motive." Sunny bit her lip. "One that does involve a criminal genius . . ." She dove in. "Uh, I must have mentioned my old boss on the *Standard*."

Will looked at her for a moment. "The one you were dating?"

She nodded. "He's up here, supposedly covering the wedding prep, but he's actually following another story." Sunny briefly outlined what Randall had told her about the Taxman.

"And your ex . . . colleague really believes this stuff?" Will looked about as willing to accept the story as Sunny had been when Randall first told it to her.

"He does," Sunny replied. "And he was asking for my help, as someone who knew the local scene."

"Then I guess I'd better talk to this Randall guy," Will said quietly. "Hear what he has to say firsthand."

Sunny dug out her cell phone, scrolling through the "contacts" lists.

"You still have him on speed dial?" Will's voice got a little sharper.

"It's my old phone from New York," she told him. "Lots of numbers from my past life are still on it." She found Randall's cell number and clicked on it. From the blurry "Hello?" she got, it sounded as if he must've zonked off right after the late newscasts. But Randall woke up pretty quickly when he realized who was calling. "Change your mind about working together, Sunny?"

"No," she told him, "but I've got someone here who wants to talk to you."

Randall agreed to meet them at a 24-hour diner outside of Wilawiport in twenty minutes.

He must've had a room nearby, because by the time Sunny and Will arrived at the diner, Randall was already at one of the Formica-topped tables, glancing around, almost bopping in place to the jukebox music. Sunny wasn't sure whether his energy came from eagerness or from the cup of coffee already in his hand. But all trace of animation left Randall's face when he spotted Will's police uniform next to Sunny.

"We were just discussing a story—a theory. Why would you go and make it official? Guess you've forgotten what it's like to be a real journalist," he said sourly.

"Oh, this isn't official," Will said as he and Sunny took seats on the other side of the table. He stared at Randall, but it wasn't his usual cop gaze. It was the look of a male checking out competition.

"Randall MacDermott, Will Price." Sunny was determined to get the introductions done correctly and politely.

Unfortunately, Randall declined to play along. "Price," he said, "the man who would be sheriff, right?" He met Will's stare with the same kind of look, then glanced back at Sunny. "And your friend on the force. I've been using other sources for local background since you weren't interested."

Great, she thought. *They're both going caveman. What's next? Is Will going to drag me out by my hair?*

But Randall donned his bland reporter's mask as he returned to Will. "I'm sure, given your political aspirations, that solving a case like this would be a big deal."

"The only thing I'm interested in is finding out who killed a young woman," Will told Randall in a flat voice. "As the case stands now, things don't seem to hang together."

Randall nodded. "Even in their scandals the Kingsburys are more staid than this."

"I understand you think there might've been an element of blackmail in Eliza Stoughton's life," Will went on, ignoring Randall's comment.

"Randall suggested the blackmailer might be out on Neal's Neck," Sunny added, then broke off the conversation as a waitress came over to get their orders. Will asked for coffee. Sunny, mindful of the late hour, ordered a lemonade. The last thing she wanted was to be kept up with coffee nerves. Their drinks quickly arrived, along with a refill for Randall, who'd taken the moment of silence to regroup. "As I said, it's just a theory." Now that his story had gotten out, he'd apparently decided to downplay everything.

"I thought you told Sunny that you had proof that this Taxman existed," Will challenged him, and Randall rose to the bait.

"I've got ten years' of files from a damned good crime

reporter and conversations with several probable victims, but nobody who'd speak for the record," he responded.

Will gave that a dismissive nod. "You also suggested that Eliza Stoughton died because she recognized this so-called Taxman, who's apparently been in business at least ten years. At this point, our main suspects seem to be the young people in the compound. For one of them to have been running this extortion racket, they'd have had to have started while still in college—or even high school."

"Not impossible," Randall argued. "Augustus de Kruk tightened the purse strings on Carson after a very free-spending freshman year. It's possible that pushed his son to extortion."

"What about Peter Van Twissel?" Sunny asked. "He's in a much lower financial bracket than the others. A little blackmail would go a long way to fund his friendships." She paused. "And if he's really a computer genius, he'd have the programming smarts to bounce payments all over creation." She looked over at Will. "You said that the surveillance cameras on Neal's Neck are recorded on hard drives. If anyone knew how to spoof a computer, it would be Peter."

She also remembered his hands, with all their tiny scars from years of circuit board accidents. Bony but strong.

Randall nodded, but admitted, "You're right. Frankly, I've been looking more at the older generations too. To me, the most likely—" He broke off, waving his hands. "I'll say it again, this is only my personal theory, there's no hard proof behind it."

"Okay, this won't be for attribution. Did I get that right?" Will asked.

"Spoken just like a veteran newsperson," Sunny assured him.

Randall nodded, leaning toward them over the table and lowering his voice. "I think it's the old man. Thomas Neal Kingsbury."

"The Senator?" Sunny frowned dubiously, remembering the patrician man at the dinner table, unconsciously posing for media cameras that were no longer there.

"*Former* senator," Randall corrected. "And the way he lost his seat, with people deserting him for a younger, more approachable rival, it's understandable that he might be a bit vengeful. He got treated shabbily by a lot of his supposedly loyal supporters."

"I know," Sunny said. "My dad mentioned that during his last campaign, Kingsbury was even reaching out to the Kittery Harbor dissidents. Not that it did him much good."

"The Senator still has some friends in Augusta," Will protested. "Enough to get a state police detachment on duty whenever he's in residence on Neal's Neck."

"But that's nothing compared to the weight he used to swing." Randall rested his forearms on the table. "When I heard stories about the Taxman, one of the things that really fascinated me was how he dealt largely in favors, dictating corporate and political decisions. It almost seemed as if the money was of secondary interest."

"Favors are the currency of politics," Will admitted. "You can see it even in the sheriff's department."

"And here I thought it was campaign contributions," Sunny said. "Or do you have to get higher up the food chain before that happens?"

Randall was still busy making his case. "To hijack both of

your metaphors, I think favors would be important currency for someone who got thrown off the food chain. Someone who used to be powerful, but who got the old heave-ho."

But Sunny could see other suspects. "Even so, what about people who are still involved in politics—like the governors? Favors could be just as crucial to them."

"Those two are politicians who won't go much farther than their respective state houses," Randall replied confidently. "Lem took his shot at being the fresh new face in the presidential race and blew it. And unless something huge changes, Tom is a long shot for the next couple of election cycles. I think they'll both end their careers as political has-beens."

"Like the Senator, but not reaching as high." Will scowled at the table. "Could the Taxman be one of them trying for some under-the-table influence?"

"And what about Caleb Kingsbury?" Sunny asked.

Randall shrugged. "A political never-was. He'd barcly gotten elected to his first term as a congressman before that scandal broke over his head. After that, he was political poison. Some people even suggest that was the beginning of the end for the Senator. Certainly, it was a big blot on the Kingsbury name."

"So, who's left? We've pretty much covered all the Kingsbury males and most of the guys in the wedding party," Will said.

"I've got a black horse," Sunny piped up. "How about Lee Trehearne?"

Both Will and Randall turned to stare at her. "What?"

"It just strikes me that an operation like the Taxman's would necessarily require a lot of information. That's what a security guy deals in, too." Sunny recalled Trehearne's furious face when she and Ken Howell had penetrated his defenses. "We know he's got surveillance stuff set up around the compound. And he'd be in a position to find out a lot of stuff, going back to when the Senator was more connected. Maybe he'd relish being the power behind the scenes."

"I hadn't thought of him," Randall admitted. "Or it could be someone on his staff. . . ."

"Or crooked NSA wonks getting transcripts of phone calls and satellite photos of people up to dirty deeds." Will was tired, and he'd obviously had enough of Randall for one night. "You've got a dandy theory, MacDermott, but nothing to back it up. I'm on shaky ground with the state police investigator as it is. If I accuse Trehearne of blackmail, or anybody else for that matter, I'll get laughed off the case. I need more than your say-so, especially when you're saying it could be any of half a dozen different people."

"I'd need access to those people to narrow it down," Randall told him. "And they're all in a private compound behind a state police barricade." He turned to Sunny. "But you, you're inside there. Don't you want to do something more substantial than the puff piece about going out on the bounding main that you wrote tonight?"

"I'm still trying to find my feet in there," she told him. "And it's not exactly easy to toss a casual, 'Hey, have you blackmailed any interesting people lately?' into the conversation."

Randall looked into his coffee cup. "I'd hoped to keep all of this on the down low until I could prove the Taxman existed." He shot a look at Sunny. "Thanks a lot for bringing the cops into it."

"If you're worried about your story leaking, I can assure you that Sunny and I will keep it confidential." Will's tone suggested that it wasn't worth spreading around.

"No, it was interesting to discuss the Taxman with a law-enforcement type—even if you dismissed my ideas," Randall said. "Maybe what I really need to do is find a professional who'll accept them."

Good luck with that. Sunny could just imagine how the no-nonsense Lieutenant Wainwright would react to Randall's theorizing. Aloud, she said, "I guess you'll have to do what you think is best. Nobody's going to hear about the Taxman from Will or me."

That pretty much ended the meeting. Will picked up the tab, and in moments he and Sunny were back in his car. "This is just what we need," Will muttered, "some amateur messing around in the case."

"Right," Sunny agreed. "That's my job."

Will glanced over at her. "It doesn't help that he's an ex-boyfriend." He took a deep breath. "It also shouldn't matter."

Sunny took the cue. Keep it work related. "So, tomorrow, you figure I should try and tackle Beau Bellingham?"

"He's a person of interest as of now," Will said. "At least you can see if what he tells you jibes with what he's telling Wainwright."

"Was he the last to see Eliza?" Sunny asked.

Will shook his head. "She was last seen on a security monitor, passing the main house around midnight."

"Did the surveillance catch her leaving the guesthouse?"

Will nodded.

"And she was heading someplace where there'd be no cameras to record whatever happened." Sunny frowned. "Beau is Carson's friend, and Carson said this was Beau's first visit to Neal's Neck. So how would he know which areas were private—and which weren't?"

"Maybe Eliza set the meeting place," Will suggested. "She was also Priscilla's friend; maybe she'd been there before. We've got a guy meeting a girl. That's pretty simple," he argued.

"Not so simple," Sunny countered. "It's a guy who's been going out with a girl—and just had a big fight with her."

"I've got three words for you," Will said. "Make-up sex. Or is that only two?"

"Then Beau Bellingham just happened to strangle Eliza after?" Sunny shook her head.

"The word you're looking for is unpremeditated," Will responded. "And after the way they made a spectacle of themselves that afternoon, it might explain a certain amount of sneaking around when they decided to bury the hatchet—or whatever. Bellingham creeps off for a booty call, things go badly, and he's left with a dead girlfriend and no alibi."

He grinned at Sunny. "I'm sure you'll figure out a way to toss that question into casual conversation."

"Sure." Sunny sighed. "And speaking of sneaking, now I've got to get back into the house without waking anybody—or disturbing whatever else they may be up to."

10

Even without an alarm clock or a schedule, Sunny still found herself waking up the next morning at the same time she usually rose for work. The old house was quiet as she got washed and dressed, so she was surprised when she padded down the stairs to find coffee, rolls, and various fixings already prepared in the kitchen—and Priscilla and Carson having breakfast. Cillie smiled as Sunny joined them at the table. "Tommy is a partner in his firm and makes his own hours, and Yardley likes to sleep in. But I guess us regular working people are programmed for early rising."

"Not that we necessarily like it." Carson smothered a yawn. "And Peter is the mad genius type who'll work on something until five in the morning and then crash all day."

Sunny saw an opening. "What's the story with your friend Beau?"

Maybe it was the matrimonial hormones speaking, but Cillie went straight into matchmaking mode. "He's single, available, and going to be a doctor."

"Um." Sunny tried to figure out an answer to that without blowing her cover as a murder investigator. "I was really asking why he seems to be asleep most of the time."

"That's because of the brutal schedule he leads." Carson shook his head. "Beau can put in eighty, even a hundred hours a week as a resident. Besides working in the hospital, he's still doing conferences and lectures by day, and he's on call every other night. When he gets some time off, the first couple of days go toward catching up on sleep."

"According to Carson, Beau should be coming out of hibernation today." Priscilla grinned.

"I gotta admire him," Carson said. "Back in school, most of us were just learning how to shuffle money. But from the beginning, Beau was on the premed track. He wanted to do something useful with his life, even if he was also our beer pong champ."

"I suspect he was also the life of the party in the frat houses." Sunny grinned. "So if we wind up doing a beer pong tournament tonight, set me up on his team."

Carson's face took on an interesting expression. "Beer pong. Do you think we could get away with it?" he asked Cillie.

"As long as the Senator doesn't hear about it," she replied. "Maybe out here by the pool. I could talk to Uncle Cale about it."

"It will have to be tonight," Carson said. "There was a text message waiting for me when I got up. My parents get in tomorrow."

Sunny's reportorial antennae quivered. "You make it sound like all fun ends then."

"No, but things will get a bit more . . . conventional." Priscilla chose her words carefully, glancing at her fiancé. "In old WASP families, in the privacy of our summer places, things tend to be a bit, well, informal."

Translation: shabby, Sunny thought.

Carson looked around at the comfortable but hardly stylish dining room. "And, while de Kruk is an old name in New York, there wasn't money behind it until my grandfather made his pile, which then Dad parlayed into the stratosphere. Our new wealth requires a lot of marble, gold plating, and publicity—plus some pretty starchy manners. As my father once put it to me, 'No goddamn SOB is going to call me gauche!'"

"Oh, dear. Will I have to dig out my long white opera gloves for dinner?" Sunny asked.

That got a laugh out of them. "No," Cillie responded, "but I think you will see ties on the guys."

"In that case, I think I'd better go home and collect some more-appropriate clothes." Sunny sighed. She'd hoped to get by with a more casual look, hanging out with Cillie and the younger set. But now she had no choice but to raid what she considered her reporter's wardrobe for anything that would pass muster with the de Kruks.

"Just let me know when you want to go, and I'll arrange for a car," Cillie said.

"Thanks." Sunny poured herself a cup of coffee, got a roll, cut it open, and spread some preserves on the two halves. The warm roll was delicious, and so was the brew. "And now, a nosy blogger question: I was thinking that today's post might be about wedding presents."

"Oh, there've been several parties already with gifts galore." Carson rolled his eyes.

Priscilla dove into the nuts and bolts. "We have a few wedding registries, though of course some people sent old family pieces."

"AKA, ancient monstrosities that they didn't want in their own houses anymore," Carson put in. "Maybe someday, when we have the space, we could have a 'dud gifts' room, where all that stuff can sit around and be ugly together. Which is sort of what they're doing right now, up at the big house."

"The gifts are here, not still in New York?" Sunny asked in surprise.

"Oh, yeah, taking up most of the old rear parlor," Carson said. "We needed the space. Some of the stuff was large, as well as ugly."

"And some of it is interesting—living history." From Priscilla's tone of voice, this was a discussion they'd had more than once. "I'll walk you over once we're finished here, Sunny. You can look the collection over and decide whether it's worth a story."

Sunny allowed herself to savor another cup of coffee before she told Cillie that she was ready. Priscilla led the way past the roadblock and along the path that led to the main house. They passed one of the ever-present security guys in his black Windbreaker. Sunny looked back, but for once this guy wasn't checking them out at all—either of them. Instead, he was talking into a microphone set on his shoulder.

As Sunny and Cillie approached the house, one of the compound's golf carts came zooming up from the opposite direction, and Lee Trehearne jumped off in front of them.

His greeting was polite enough, especially to Priscilla, but he looked at Sunny as if she were a one-woman torch-waving mob advancing on the house.

Hmmm, Sunny thought, *I guess I know who that guy we passed was talking to on his radio.*

She went to go around Trehearne, but he stepped into her path, saying, "Well, Ms. Coolidge, what brings you here?"

"Priscilla is bringing me to take a look at the wedding gifts," Sunny replied. "I'm planning on doing a blog post, maybe taking a few pictures. . . ."

Trehearne's lips quivered a little. "The gifts that my people are supposed to keep secure?"

Here's a chance to extend an olive branch, Sunny thought. "Well, sure. I think your security efforts deserve some good press. We could have you and some of your guys in the pictures, too. Let any bad guys out there know what they're up against."

"The idea is not to let them know anything about the compound," Trehearne said.

"It might help discourage them a little," Sunny countered pleasantly, "if they knew the house was surrounded by surveillance cameras, for instance."

"That's possible," Trehearne admitted. Then his eyes sharpened. "Who told you about the house surveillance?" His tone suggested that whoever had opened his mouth wouldn't have a job much longer. Sunny drew a deep breath. The last thing she wanted to do was get into an argument with this guy. "Look, Mr. Trehearne, I don't want to give away any security secrets. I'm just looking for a nice story to humanize the proceedings here."

"Really, Lee," Priscilla joined in, "do you think anyone's

going to come in and steal the crystal and silverware? Besides," she gave a little shudder and said as an aside to Sunny, "as for some of the old family pieces that came our way, I'd never admit it in front of Carson, but I wouldn't exactly be heartbroken if some of those monstrosities magically disappeared."

She continued on her way into the house, Sunny behind her, and Trehearne right behind them both. Sunny's wise-cracking alter ego immediately sprang to life. *What's his problem? Is he afraid you're going to slip some soup spoons into your pocket?*

Sunny had only a hazy idea of the layout of the mansion. The only parts she knew were the entrance hall and the route to the dining room. Now she followed Priscilla into one of the wings and down a long hallway, then took a right and came up to a pair of beautiful old sliding doors with yet another security guy standing in front of them. He drew himself up to attention, shooting a "What do I do now, Boss?" look at Trehearne.

The security honcho sighed. "Open the doors, Alvin. Ms. Kingsbury wants to inspect the gifts."

After this buildup, Sunny was anticipating something on the order of Ali Baba's cave. And as Alvin the guard pushed one of the doors aside, the view seemed pretty damned close. The first thing Sunny saw was something that looked like a lazy Susan on steroids—or maybe hit by gamma rays. It was a sort of buffet centerpiece that rose almost three feet high. In the middle was a basket in the form of a Chinese pagoda, surrounded by a framework of a good dozen arms disguised as sinuous tree limbs, each holding out serving dishes. Altogether, the thing was larger than Sunny's kitchen table.

Priscilla stood beside it with a critical glare. "It's a solid silver epergne, more than two hundred years old, and takes up more space than some pieces of furniture," she said, echoing Sunny's thoughts. "What are we supposed to do with it?"

"Well, it's got lots of room for chips and dips at a party," Sunny suggested. "Or you could put in plumbing and have private bird baths."

Cillie laughed at that. "I like the idea. But no, we'll probably hide it somewhere, then spring it as an awful surprise when the next generation of the family gets married."

They went around the huge, ornate, and heavy serving tray to a table filled with crystal glassware of all descriptions. Sunny stared. "Now I get it. If you're going to have a party big enough to use all those glasses, one of those silver thingies isn't going to be enough."

Cillie ducked her head in embarrassment. "Having every kind of glass is sort of a de Kruk thing. They're completists." She moved over to a small wooden chest. "Now this is an heirloom I actually like. I'm hoping it will be our everyday silver." She opened the top to display a dully gleaming set of knives, forks, and so on, all of them looking old enough that George Washington could have eaten with them.

Sunny hefted a soup spoon heavy enough to brain someone. "Solid silver again, huh? Well, you'll burn calories just by hefting these things while you eat."

They went through the rest of the wedding loot. The

chinaware was modern, and some of the "old gifts" were hilarious, like the moose head that was supposedly a hunting trophy from Teddy Roosevelt, or the shark-tooth necklace some Kingsbury ancestor brought back from a missionary stint in the South Seas. Sunny pulled out her digital camera and shot a few pictures, starting with a photo of a glowering Trehearne next to the oversized epergne, for scale. Other shots featured a smiling Priscilla holding up various items.

By the time she finished with the photography, Sunny had the rough outline for her post already in her head. She thanked Priscilla, smiled at Lee Trehearne and Alvin, and headed back to the guesthouse and her computer. Then it was a case of generating her story and weaving in appropriate photos. By the time she was done, they were well into the day, but Sunny was pleased.

I bet Ken will like it, too, she thought. Which reminded her that she should go for more local color, something the *Courier*'s readers might appreciate. *Maybe I can talk to Fiona Ormond and get a list of local companies involved in the wedding. I'm sure there must be some; Priscilla would have wanted to use them, even if the snooty de Kruks might not have considered it.*

As Sunny typed in a reminder note to herself, someone knocked on the door to her room. Cillie stood in the doorway, dressed in a damp bathing suit and her terrycloth beach wrap. "I hope I'm not disturbing your work," she apologized.

"Just finishing," Sunny said.

"Oh, good." Priscilla paused for a moment, then lowered her voice. "Uncle Cale volunteered to get some supplies for the—um—activity you suggested, and he asked if you wanted to share the ride. I wondered if you wanted to use it as an opportunity to go back to your place and get some more clothes."

Sunny had a brief flash of being forced to sit down to dinner with the de Kruks in her old bathing suit, and sighed. "I suppose the sooner I get some more stuff together, the better."

"Uncle Cale said you could meet him in the parking area with the golf carts in, say, half an hour. Is that okay?"

"Yes, I'll be done and ready." Sunny watched Cillie set off down the hallway, and then shut the door. She returned to her computer, and sent an e-mail to Ken that her blog post was ready to go. Then she got out her cell phone. Her dad sounded as if he'd been roused from a nap, but he was happy to hear from her. "Are you going to be discontented with your old room now that you've been sleeping in the lap of luxury?" Mike teased.

"The furniture in my old room is probably newer than the stuff in here," she told him. "Is everything okay?"

"Yeah, I had a salad supper last night, afraid the food police would come in and bust me if I had a hamburger." Mike paused. "You're missed—not just by me, but by your furry friend. He's been moping around, barely touching his food. Spends most of his time by the living-room window. If I didn't know any better, I'd think he was watching for you."

"Shadow was pretty upset when I left," Sunny said. "But that sounds more like dog behavior. Something that I'd expect from Toby—except he'd probably chew off the windowsill while he was waiting."

Mike laughed, but his heart wasn't in it. "That dumb dog," he growled.

"But I wasn't calling to make cracks about Toby," Sunny said. "I have to come home and get some more clothes. The de Kruks are arriving tomorrow, and apparently that means the dress code gets stricter."

"Well, I'll be glad to see you," Mike told her. "As for the furball, we'll just wait and see."

About twenty minutes later, Sunny walked along the path that led to the miniature parking lot with the golf carts and found Caleb Kingsbury leaning against one. "I hope we're not climbing aboard that jalopy to go into town," she told him. "It's a little open for my taste."

He laughed. "No, the real cars are over there." He pointed into the distance. "But I figured it was easier to meet you here than give directions." He and Sunny strolled along in the direction he'd pointed. Clothes on her mind, Sunny noticed that Cale himself was wearing a faded T-shirt and a pair of disreputable cargo shorts. The only decent things on him were a new-looking pair of Top-Siders.

"I see you've dressed to meet your public," Sunny said as they reached an area, shaded by trees, where several town cars were parked.

He turned with a grin. "What, I'm not fancy enough to go to a wholesaler's to buy beer?"

There's one local business I can't link to this wedding, Sunny thought. A source for champagne, maybe, but a beer supplier—no. Cale Kingsbury wasn't finished yet. "Did Cillie mention that you're expected to download an official set of rules for this beer pong tournament?"

"Wonderful." Sunny rolled her eyes. "I only said that

as a joke, you know, and now it seems to have taken on a life of its own."

"Oh, just go with the flow," Cale told her with another grin. "So many places have their own house rules. This will avoid arguments."

Which you don't want when there's a lot of beer being consumed, Sunny silently agreed. "Okay." She sighed. "I'll take care of that after I come back from upgrading my wardrobe."

"Oh, right. Got to clean up for the de Kruks." Cale looked down at his grungy outfit. "I know I have one suit aboard the *Merlin*. Hope I've got some other presentable stuff stowed away. Otherwise, I'll have to dig out something that's been sitting around for God knows how many years." He patted his stomach. "Will it still fit?"

"More to the point, will you be able to get the smell of mothballs out?"

"Maybe if I hang them from a yardarm in the fresh air," he said as he bypassed the shiny black town cars for a much humbler and nondescript station wagon. Jingling the keys, Cale opened the passenger side door. He handed Sunny in like the practiced gentleman he was, then went around to the driver's side and climbed aboard. Inside the enclosed space, Sunny got a strong whiff of Cale's cologne and grimaced unintentionally. He instantly looked contrite. "A little too much? I'd been working up a sweat on the boat and splashed some on."

More like bathed in it, Sunny's cranky side suggested.

"It's an interesting scent," she said aloud.

"It's sandalwood, and a bunch of other spices. I've worn it for years, ever since a lady friend bought it for me at a little place in Paris. My father gives me grief about it. To him all a gentleman needs is a discreet dab of bay rum."

"Well, times change," Sunny said.

He started the car, and soon they were passing the troopers and the roadblock. Some people suddenly darted at them from across the street, and Sunny saw the cameras a second too late. She noticed that Cale had arranged one hand to cover the bottom half of his face.

Great, she thought. *They probably got me with my mouth hanging open.*

"Sorry, should have warned you," he apologized. "I keep forgetting you're not used to this, being from the other side."

"You make it sound like the dark side," she said.

"I guess it's all in the way you see it," Cale replied. "How is it going, by the way? Cillie seems to like you."

"And that's even before I suggested a nice round of beer pong."

Cale refused to be deflected. "How about the others?" he asked. "I saw Tommy Neal giving you the 'I'm too important to notice you' routine yesterday. Is he acting a bit more human today? Is Beau?"

"I'm still wondering if I'll ever get to see Beau fully awake," Sunny replied.

"He strikes me as a nice kid. So does Carson."

Sunny nodded. "He and Priscilla seem to get along well."

"Yeah, that's a pleasant dividend when they're trapped in something more like a business merger than an engagement." Caleb frowned.

Sunny glanced at him.

"Not for attribution," he said.

She nodded, but pushed. "You're suggesting . . ."

"I'm suggesting that Augustus de Kruk finally realized he's carrying too much baggage to ever be president." Cale shook his head. "I think he finally got the point at one of those political dinners. He wasn't up on the dais to be roasted, but it seemed like every speaker sent a zinger his way. For a guy who spends a lot of time on television, he was lousy at acting as though it was all in good fun. Carson, on the other hand, came off looking pretty good on Augustus's reality shows. Not just a pretty face, either—he gave the impression of being a capable executive."

"So you think Augustus has decided to set things up for Carson, politically?" Sunny asked.

"He's not going to have the boy run for office next Tuesday, but yeah, I suspect Augustus went looking for a little political oomph to add to Carson's image. And as it turned out, we Kingsburys had a girl who was the right age." Cale turned to her, his face dead serious. "My father is no spring chicken anymore, and he's determined to have his blood in the White House before he goes. He'd rather it was one of her brothers, but he's old-fashioned enough not to even seriously consider Cillie for the starring role. He'll settle for First Lady. So yeah, it's not a shotgun wedding, but Cillie and Carson were strongly encouraged."

"Then I suppose it's a good thing they like one another." Sunny sighed. "Was it this way in Camelot?"

"You mean the Kennedys and the Bouviers?" Cale asked. "I've heard stories—"

Sunny waved that off. "No, no, I meant Arthur and Guinevere. Although maybe all that dynastic stuff would have seemed a lot more natural, way back when."

They made polite chitchat for the rest of the drive to Sunny's house. She apologized for taking Cale out of his way, but he waved off her concerns. "I want to do my shopping as far away from Wilawiport as possible," he said as he held the door for Sunny. "How long do you think you need?"

"Could I have an hour?" Sunny asked. "I'd like to visit with my dad."

*

Shadow knew how to wait, if he had to. He'd done it before, hunkered down in front of mouse holes, waiting for the prey to emerge. But it had been a while since he'd had to do that. And this wait seemed to stretch on for a long, long time.

He skimped on sleep, which was a very bad thing for a healthy cat. Shadow knew that, when he found himself nodding off in his water bowl. Bad, bad, bad.

The Old One tried to be nice to him, feeding him and talking to him. But it wasn't the same as having Sunny around. And when the Old One settled himself on the long, soft chair, it just about drove Shadow crazy. He began to consider one of the things that made light on the table beside the sleeping two-legs. A little determined pushing, and it would fall to make a wonderful crash, sure to wake the Old One. If Shadow couldn't sleep, why should this human get to?

Finally, Shadow was so tired, he decided to try for a light doze. He scrambled up onto the pillows away from the snoring Old One, then stretched to climb onto the very top of the couch, beside the window. The sun was coming in and it was very comfortable, but Shadow didn't care about that. He wanted to see and hear what was going on in the front of the house, and this was the best place to do that. He draped himself along the top of the couch and peered out the window with eyes that grew heavier and heavier until finally his head slid down.

Just a short nap, he told himself, *a little doze.*

But when his eyes opened, the sun had moved quite a distance in the sky. Shadow blinked. What had wakened him? It wasn't the Old One, who made his usual noises. No, it was the rumble of an engine. Shaking himself awake, Shadow saw a go-fast thing come up the driveway and stop. A strange two-legs got out and opened a door. Then Sunny came out!

Shadow gave a stifled mew of excitement and dashed for the door. He heard the rattle of keys, and when the door opened, he raced around Sunny in a dance of welcome. She'd come back! She'd come home!

But even in the middle of his greeting, he caught that spicy, strange scent he'd found on Sunny before. And it was much stronger. Shadow faltered. What was going on here? Everything seemed all right. Sunny and the Old One sat down and talked. But Shadow moved restlessly around, marking Sunny's shins and ankles. Couldn't the Old One smell the strange scent? Especially the hint of male beneath it?

Maybe not, Shadow thought. *With all the stinks the Old One gives off, maybe he can't smell anything anymore.*

After a while, Sunny looked at the thing on her wrist. That was always a bad sign. When humans did that, they often jumped up and started running around, ignoring cats.

Sure enough, Sunny got up. Shadow followed, determined not to let her out of his sight. But when she climbed the stairs and got to her room, she closed the door in his face!

Shadow raised a paw to claw at the wood, but he knew that wouldn't do much. Instead, he went across the hall and hid inside the room of tiles, barely letting one eye peek around the door frame. It was cool in there—cold, really—but he kept his post.

It was worth it! After a while, Sunny came out, and Shadow all but sprang across the hall, getting into the room before Sunny closed the door. He stretched up to look over the top of her bed—and his worst suspicions were confirmed. She had piles of clothing up there, not fresh from the wash, but with dead smells from sitting in a closet. He had to get very close to get any scents at all. What did she want with these old things? Was she going to get rid of them?

He heard Sunny's footsteps in the hall and darted under the bed, peering out as she came into the room. Worse and worse. She came in with another one of those big things for carrying clothes and put it up on the bed, then began putting things in it. Shadow stayed hidden until she turned away to the closet. Then he made his move.

She's not leaving without me this time, he thought.

11

Sunny lugged the soft-sided suitcase down to the front hall. It was a bit unwieldy on the stairway, a little heavier than she'd expected. She hadn't packed all that much, really—she'd just chosen the large case because she didn't want the outfits to get crushed. Out of the clothes she'd arranged on the bed, she'd finally picked a pair of suits, one with pants, one with a skirt, both dressy without being too sedate. Then she went back to the closet and took out a party dress, its coral color a bit bolder. It worked well with Sunny's hair and her tan, but didn't show off too much. Along with the necessary accessories and the things she had up at Neal's Neck already, Sunny hoped those outfits would take her through the next few days.

As she reached the foot of the stairs, she held the bag high, alert for Shadow. *We are not going to have another game of detach the cat this time, buddy.*

But Shadow was nowhere to be seen.

Still holding the bag awkwardly to avoid a sneak attack, Sunny went into the living room, where Mike sat on the couch.

"Shadow in here?" she asked.

Her dad shook his head. "I haven't seen him since he took off up the stairs after you."

"I had to keep him out of my room while I was packing." Now she felt guilty about it. "He went a little crazy with the bag I took yesterday."

Mike shrugged. "Well, he didn't turn up here."

Maybe he's sulking, Sunny thought as she went down the hall to the kitchen. Often when Shadow got in a mood, he'd scowl down at the world from a perch up on the top of Mount Refrigerator.

But Shadow wasn't there, either.

Now Sunny found herself torn. She didn't want a scene like the one they'd gone through the last time she'd left. But she didn't want to go without saying good-bye to Shadow, either. She was debating whether to check out a few more of his hideouts when the doorbell rang. That took the decision out of her hands. She came down the hall to see Mike at the door, speaking with Cale Kingsbury. Usually her dad would be more animated when talking with anyone with a connection to local politics, but Mike was politely silent as Cale chatted.

Polite—or maybe a bit standoffish? Sunny suddenly wondered. Years may have passed since the scandal that brought Cale Kingsbury down, but that didn't mean it had been forgotten hereabouts. One of the more potentially negative aspects of the Kittery Harbor Way.

Either Cale didn't notice or he'd gotten used to that reaction. Or both. He greeted Sunny and took her bag, said good-bye to Mike, and then escorted her back to the car. Cale deposited the case in the back of the station wagon beside his load of contraband (hidden from view under an old picnic blanket) and then held the door for Sunny. As he slid into his seat, his face had a cat-who-ate-the-canary expression. "This is gonna be fun tonight."

"You know, it started out as a joke, but now it's taken on a life of its own," Sunny said. "Sounds as though you're looking forward to this game more than Cillie and Carson are. I thought you were just the facilitator."

"And you're the instigator," Cale reminded her. "But I think it's the right thing. The kids need to cut loose, and this is a fairly benign way to do that. Besides, I figure buying the beer buys me an invitation, too." His grin was infectious, and mischief danced in his eyes. "I got this Belgian ale, very high-octane. It's gonna be a blast, and I intend to be there as soon as I can ditch the grown-ups."

He sounded so much like one of Sunny's college boyfriends, she had to laugh.

They discussed the finer points of beer pong for most of the ride up to Wilawiport, with several disagreements over things like defensive deflections and penalties.

"That's why you've got to download a set of rules from someplace," Cale said. "Then they'll be there in black and white. People will be stuck with them."

"All right, all right," Sunny capitulated. "I'll take care of it after I get up in my room."

The town car rolled past the roadblock, with no paparazzi jumping out of the bushes. Sunny felt a little disappointed. She'd been prepared this time, putting on large sunglasses and a baseball cap with a long peak.

They came to a stop outside the girls' guesthouse. As Sunny got out and Cale got her bag, she asked, "Where will you hide the supplies? I don't think you can just slip them into a refrigerator."

"I've got ice and a couple of those Styrofoam chests." He kept his voice down, glancing over toward the road-block. "We're a little too close to the outside world to go unloading things here."

Shaking her head, Sunny took her bag and lugged it up to her room. She'd barely deposited her burden on the faded quilt bedspread when she heard a knock on the door. It was Priscilla.

I suspect that Trehearne's not the only one using the security guards to find out who's where, Sunny thought. Cillie just about confirmed that with her first words. "I heard you were back, and I wanted to catch you. It's Beau's turn to do the lunch run, bringing sandwiches and stuff from the kitchen of the big house. If you just sort of bumped into him over there, you could spend some time alone with him."

Great, Sunny thought. *Sounds like I'm being set up with a potential murderer.*

Priscilla quickly convinced her otherwise, though, her expression darkening as she spoke. "I haven't forgotten why you're really here—so I talked to him a little bit." She waved her hands. "Not telling him about why you're here, just saying that he couldn't lie around ignoring you. This will give the two of you a chance to talk. From the way you asked about him at breakfast, I'd have to be pretty dense not to realize that you're interested in Beau, and I don't mean romantically. I shouldn't be surprised, after the way he and Eliza got into it the afternoon before—" She broke off her words.

Sunny nodded. "Do you know what the two of them were fighting about?"

Priscilla shook her head. "We're supposed to be too well-bred to eavesdrop—and of course, there was music playing. By the time it got loud enough for me to notice, they'd sort of gotten to the generic insult stage. He called her a social-climbing bitch, she said he was just a general bastard. That sort of thing."

Sunny frowned. So it sounded loud, but not exactly personal. Neither Beau nor Eliza seemed to be throwing actual dirt in each other's faces. *Well, that social-climbing comment was a bit sharp, but it's kind of hard to imagine a spat like that leading to murder,* she thought.

Still, Beau was Will's prime candidate, with at least a possible check by his name when it came to opportunity. She ought to take a shot.

"Okay, just let me unpack," Sunny said. It wasn't so much about hanging up her things as it was making sure those suits got a proper airing. She'd already twitted Cale about him smelling like mothballs; no way was she going to sit down with the de Kruks in a cloud of eau de cedar.

Cillie bit her lip. "I don't think there's time. I stalled him as long as I could, waiting for you, but Beau was starting for the kitchen when I headed up here."

"Then I'd better catch him." Sunny followed Priscilla outside, thinking, *Another plan shot to hell.*

She managed to catch up with Beau on his way back down the path between the big house and the pool. He was carrying a big cardboard carton easily enough, but just as Sunny came up, a breeze sent a couple of bags of chips airborne. Sunny darted to pick them up. "Let me give you a hand."

"Oh, thanks," he said, "Sunny."

There was a barely perceptible pause before he used her name. Had he been trying to remember it, or debating whether to use it?

"Put that thing down for a minute, and let's see what I can help carry," Sunny suggested.

Beau dropped to one knee, setting the carton down on the graveled walk. The breeze plucked at the Hawaiian shirt he wore over another green scrub shirt—or maybe the same one Sunny had seen him in yesterday.

"Maybe I shouldn't have asked for the chips," Beau said. "They had to put them on top, otherwise they'd get crushed. But I figured we'd better have some munchies around for later." He gave Sunny a closer look as he knelt with the carton. "Did you really suggest beer pong?"

"Guilty as charged," Sunny replied.

"What, are you trying to get us all drunk so we'll talk about stuff we shouldn't?" He broke off, running a hand across his eyes and then down his face. "Sorry, that didn't come out very well. Carson and Cillie told me you're a reporter, doing stories about the wedding planning and stuff. But after the whole mess with Eliza . . ."

Take the opening, Sunny decided. "How did you meet her? I understand she was in Priscilla's crowd."

"She is—was," Beau corrected himself. "We hooked up when Carson and Cillie began getting serious. One of those big de Kruk mob scenes. How many parties have you attended where they've got a stage manager shepherding you in front of the cameras right on schedule to make the evening news? But we hung out and then dated a bit when my schedule allowed. Frankly, I think she was on the rebound. She'd been engaged, but it all blew up. She didn't like to talk about it."

He blinked, as if dealing with an unpleasant memory. "But Eliza was really on my case to be my plus-one when I got the invite to this get-together. I thought it was kind of pushy, but Carson and Cillie were cool. To tell the truth, I was really looking forward to taking a break up here. Carson said it would be nice and quiet."

"But it didn't turn out that way?"

Beau's face tightened. "So now it's about that stupid fight? Does everybody know about that? Will I see my face on *Eagle Eye* while they play detective and wonder if I'm 'involved' in Eliza's murder?"

"I can't promise what *Eagle Eye* will do," Sunny said. "As you pointed out, I am a reporter, but there is such a thing as off the record. If you say that up front, reporters can't quote you. Not all reporters follow that as strictly as they should nowadays, but those are supposed to be the rules."

"Why would you even tell me that?" Beau frowned.

"Because I think you're going to need a crash course in dealing with reporters." Sunny gave it to him straight.

Beau paused for a moment. "You mean they think . . . ? Sure they do. That detective guy seemed like just a schlubby-looking older guy at first, but he's like some of the surgeons in the hospital. Put a scalpel in their hands—"

He stopped again. "Does that detective think I killed Eliza?"

"I can't reveal my sources," Sunny told him.

Beau turned round to sit on the grass, his head in his

hands. "This is like a nightmare. I came here to chill out." He looked up at her. "You don't know what a pressure cooker a medical residency can be. Becoming a doctor is sort of like joining the biggest fraternity there is, but getting there, they don't just put you through hell week, it's more like hell years. I've put in a hundred and twenty hours a week sometimes."

Sunny nodded. Carson had said something along the same lines.

"So I come up here, Carson's told me how quiet and secluded the place is, and all I really want to do is sleep. I mean, I know I'm supposed to stand up for Carson on the wedding day, and I'll do whatever they want of me. But my whole plan for coming up here was to veg out. With Eliza pestering me, I was kinda down to my last nerve, and the minute we got here, Eliza started getting on it."

"Why do you think that was?"

He looked down for a moment, then up at her again. "I couldn't say, but she was in a foul mood even on the way up here. Carson had one of his dad's private planes fly us up from New York—Carson, Peter, me, and Eliza. I thought she'd be delighted at such a sweet setup. Instead, she was rude to the cabin steward and drank a lot. All I wanted to do was sleep. We were going to be in the air for about an hour and a half, and I intended to get some rest."

"And?" Sunny asked.

"It seemed to drive her crazy that I wasn't paying attention to her. Eliza insisted on talking to me, even when I was dozing off. She kept it up when we got to the compound. And when we were around the pool, she even got worse. She kicked me to wake me up, and I told her to knock it off. Instead, she jumped down my throat."

Beau took a long, deep breath. "Maybe I could have handled it better if I hadn't been so burnt out. But when she began screaming at me, I started shouting back." His shoulders slumped. "It's not as though I was the only one—just the one who got it the worst. Eliza also got into it with Carson and Tommy Neal, too. I thought I was pretty tightly wound up when I joined up with Carson to come here, but now I'm wondering if maybe Eliza was worse." *If Eliza was being blackmailed,* Sunny thought, remembering Randall's theory, *that might've made her a little touchy.*

Beau stood up. "So that's the story. I liked Eliza—not an undying love thing, but she was cool, and pretty, and we had some good times." He looked down at his hands. "It's not like I had any reason to want to murder Eliza. Guess it sounds kind of corny, but the whole reason I wanted to become a doctor was to help people, not to kill them."

"Well, you can't help it if the police suspect you," Sunny said, feeling a sudden surge of sympathy for the big guy. "I suppose they've been pretty careful with you, since you're on a big shot's home turf. They'd get a lot tougher if they had some strong evidence linking you to the crime. Don't get yourself in trouble with them by telling them lies. And if they do start questioning you seriously, remember you're allowed to get a lawyer. And stay quiet until one gets there."

Beau Bellingham bent down to get the carton of food. "I didn't think I'd be saying this, but thanks, Sunny."

Don't mention it, Sunny sourly thought as she collected the bags of chips. *I do this for all the murder suspects I bump into.*

*

Shadow absentmindedly licked one paw. One of his claws had broken in his struggle to escape from Sunny's bag. After being squashed, carried, and then left in a cold, dark place, he had wormed his way to the top of the bag. It had one of those open-close things the two-legs used, a little piece of metal on a long track. He'd dealt with them before.

But he'd never had to open one from the inside. Just getting hold of the little piece had been a struggle, and moving it had resulted in the painful break. Annoying, but not too bad. There wasn't any blood.

He'd gotten the bag a little bit open, but then he'd been interrupted by sudden light, getting picked up, carried . . . and squashed down again.

He'd landed heavily on a bouncy surface—a bed—and heard Sunny's voice. But by the time he'd gotten a paw out and opened the bag enough to squirm out, Sunny was gone.

Searching this new house had not been good. Everything was old and dusty, and even the air smelled dead. Even worse, he hadn't found Sunny.

So Shadow found a way out and began exploring outside. There were fewer houses around here than at Sunny's place—or was that Sunny's old place? Was this Sunny's new place? There was plenty of grass and some bushes, quite a few interesting smells that had distracted his search. But he only caught a few brief whiffs to show that Sunny had been in various places.

Then Shadow's stomach began telling him it was time to eat. He'd walked a long way to some of the other houses nearby, hoping to find one of those bags that humans filled with old food. It might not be the best tasting, but it would fill him up.

The problem was, the two-legs around here locked those bags up in strong containers. He began to lose hope as he approached the back of yet another house to see a human female standing behind a glass door. When she saw Shadow, the two-legs knelt down to peer out at him.

Shadow stretched up, resting his forepaws against the glass to get a better look. Suddenly he watched a flurry of motion as another cat, a She by the size of her, appeared, flinging out her paws and raking at the glass with her claws.

This stupid She wants to scare me away, Shadow thought. He'd seen this before, cats who were very brave so long as there was a door or window between them. He could understand not wanting to share a special two-legs with some wanderer. Sometimes Sunny had annoyed him by feeding some passing freeloader. But no self-respecting cat should threaten what she—or he—couldn't do. Claws were real . . . and so was blood.

Sure enough, when the human opened the door, the brave warrior-She disappeared. But happily the two-legs brought out a paper plate with some food on it. Shadow took a bite. It was unfamiliar, and rather rich. His stomach would probably make noises later. But he ate, taking small bites.

And as soon as the door had shut, those white paws and claws appeared again. He didn't even bother to pretend-fight. As soon as he had enough, Shadow trotted along. It looked as though he'd be stuck around here for a while. He still had to find a safe place to rest.

*

As the day progressed, Sunny found herself looking forward to the clandestine beer pong tournament. If someone had told her a week ago that she'd be spending the day lounging beside the private pool in a million-dollar compound, she'd have had a hard time believing it. She'd have given this someone an even harder time if they'd suggested that such an R&R setting would get on her nerves.

The fact of the matter, though, was that she felt restless. She swam, she sat in the sun for a while, she chatted with the wedding party, she had something to drink—something non-alcoholic, she didn't want to get a head start on the evening's competition. Carson, Priscilla, and the others were perfectly nice—even though Beau was still mainly catching up on his sleep. But there were odd silences, sudden stilted moments that showed no one was really comfortable.

Then it was time to change for dinner. Sunny returned to her room to discover her travel bag still lying on the bed. She'd been so distracted, she'd forgotten to come back and hang everything up.

"Wonderful," she muttered. "Everything is probably all creased now." Would she be able to get hold of an iron?

But when she opened the bag, she not only found creases, but cat hair all over everything.

I guess keeping him out only worked so far, she thought, *and this is the way Shadow punished me. That crazy cat! Now I've got to find one of those sticky roller gizmos before I can iron anything.*

She hung up the garments, keeping them far away from her other clothes, then dressed for dinner and put on her company manners, and went to deal with the "grown-ups," as Cale called them.

Dinner was another tedious affair. Conversation seemed to die around the Senator, except for topics like politics. Mrs. Kingsbury tried a couple of times to talk about the upcoming wedding, but even Fiona Ormond couldn't keep the talk going. Sunny was a little surprised to learn that either Cillie's grandmother was computer-literate or had somebody on staff who was, because she complimented Sunny on her blog post about the wedding gifts.

At last the meal ended, and people began to drift away. Sunny went back to her room to collect the beer pong rules she'd printed out earlier. When she emerged, she encountered Priscilla, her eyes sparkling and conspiratorial.

"Everybody's looking forward to this," she said in a hushed voice, as if her grandfather could hear her from hundreds of yards away. Downstairs, they met the Neals, who looked livelier than Sunny had seen them thus far. Tommy even said hello and chatted a bit as they walked over to the pool.

The sun was going down, and there were long shadows. But only a couple of lights were on, mainly in the area around the cabana, where Carson, Beau, and Peter were manhandling a decrepit-looking old Ping-Pong table out onto the deck surrounding the pool.

"That was down in the basement of the big house," Cillie said. "I don't know how Uncle Cale managed to smuggle it out here."

Tommy joined the guys in setting up the table. "This will make the game simpler," he said. "It's the regulation size."

Sunny held up the rules. "Okay, I assume you all know

the basic idea of the game. Each side fills a certain number of cups one-third of the way with beer. Teams take alternate turns tossing or bouncing a Ping-Pong ball into their opponents' cups."

Sunny stopped. "We've got the table. Have we got a ball?"

Peter Van Twissel held up a crisp new package of Ping-Pong balls and a sleeve of plastic cups. "It looks as though Cale took care of everything."

"Good." Sunny resumed reading. "Each member of a team gets one shot. Whether a toss or a bounce, the shooter's elbow must remain below the level of the table. If a ball lands in a team's cup, one of the team members must drink that cup. If the ball lands in that cup again, the game is over, and the losing team must consume all of the cups remaining on the table. So, if the enemy's ball lands in a cup, it's a good idea to drink it right away, rather than risk a double hit. You can toss or you can bounce the ball toward your opponents' cups. But if the ball is bounced, the opponents can try to deflect it away."

"That's not the way we played it at school," Carson objected.

"It's the way we played it," Cillie replied.

"And this is why I was advised to download something." Sunny waved the paper in her hand. "In case of arguments, these are the rules we'll go by." She went back to reading. "Twice in the course of a game, a team may rerack its cups. There's a diagram showing how they can be arranged. If a ball circles the rim of a cup, the defending team can try to flick it away. Of course, if you spill the cup, it counts for the other side. If one team clears all the opposing team's cups, the opposing team still has a turn. Each member of the team is allowed to keep shooting, until he or she misses. When all the team members have missed, and there are still cups on the table, they have to share the beer in those cups."

She looked around. "So now we consider the question of teams. We've got an odd number of people—"

"Count me out," Beau Bellingham said. "I'm not up for a night of drinking."

"Well, Cillie and I will be a team," Carson said.

"And Yardley and I will be one," Tommy Neal announced.

Peter looked at Sunny. "I guess that leaves you and me."

Sunny shrugged. "Next question—how many cups?"

They decided on six, which would make for a quicker game. Carson and Tommy went into the cabana, emerging with a heavy cooler. Peter had already unwrapped the package of plastic cups. The guys opened a couple bottles of beer and began pouring.

"They should be in a triangle," Sunny called, "with the wide end flush with the end of the table."

"So who goes first?" Cillie asked.

"One member of each team come to this end." Sunny opened the package of Ping-Pong balls. Cillie, Tommy, and Peter joined her. She gave each of them a ball. "Now, without looking at the cups, toss your ball toward them." Priscilla and Tommy both managed to get a ball into a cup. Peter missed altogether.

"So, Peter and I will play whoever wins this game." Sunny said as Carson retrieved the balls. "Cillie, you and Tommy toss to see which team goes first."

This time, Priscilla missed while Tommy hit, so the game proper began. It was a close-fought battle, but in the end, the Neals eliminated all of Carson and Cillie's cups while two of theirs remained. The de Kruk-Kingsbury alliance drained the cups, and while the field of battle was being restored, Beau stood up. "Sorry, guys," he said. "It's been fun, but I think I'd rather sack out." He gave Peter Van Twissel a tap on the arm. "Good luck, bro. You, too, Sunny."

They didn't have much, though. The game quickly developed into a slaughter. Sunny managed to clear three of the Neals' cups, but Peter missed every shot. "I'll drink the extra one," he said, his voice gallant but a little slurred. The Belgian ale was already hitting him pretty hard.

Priscilla and Carson pulled off a victory in the next round, and proceeded to roll over Sunny and Peter in the next. This time, Peter managed to land one of his tosses not in the cup, but in the pool.

Tommy and Yardley Neal fought their way back to victory in the next go-round and made mincemeat of Sunny and Peter. This time, he attempted to block a bouncing ball and managed to spill two of their cups down the front of his pants. As he stood blinking down at the spreading stain on his khakis, Cale Kingsbury came strolling around the pool. "That doesn't look good, Van Twissel."

Peter jerked his eyes up to Cale's, an ugly expression on his face. "I don't need you to point out the obvious."

Apparently, all that beer he's taken on has made for a real Jekyll and Hyde transformation, Sunny thought as she took in the scene. *Drunk, humiliated, angry—and now he's found a focus.*

Cale tried to smooth things over. "I just thought that maybe you'd want to take a break. I could pinch-hit—"

"Don't talk down to me, old man!" Peter's bony, capable hands clenched into a pair of dangerous-looking fists as he took a furious step forward. "I don't—I don't—" He suddenly stopped, his hands loosening to clutch at his stomach. "I don't feel so good."

"I think what you need is a chance to lie down," Cale said.

At least he didn't say, "sleep it off," Sunny thought. *Otherwise, he might have set Peter off again.*

"I'll help him back." Carson put a supporting arm around Peter, whose face had gone from brick red to off green in mere moments.

"Yeah," Priscilla said. "I think you'd better hurry."

Carson guided Peter in a quick, if wobbly, walk. After they were through the gate Cale glanced around the remaining members of the party.

"So what do you say?" he asked. "Should I pinch-hit for Peter?"

By now, everybody had drunk enough beer to be in an agreeable mood, although Sunny warned Cale that he was probably boarding a sinking ship. She had him read the rules, which had gotten a bit smeary thanks to spilled beer, but he was able to understand enough. He took his position beside Sunny as Tommy Neal attempted to bounce another ball at their two remaining cups. Cale's hand darted out to flick the ball away.

Then it was their turn. Sunny and Cale both successfully landed their shots, reducing the Neals' cups from five to three.

"That's the closest score you've had in a while," Carson said when he finally returned through the gate.

"How is Peter?" Sunny asked.

Carson shrugged. "I put him in bed with a large bucket—just in case. But he passed out before he got sick."

"Are we playing doctor or beer pong?" Tommy demanded, turning them back to the game. He and Yardley tried to make a comeback. Tommy managed to land a toss, reducing Sunny and Cale to a single cup. Then Yardley tried to bounce the ball at the lone survivor.

"De-fense! De-fense!" Carson and Cillie chanted, and Cale came through, flicking the ball away.

Now it was Sunny and Cale's turn. He tossed his ball unerringly into one of the Neals' remaining cups. *Course, it's easier for him,* Sunny thought. *He's sober.*

She went to toss her ball, and her foot slipped on spilled beer. Her shot looped high, hit, and flipped up, catching an astonished Tommy in the forehead . . . and dropped into the cup.

"We won! We won!" Sunny jumped up and down, waving her arms in triumph.

"But we won the most games." Yardley tried for dignity, but she was swaying a little as she spoke.

"I'm just glad we won one." Sunny stopped jumping. She was beginning to feel the beer, too.

"I think it's time we called it a night, before one of us falls into the pool." Priscilla bit her lip, belatedly realizing her comment was a little too close to what happened to Eliza. Nobody else said anything, but Sunny could feel that cloud of constraint setting in again.

She looked at her watch. It was getting late. Will would be getting off soon. She should share what Beau had told her about his fight with Eliza.

They dragged the damning evidence into the cabana, cleaned up what they could, and headed down the path to the guesthouses. Cale waved a silent good-bye as he set off in the opposite direction to the mansion.

"I think I'm going to take a little walk," Sunny said when they got to the front of the girls' house.

Priscilla laughed as she held onto Carson's arm. "Trying to clear your head?"

"It wouldn't hurt." Sunny watched Cillie, her fiance, and the Neals go in, then turned to pass the roadblock. A quick turn at the first intersection, and yes, there was Will in his police cruiser. She got in on the passenger side, and he set off through the neighborhood. "You look a little wobbly tonight," he observed. "Were you trying to dig up clues over brandies by the fireplace?"

"More like trying to get the suspects to let their hair down over beer pong," Sunny admitted. "Not much to report there. But I got Beau Bellingham alone earlier. We talked about his relationship with Eliza and that fight they had."

Sunny stopped, realizing that Will wasn't listening. He'd slowed the car and was peering off into the distance. This was a quiet residential block in a part of town that didn't run to streetlights. Whatever he was staring at stood in an even deeper patch of shadow from a huge pine tree. "That's Nesbit's car," Will said.

Now Sunny looked harder, barely able to make out the fact that a car was parked in the shadows. She knew that the sheriff often drove an unmarked county car, but how would Will recognize it all the way over there?

"It's the whip antenna," Will explained as if he'd overheard her thought. "I just caught the silhouette, but that's something we all keep an eye out for. It means the boss is around."

He drove up behind the mystery car, his headlights revealing that someone was behind the driver's wheel. The driver didn't turn around, though.

Will stopped the car and got out. He looked in the window and recoiled, trying to stop Sunny as she got out to join him.

But he was too late. She got an eyeful of Frank Nesbit's trademark mustache and pale face, now twisted in a rictus of pain and surprise, his glazed, staring eyes—and of the bloody wound across his throat. All the beer Sunny had drunk made a sudden attempt to leap out of her stomach, and she stumbled back, fighting for control.

Will would kill me if I threw up on his crime scene, some part of her brain commented.

Will stepped back and took out his flashlight, playing it over the interior of the car. Sunny wished he hadn't. All it seemed to show was drying blood all over.

"I think he knew whoever did this." Will turned to Sunny, took in her pale face, and went to her, but she waved him off.

"I'm okay." She gulped heavily. "I think." Then she asked, "What makes you say that?"

"He let him get close enough to slit his throat," Will's face was grim. "I know that Nesbit always carried a gun in a shoulder rig. He said it was one of the perks of the job. But when I looked now, his jacket was zipped closed. If he'd had any suspicions at all, he'd have wanted free access to his weapon. That jacket would have been open. Instead . . ."

Will shook his head. "It looks as though he made the mistake of bringing a gun to a knife fight."

12

The quiet neighborhood was neither quiet nor dark for long. Large floodlights threw a harsh glare over Frank Nesbit's car, and a steady rumble came from the gasoline-powered generators providing juice for the lights. Radios chattered from shoulder-mounted units on state troopers as well as from several state police vehicles; along with the red flashers, it was like a scene from a movie. Troopers moved around setting up a perimeter, and Sunny spotted Ben Semple's shocked face beyond the crime-scene tape.

"Ben Semple already called in the news to headquarters in Levett," Will told Lieutenant Ellis Wainwright. "They're rousting Captain Ingersoll"—who Sunny recalled was the sheriff's second in command—"out of bed to get over here."

Wainwright nodded. "In the meantime, I'm hoping you

can give me some answers. What the hell was Nesbit doing here?"

"I have no idea," Will replied. "He didn't share his schedule with me. As far as I know, he had no reason to be around here at this time of night." He hesitated for a moment. "I'd say this was a good spot for a quiet meeting, though."

"Mmmph." Wainwright made an indeterminate noise and glanced at Sunny. "As you were doing with Ms. Coolidge."

"She came out to share anything she'd heard in the compound," Will said stiffly.

"Anything that didn't fit in her blog, I suppose," the state police investigator cut in. "Lee Trehearne is still unhappy with the way you publicized the wedding presents."

"Did you read the post? Do *you* think I endangered the security of the gifts or the house, Lieutenant?" By now, Sunny's nausea had transformed into anger. "I tried to point out what a good job Trehearne's doing, but the fact is, he just doesn't want me around. Does the same go for you?"

"I guess that depends on what you can tell me about the movements of any of the people in the compound," Wainwright replied. "You were spotted with Priscilla Kingsbury, Carson de Kruk, and several of their friends at the guesthouses before you set off on your little walk to meet Constable Price here. What were you all doing prior to that?"

"We were having a little . . . entertainment." Sunny silently cursed her beer-thickened wits. How much would she have to tell?

Wainwright gave her a cool but penetrating cop's gaze. "Yeah. I could smell the 'entertainment' on you. At a guess

I'd say it was some kind of drinking game. Who was participating?"

Sunny could feel her face growing warm. And Will was no help, studiously keeping his eyes averted. He was leaving her on her own—or, rather, silently telling her not to cover things up.

"Beau Bellingham left after the first round. He said he wanted to get some sleep." Sunny didn't need a scorecard to realize that her statement would put another check mark under "Opportunity" for Beau. As for motive . . . "What could he possibly have against Sheriff Nesbit?"

"Just tell me who was present and who wasn't." Wainwright's voice was cold.

"Carson and Priscilla were playing, and so were Tommy and Yardley Neal. Peter Van Twissel was on my team, but he, um, wound up a little under the weather—"

"Or in the bag," Wainwright muttered.

"So he went to lie down," Sunny finished a little defiantly. "Then Caleb Kingsbury came to join us for a while."

"Sure," the state police investigator said. "The fun-loving Kingsbury."

That got a flicker of interest from Will's poker face.

Now he probably wishes we'd had more time to talk before this whole circus hit, Sunny thought.

She took a deep breath. "Lieutenant, I'm sure you know that Augustus de Kruk and his wife are arriving tomorrow. Carson, Priscilla, and the others were just hoping for a last blowout before things got more, well, formal. This was their only chance to let off a little steam."

Wainwright looked at her shrewdly. "And maybe a

chance for someone to let something slip, thanks to the beer."

Sunny gave a small nod of concession. "But no one said anything. Maybe you should talk with Caleb. He was with the older generation of the family."

"And I'm sure they'll all stick together," Wainwright growled. "At least as far as they'll tell us."

"Don't knock yourself, Lieutenant," Sunny joked, but she couldn't hold on to her flippant attitude. More somberly she added, "Do you really think these two things are connected?"

"Two people get murdered, a few blocks from one another, and a couple of days apart . . ." Wainwright's rumpled face added a few wrinkles. "The proximity is suggestive, and I don't mean that in a dirty way."

"But what connects a girl up here from New York City to a sheriff who barely leaves Elmet County?" Sunny demanded.

"The Kingsburys, for one," Lieutenant Wainwright said. "Lord knows that Frank was about as plugged in as anyone in the county." He turned to Will. "Given your relationship with Frank, you should get ready for people looking into you."

That jarred Will a little. "Hey, I was only running against him for sheriff. It wasn't a blood feud."

"He stuck you out here in the boondocks while he was busy campaigning," Wainwright pointed out.

"So people will think I killed him because he wouldn't let me speak to the local rotary clubs?" Will shook his head as if a mosquito were buzzing around his ears. "That doesn't make any sense."

"You're the one who found him, after picking up a witness for yourself." Wainwright scowled again. "I'm not saying anything, Price, I'm just throwing out a few facts. You should think about how they might be interpreted." He paused for a moment as Captain Ingersoll arrived in a patrol cruiser with sirens blaring. "Is this Ingersoll politically connected?" he asked Will.

"I don't think so," Will said. "He's a pro, worked with my dad before Nesbit took over as sheriff. Kind of a hard-ass, from what I remember. These days, he seemed to be the brain Nesbit would pick when he had to think about policing."

"Okay." Wainwright turned a poker face on Will. "And how do you think Ingersoll would feel about you being his boss?"

"Um." Will closed his mouth with a snap. "Not very positive, I expect."

Wainwright gave him a wintry smile. "Welcome to politics, bunkie."

Captain Ingersoll was a big, florid man who very evidently had been fast asleep about forty minutes ago. Sunny wouldn't have been at all surprised if he actually still had on his pajama top under the zipped-up green sheriff's department Windbreaker he wore.

I wonder what his first official action will be? she thought.

She didn't have to wonder long. Ingersoll strode right up to Will. "Constable Price, you're hereby relieved of your liaison duties here." The captain had a hoarse, breathless sort of voice that made Sunny want to start coughing in sympathy. "After you've rendered any assistance Lieutenant

Wainwright requires, you'll return to your normal duties at the beginning of the next shift."

*

One pair of eyes unblinkingly took in the activities in the almost unbearably bright circle of lights. Shadow crouched beside a bush in a big flowerpot—a very big one, it had to be twice as tall as he could stretch his body, a long jump to get to cover. He'd wedged himself into a tight space beside the giant flowerpot, and had slept for a while, but had been awakened by go-fast things making horrible screaming noises as they rushed along, then screeching to a stop. And the too-bright lights with their too-loud noises had made further sleep impossible.

It took him a while to realize that Sunny was also down there in the circle of light. Shadow's first thought when he spotted her was to run straight to her. But there were other two-legs around her, and when he saw the way she held herself and moved, Shadow knew she wasn't happy. Maybe this wasn't the time. Because the absolute worst thing that could happen would be if he came up to her, and Sunny pushed him away.

So he hunkered down and simply watched.

I know Sunny is around here, he thought. *I can always find her again.*

*

After getting the official brush-off from Captain Ingersoll, Will made arrangements to submit a statement in the morning. "Do you want me to do this at the station in

Levett, or should I go to the Troop *A* barracks in Alfred?" he asked Wainwright.

"Go to the barracks. You, too, Ms. Coolidge." The state police investigator glanced over at Captain Ingersoll. "No reflection on you, Captain, but I'd like this to stay in-house."

"Understood," Ingersoll replied. "But I'd appreciate it if you'd keep me in the loop. And, of course, feel free to request any assistance we can offer." His reddish face deepened in color. "For the time being, you can consider *me* the local liaison."

Sunny had a sudden ridiculous vision of the oversized captain directing traffic outside the Kingsbury's compound and had to bite her lip to keep from laughing inappropriately. *Hold it together,* she told herself firmly.

Wainwright was diplomatic, saying, "Thanks, Captain, I appreciate that." He turned to supervise his troops with Ingersoll on his heels.

"The troopers along the perimeter will have more than nosy neighbors to deal with now," Will noted as the first news crews arrived along with the state police crime-scene team.

Will didn't seem all that upset about being removed from his post; when Sunny asked about it, he replied, "Why would I complain about *not* being a fifth wheel?"

Then he frowned. "Although there's a ripe smell of politics in this already. Wainwright had a point. If Ingersoll thought I had a chance of ending up as his boss, would he have handled that scene the way he did?"

"Well, he was very formal," Sunny said.

"Yeah, in a superior officer talking to a subordinate sort

of way." Will's frown deepened. "Ingersoll isn't a politician like Nesbit, but with all the years he's spent in Levett, he's got to know at least some of the powers that be. I guess he must have told them what happened, and they're already coming up with something."

"What could they come up with on the spur of the moment?" Sunny was ready to argue some more, but her cell phone gave off the pinging sound that meant she'd gotten a text. "Excuse me," she said, opening up the device.

The message was brief:

MUST SEE YOU BOTH. URGENT. CHK CROWD.

It came from Randall.

Silently, Sunny showed the screen to Will. Together, they began to scan the faces around the perimeter.

"There he is." Will nodded toward the middle of the street, near where his car was parked. Randall stood right next to the yellow police tape. He gave a little wave, keeping his hand in front of his chest so it wouldn't be noticed by others.

"Do you think we should talk to him?" Sunny asked. "Or do you think he's only trying for the inside scoop?"

"You know him better than I do," Will responded noncommittally.

"Okay, then, I think we should see what he has to say." Sunny quickly texted back: FOLLOW US.

She showed the message to Will, who nodded. They caught up with Lieutenant Wainwright, and Will said, "If you have no further use for us presently, I'll take Sunny back to the compound and head home."

Wainwright nodded, barely looking at them. Will led Sunny back to his cruiser, then he had the job of turning the car around in a pretty tight space. Troopers were already shooing onlookers away and holding up the crime scene tape as Will nosed his way out. Once the mob scene was behind them, Will proceeded at a sedate pace, barely faster than a brisk walk, for a few blocks before pulling over.

Sunny peered into the darkness behind them, the only illumination coming from the red glow of their brake lights. After a moment or two, a walking figure came toward them—Randall MacDermott.

Will flicked a button to unlock the cruiser's rear doors, and Randall slipped into the caged backseat.

"Sorry for the accommodations," Will said.

"It's not the first time I've wound up back here," Randall replied. "Not so much in recent years, though."

"You said you needed to see us," Sunny prompted. "What about?"

"First, I need to make sure I've got the facts straight," Randall said. "The dead person back there—it's Frank Nesbit, the sheriff, isn't it?"

"What makes you think so?" Will replied cagily.

"Because I recognized his car. I spoke to him earlier this evening." Randall's voice sounded a little tight, as if he were having a hard time getting the words out. "I told him about the Taxman."

"You what?!" Sunny burst out.

"I told you that I was looking for a professional who'd take me seriously," Randall defended himself.

"And you just happened to pick the guy I'm running against." Will shook his head. "How did he take it?"

"The sheriff was a lot more interested than you were." Randall shifted on the seat. "He asked a whole bunch of questions."

"Were they cop-type questions, or politician questions?" Will asked.

"Or were they blackmailer-type questions?" Sunny spoke up, catching looks from both Will and Randall. "Look, we were just standing over Nesbit's body wondering about any possible connection between him and Eliza Stoughton. What if he was the one who was blackmailing her?"

"And then she came back from the dead to kill him?" Will asked in disbelief.

"Obviously not, but maybe Eliza mentioned it to someone else, who went after Nesbit. You always said that Nesbit was more of a politician than a cop, Will. In either job, he was handling a lot of secrets."

"Not to knock your theory, Sunny," Randall interjected, "but the Taxman has put the bite on people all over the country. Do you think your sheriff had access to information on that scale?"

"When you put it that way . . ." Sunny sighed.

"I think the answer you're looking for is 'no,' " Will finished for her.

"You don't have to rub it in," she told him. It had been a decent theory while it lasted.

But Will wasn't finished yet. "And I hate to knock *your* theory, Randall, but Nesbit's death doesn't necessarily connect to your mythical Taxman at all."

"Sure," Randall replied. "After I talked to him, he died of natural causes. Looked like a lot of blood for a heart attack," he deadpanned.

"Nesbit could have died because of the case we already had on the table," Will said. "It's a high-profile affair, and if he cracked it, that was a guaranteed four more years in office. Maybe he was following some lead he'd dug up, and things went south."

Randall wasn't giving up so easily. "And I think there's more to it than just another case. You say the sheriff was a politician. That probably means he knew the local political dirt, maybe even something about the Kingsburys. What if he was trying to get information out of another blackmail victim?"

Sunny said nothing. She was tired, but the alcohol had burned off and her mental facilities felt very clear. Too clear, maybe—she was putting things together into a picture she didn't like.

The sheriff might've been more of a politician than a cop, but he wasn't a complete idiot, she thought. *If he assumed he was going to talk to a murder suspect, wouldn't he have been warier? Wouldn't he have kept his gun handy?*

But if, as Randall suggested, it were a blackmail victim, Nesbit might not have seen the violence coming. He might easily have gone to a secret meeting, maybe a political meeting, with his jacket all zipped up.

If that were true, then Lieutenant Wainwright, Will, and all the other cops were going at the case all wrong. They thought that Eliza Stoughton's death was the result of an unpremeditated attack by someone personally associated with her. Whereas if Randall was right, Eliza had been being blackmailed by someone with a number of pigeons on his string. Sunny hadn't considered it before, but given all the people assembling for this get-together, another blackmail victim could be present. How would such a person react to Eliza asking about ways to get out of the Taxman's web? Maybe he shut her up to keep her from drawing attention to the extortion scheme. And then, when Nesbit tried to follow up . . .

Sunny shuddered, but stayed silent. *That means that someone on Neal's Neck has a secret worth killing for—twice.*

13

The late hour had become even later, well past midnight, by the time Will delivered Sunny to the checkpoint at the edge of Neal's Neck. She noticed there was only one state trooper now standing beside the sawhorses.

That roused a comment out of her tired brain. *I guess if the ninety-nine percenters were going to attack, this would be the time to do it. Hope Lee Trehearne has his own private troops on high alert.*

She gave Will a good-bye kiss and started around the roadblock, heading for the guesthouse. That's when Sunny discovered someone else was still awake and alert. Priscilla Kingsbury rose from where she'd been sitting on the fieldstone steps leading up to the front door. Apparently she too had shaken off her tipsiness. Her face was sober and concerned.

"Are you all right?" she asked in a low voice as Sunny approached. "We heard sirens, and the trooper on duty said that a cop had been found dead in his car. It wasn't your—your friend, was it?"

Sunny shook her head and Cillie heaved a sigh of relief. "I stayed up to see you. I was afraid—"

"It was Sheriff Nesbit." Sunny's voice sounded harsh in her ears.

Priscilla's face showed her shock. "I used to meet him, sometimes. It sort of came with the territory, working in this county—especially with his wife working on the food pantry with the 99 Elmet Ladies." She shook her head, still digesting the news. "He seemed like a nice man."

Yeah—nice to a Kingsbury, said Sunny's brain reflexively, but she didn't voice the unkind thought out loud. She hadn't liked the man much, but nobody deserved Nesbit's fate. Besides, there were other things she needed to warn Cillie about.

"You remember the state I was in—hell, the state we *all* were in?" Sunny said. "Seeing the sheriff dead shocked me sober, but Lieutenant Wainwright could still smell the beer on me. He even asked what drinking game we'd been playing. So don't try lying when he asks what we were doing earlier. It won't look good."

"But why would he ask—" Cillie broke off, if possible, looking even more shocked. "He can't think that anyone here—"

"To quote the man, 'The proximity is suggestive.' He can't ignore looking for a connection when two people get killed barely a couple of blocks apart."

But Cillie's concerns were closer to home. "If Grandfather finds out about the beer pong, he won't be happy."

That should be the least of our troubles, Sunny thought. But all she said was, "You'd better tell the others, too. I suspect tomorrow is going to be a long day."

*

Her prediction proved only too tiresomely true. Sunny got only a few hours' sleep after a marathon phone call with her father discussing what had happened to the sheriff. Mike's enthusiasm for politics diminished considerably now that it had turned from bare-knuckles to bloody. He wanted her off Neal's Neck, but she argued to stay. What kind of reporter would she be, turning her back on a mystery—and a story like this?

She won that difference of opinion, but it didn't feel much like victory, dragging herself out of bed to head down to the state police barracks. The good news: the clothes she'd unpacked yesterday didn't smell as stuffy, and Priscilla had been able to get hold of a lint roller and an iron for Sunny to use. The bad news: Sunny had to wear one of her limited supply of suits for her trip. And Lee Trehearne was on hand to see her off in one of the compound's town cars, his expression mixing a self-satisfied "I told you so" with violent dislike.

Just the memory of Trehearne's evil eye kept Sunny sitting in a stiffly uncomfortable pose until she was about half a mile away from the compound. *Don't relax too much,* she warned herself as she finally sank back into the upholstered seat. *You don't want to doze off.*

To keep herself awake, she mentally edited the statement she was going to write down for the troopers. Sunny decided to tactfully evade the subject of beer pong, and merely say that the younger members of the gathering had been entertaining themselves by the pool.

They arrived and Sunny asked her security guard/driver to wait while she took care of her business inside. If they decided to hold onto her for questioning, she could send the car back then.

Sunny had half expected to find herself in an interrogation room with a pad and pen. Instead, a young trooper led her to an empty office with a desk. She sat down to work on her story. Will had said that the blood at the murder scene was still fresh, so Sunny contained herself to the events of that evening. She mentioned that Beau Bellingham had left the group fairly early, and that Peter Van Twissel had departed some time afterward, accompanied by Carson. She couldn't put a time to the bridegroom's return, having been too busy launching her big beer pong assault to check her watch.

I hate to flag them as possible suspects, Sunny thought, *but this is too important to start fooling around.*

She wondered what kind of alibis Cale could offer for the rest of the family.

After a final read Sunny decided she'd done the best she could. She signed the statement, turned it in at the front desk, and found herself dismissed with the warning that Lieutenant Wainwright might want to talk with her again.

Sunny's eyes did sink closed on the sixteen-mile return ride, but she made a determined effort to rouse herself before she arrived back at the compound. She needn't have bothered. The guesthouse was empty except for a note

from Priscilla inviting her to breakfast in the boys' accommodations. Sunny went over there to find most of the
guests around a large and somewhat scuffed dining room
table. *Apparently the furniture gets harder use here in
boy-land,* she thought.

Peter certainly looked the worse for wear. He was hor-
ribly hungover, extremely apologetic for his embarrassing
behavior the night before, and barely able to stomach any
breakfast. He had to excuse himself hurriedly when
Tommy Neal suggested he try hitting one of the leftover
bottles of beer as hair of the dog.

Sunny looked after Peter with a certain amount of sympathy. But that soon faded as she found herself considering
Peter Van Twissel in quite another light. He'd shown himself to have quite an ugly streak when he drank beyond his
limits. How much had he imbibed on the day that Eliza
Stoughton was killed? He was the only male in the party
that Eliza hadn't wound up fighting with—at least, not in
public. So motive was open. As for means, Sunny remembered how strong his bony fingers had looked—and how
easily they'd curled into fists. As for opportunity, well, she'd
thought of that before. Assuming he was aware of the surveillance cameras, he certainly had the computer savvy to
wipe any evidence from the hard drives.

But seeing him pale and hunched over this morning, he
seemed as though he couldn't harm a fly. Most likely, the
fly would win. Could Peter really look so natural after
killing two people? For that matter, could he have dragged
himself out of bed to meet with Frank Nesbit? Or could
the sick bit have been an act? Peter had seemed pretty
drunk; even his nasty side had seemed real enough.

Carson came in to apologize for Priscilla—she'd been hijacked by Fiona Ormond for wedding business. "I think they're talking about cakes, and Fiona wanted Cillie's opinion of the local bakeries." He paused for a second before asking, "How did it go with the state police?"

Sunny kept her answer brief, just mentioning the pen and pad. She wasn't about to give another impromptu course on dealing with police interrogations.

Speaking of which . . . Sunny shifted her gaze to the front-runner in the suspects sweepstakes. Beau Bellingham was awake but still wearing the same rumpled surgical scrubs he'd probably slept in. *Did he not own any other clothes?* Sunny wondered. *It's not like he's on call out here.* When anyone spoke to him, he replied in monosyllables. His expression was stiff, almost sullen, but the way his eyes darted around the room showed that he was on edge.

He knew already that the cops had their eyes on him, Sunny thought. *Having another flimsy alibi isn't going to help, even if he doesn't have much in the way of obvious motive.*

During the course of the day, each member of the group was brought in for a talk with Lieutenant Wainwright. Otherwise, they worked quietly to clean up the area of last night's party, collecting the empty bottles, rinsing them out, and adding them to the recycling boxes outside the kitchen of the big house. The Styrofoam ice chests could be broken up and put in the trash, after the water remaining from the ice had been poured off. A generous collection of full bottles also remained, which wound up in the refrigerators of the guesthouses. Carson reported that the Ping-Pong table was already gone when he went to scout the area after rising. Cale Kingsbury must have been up and on the move even earlier.

Of course, Sunny had another job as well—getting out another blog post. The hard-news reporter she'd been wanted to focus on the murder near the premises. *Kind of hard to shoehorn a subject like that into coverage of a festive event,* she thought.

While she sat in her room, wrestling with trying to tie the two diametrically opposed concepts together, Priscilla popped her head in. "Just wanted to check how you were doing." She made a game attempt at smiling. "After last night, I figured you might want to rest a little more."

Inspiration struck. "You said you knew the sheriff when I told you what happened," Sunny said. "How about the rest of your family?"

"Well, Grandfather had some dealings with him. Political fund-raising dinners and, of course, security for the property here. In fact, he's going to issue a statement about the sheriff in an hour or so."

"How about your brothers and your uncle?"

"They knew him in passing, I guess."

Sunny nodded. "Here's what I'd like to do for today's blog post. I don't think we can ignore what happened last night. So I'd like to have each member of the family—the folks from Maine—respond to this new tragedy, losing a neighbor during what should be a happy time."

Cillie might work for a nonprofit foundation, but she came from a family of politicians. "That might work pretty well."

"Great," Sunny told her. "Let's go listen to your grandfather and see if we can crib anything from his statement."

It seemed like déjà vu all over again. Sunny stood in the

same grassy area, facing the hastily assembled platform. This time, though, she was hiding behind the stand of bushes with Priscilla Kingsbury instead of Caleb. Sunny had been fast asleep for the Kingsbury's official statement regarding what they called Eliza Stoughton's "mishap." Ken Howell had attended, however. According to him, the Kingsbury lawyer, Vincent Quimby, had done the talking. She spotted both Ken and Randall in the crowd of the usual media suspects.

A moment before the appointed hour, a golf cart appeared on the path from the big house—the cart with the senatorial seal on the windshield. It came to a stop, and Senator Thomas Neal Kingsbury emerged, with Lee Trehearne behind him. The Senator stood very erect in his summer-weight suit, but his steps were careful as he climbed onto the platform. Trehearne attended him like a mother hen until Kingsbury finally waved him away. For the first time, Sunny got a sense of the man's age. *Maybe he really is just hanging on until he sees a relative in the White House,* she thought.

As he approached the microphone set up at the front of the platform, the Senator's habitual quirks kicked in. But this time, his studied poses and vocal cadences made sense. There really were cameras on him.

"Thank you for coming," he said. "I'll keep this brief. You all know my family has gathered here for a wonderful event. We're all very saddened by this senseless tragedy. None of us has any idea why this terrible thing happened to Sheriff Nesbit, or how. What I do know is that Frank Nesbit was a fine public servant and a good man."

Yup, Sunny's cynical reporter alter ego commented, *just like every other dead politician who wasn't caught with his hand in the cookie jar.*

"Along with all of my family, we extend the most heart-felt condolences to Frank's wife Lenore. It's a very sad business." He stood looking saddened for a long moment, about enough time for a TV reporter to recapitulate when and where the statement was being made in the cutaway back to the studio. Then Kingsbury said, "Thank you very much. No questions, please."

Of course, that didn't deter the more hard-boiled press professionals. They responded about the same way Shadow would on being offered a plate of prime tuna. Randall Mac-Dermott was the first reporter who managed to pitch his voice to cut across the noise and be heard. Whatever his other shortcomings—and Sunny had a long list—he was a real reporter, she thought admiringly. "Senator," he called, "do you think there's any connection between the sheriff's murder and the death of the young woman on your property?"

The look Kingsbury sent Randall would have quelled a lesser man. Then the Senator pulled himself together and walked back toward his golf cart, not even dignifying Randall's shot with a "no comment." In a moment, he was gone.

"A little on the brief side, but you can see how he handled all the main points," Sunny told Priscilla. "I think you'd want to work some personal recollection into whatever you say about the sheriff. You're here working for the foundation. Is there something he might have done to help?"

"He twisted some arms when it came to fund-raising," Cillie said as she led Sunny over to the big house. "Let me see if I can come up with a better way to say that." They found the older generation preparing for lunch. Cillie's older brother Tom frowned when Sunny made her pitch but nodded his head as he thought it over.

"Okay if I do this off the cuff?" Tom Kingsbury asked. Sunny held up a small cassette recorder. "It's been a while since I was involved in politics up here in Maine, but I certainly remember Frank Nesbit. He was a good friend and supporter to my grandfather—loyal, too. He stuck it out on the Senator's last campaign, and when Cale lost on his reelection bid." Tom suddenly stopped. "Better cut that. We don't really talk about my grandfather's last campaign, so many people turned their backs on him. Same thing with Uncle Cale's stint in Congress. Can I start over?"

Sunny nodded. Tom frowned in thought for a moment, then said, "It's been some time since our family took part in politics here in Maine. But I remember Frank Nesbit, and not just as a good friend and loyal supporter of my grandfather. As sheriff, he represented everything that local public service should be about. I'm sorry I didn't get a chance to see him on this trip, and sorrier still for what happened to him. We Kingsburys would all like to express our sympathy to Frank's family." Tom cocked his head. "Okay?"

"That's fine," Sunny said. "Thanks, Governor."

When they approached the eldest brother, Lem, he turned to his wife. "Deborah, do we have anything to say?"

She responded with a prompt but obviously prepared party line. "We join with the Senator in his sorrow at the loss of a good man like Frank Nesbit. While his life was an example of public service, his death shows how dangerous law enforcement can be. Family to family, we grieve with the Nesbits."

The Senator himself declined to add anything. He gave Sunny a moment's frowning consideration, and then said, "I've already made a statement on that subject."

Case closed, Sunny thought. *Go away.*

She thanked the Senator, then she and Cillie beat a quick retreat. On their way out of the house, they bumped into Cale Kingsbury. When Sunny asked him for a statement, he waved her recorder away. "Nothing I have to say would carry any weight. You had more contact with the man, Cillie. If you can say he helped with the foundation in any way, that would be good enough for me."

It took a while to weave together the more professional pronouncements from the Kingsburys with Priscilla's more heartfelt memorial, but in the end Sunny was pleased with the results. Along with a nice portrait of a subdued Cillie and one of Ken's shots of the Senator at the mic, it made for a nice, respectful posting. Once that was accomplished, Sunny felt justified in putting her feet up for a while and trying to catch up on some of the sleep she'd lost. The afternoon shadows were stretching more toward evening when she awoke. Her drowsy eyes seemed to see a familiar silhouette outlined against the window. *Shadow?*

But when she blinked herself alert and sat up, the cat was gone.

*

Shadow picked himself up and walked out of the soft bed of flowers where he'd fallen. He'd wandered around this new place for so long without finding Sunny that he'd begun to lose hope. Why would Sunny come here? There didn't seem to be much of interest to be found here. He'd come across a place where there was loud music and a big pond of splashing water. He'd seen those places before and never thought they were any good. For one thing, the strong, nose-twisting stink that came from the water made it hard to scent anything else. He'd have left right away except that there was a two-legged female there who had petted him gently and had given him some food.

She was nice, but she wasn't Sunny.

He'd finally drawn away and went back to the house where Sunny had left him earlier. Getting in wasn't as easy this time. The doors and all the windows on the ground floor were closed. He'd been experimenting with the upstairs when he'd gotten a trace of an unmistakable fragrance. Working his way carefully along the roof, he'd approached another window and looked inside. There was Sunny, lying on a bed, asleep!

Shadow had immediately set to work on the screen in the window, trying to pull it aside so he could enter and wake Sunny up. But he'd foolishly used the paw with the broken claw. A sudden jolt of pain had made him jerk back—not a good thing when dealing with the tricky footing of a roof.

He'd found himself tumbling backward, and then there was no roof under his paws, only air. Nothing for his claws to catch hold of. And then he'd impacted on soft earth and sweet-smelling flowers—although a few of them would never be the same after he'd landed on them. Shadow got back on his feet, shook himself, and sneezed. Then he pranced out onto the grass, his tail held high. *Just in case anyone saw me,* he thought, *I'll act as if I planned to do that.*

*

Sunny managed to get in a decent nap before Cillie Kingsbury appeared at her door. "Carson got a call. His parents are in the air. They expect to land in about an hour."

The news shouldn't have startled Sunny. She knew the de Kruks were due to arrive today. So why did her stomach suddenly tighten the way it used to when she was going off to interview someone for a big story? She was just a spear-carrier in this particular opera—nothing but window dressing.

And speaking of dressing, she had just enough time to take a shower and change into her other suit before rejoining Priscilla downstairs. A moment earlier, Sunny had been admiring her reflection in her cinnamon-colored suit. She'd made more of an effort to get active lately, and the results had shown. Her suit wasn't tight, the skirt was just the right height, she'd even felt stylish. Compared to Cillie's outfit, however . . . Well, Priscilla's left shoe probably cost more than Sunny's whole outfit combined.

But if Sunny felt a reporter's buzz, Cillie radiated nervousness.

"Come on," Sunny told her. "You look as if you expect them to eat you. Haven't the de Kruks been here before?"

"No," Cillie replied. "And now that they're almost here, everything looks so moth eaten."

"Well, you look nice." That was an understatement. Priscilla wore a deceptively simple aquamarine dress that flattered her short, sandy blond hair. The jewelry she wore with it was silver—old silver, with a patina, probably a hand-me-down from some Victorian ancestor.

"So do you," Cillie said. "That's a nice color for you."

Sure—when you can't compliment the clothes, compliment the color. With a determined mental effort, Sunny shut her interior critic down. She wasn't the center of attention here, the bride was. "I'd tell the de Kruks that the place is like your jewelry—old with a story behind it."

Cillie touched her necklace. "It was my great-great-grandmother's. How did you know?"

"Because it looks like a family piece. Augustus de Kruk's family line may be old, but their money is new. The Kingsburys, though, have history. To be crude about it, isn't that what they're marrying into? Even if that includes the silver monstrosity in the rear parlor."

Sunny's irreverent analysis shocked a laugh out of Cillie, and seemed to put her on a more even keel.

"So where will you receive the guests?" Sunny asked.

"Down in front of the big house," Priscilla replied. "I suppose we'd better start collecting people and get a move on."

They came downstairs to find that Carson had already shepherded the rest of the younger guests out onto the road. He wore a cool gray suit with a muted check. Its skinny lapels and tailored fit flattered his slim build. Tommy Neal was more businesslike in navy blue. Peter Van Twissel had a suit much the same color, but his was definitely off the rack and didn't fit him as well. And with his khaki slacks, off white jacket, and shaggy hair, Beau Bellingham looked like a beach bum crashing the party. Yardley Neal was a symphony in beige—clearly an expensive ensemble, but in a color that didn't necessarily suit her.

"Shall we get the show on the road?" Carson suggested.

They'd barely started on the path when they had to draw off to let a motorcade of two town cars and a Range Rover pass them on the way out. Sunny caught a glimpse of Lee Trehearne in the lead vehicle, barking orders into a microphone.

"There goes the welcoming committee," Cillie muttered.

When they arrived at the mansion, only Cale Kingsbury stood outside. "Too much hot air in there," he told Sunny with a grin. "The Senator is still working on his welcoming speech." He got a little more serious when he saw Priscilla, taking both her hands and stepping back to admire her. "Pay no attention to your broken-down old uncle," he said. "Except when he tells you that you're a lovely young woman." He turned to Carson. "And you, my friend, are a lucky young man."

Actually, Cale didn't look too broken-down. He wore a summer-weight tan suit with a slightly darker knit tie. Only the width of the tie and the lapels suggested that his suit wasn't as fashion forward as some of the others.

Sunny wouldn't have minded a chance to talk with Cale, but she didn't get much of a chance. He circulated among the members of the wedding party, chatting and joking. *And certainly bringing down the tension level,* Sunny had to admit.

The rest of the Kingsbury clan emerged, the males in almost identical navy blue suits, although the Senator's had a pinstripe. The female side of the party all wore pastels.

A security guard stepped up to whisper in the Senator's ear. "They've arrived," the Senator announced, and everyone began to sort themselves out along a fieldstone retaining wall in front of the house. Now that Sunny came to think of it, that wall had served as a background for numerous family photos she'd seen around the place.

Sunny quickly positioned herself away from the

developing reception line. *Spear carrier,* she reminded herself. *Window dressing.*

Still, it was an impressive little ceremony as the de Kruks, Augustus and his wife Magda, arrived. The Senator welcomed them, looking almost natural as he shook hands with the Emperor Augustus. Then came the political glad-handing with the governors, Lem Junior and Tom and their ladies, Deborah and Genevieve. After that, Carson and Priscilla offered handshakes and hugs, ending the formalities.

Augustus de Kruk glanced around. With his shining dome, beaky nose, and piercing eyes overshadowed by heavy brows, he really did look like a bald eagle, the alter ego used in so many op-ed cartoons.

Personally, Sunny had never responded well to the "look of eagles" she read about. To her, what eagles were usually looking for was their next meal. Certainly, the Emperor Augustus was quick to pounce when his eye fell on Beau Bellingham. "I hope you'll be getting a haircut before the wedding, young man." Augustus's trademark growling voice, which he'd used to blight a hundred reality-TV careers on his various business shows, rumbled out as if the big man were perfectly willing to make his record a hundred and one.

Beau looked as though he'd been slapped, putting a hand up to his blond mop. "Oh, uh, of course, sir."

The Emperor nodded. All was right with the world.

Priscilla suddenly appeared beside Sunny, hooking her arm and bringing her forward to the imperial presence. "Augustus, I'd like to introduce Sunny Coolidge. She's a reporter, sort of embedded with us for the wedding."

That ignited a spark of interest in de Kruk's predatory eyes.

Sure, Sunny thought, *he always was a publicity hound.*

"I wouldn't have expected that, Priscilla," Augustus said. "Such an interesting idea. Which media outlet do you report for, Ms. Coolidge?"

"The *Harbor Courier,* a local paper," Sunny replied. "Because first and foremost, this is local news."

"Mmm-hmmm." The interest in de Kruk's eyes blinked off as if a switch had been flicked when he heard that Sunny didn't represent a national media outlet.

The Senator's wife decided the moment had come to offer some concrete hospitality. "We have a little light meal prepared," she offered. "Or, if you would prefer to freshen up after traveling—"

Her polite speech was interrupted by a near shriek from Augustus de Kruk. "What—what is that *animal* doing here?" His famous rumble came out more like a falsetto, and his hand trembled as he pointed over evcryone's head.

Like everyone else Sunny swiveled to see what had upset the big man. Then she had to stifle a large gulp.

"That animal" was a cat, peering down with interest from the top of the fieldstone wall.

And that cat was Shadow.

14

At the first sign of trouble, Lee Trehearne had come at a run, then he halted, staring back and forth, struggling with how to resolve the situation. Augustus de Kruk kept cowering back, shouting, "Shoot it! Somebody shoot it!"

That seemed a somewhat extreme reaction to a cat that was doing nothing more aggressive than staring at him. Sunny kept her mouth shut, however. She had a strong suspicion that things wouldn't go well for her if de Kruk discovered that the animal causing his apparent nervous breakdown was her cat. And knowing Shadow, he was just as likely to seal the deal by leaping down into her arms. Still the situation seemed surreal enough that Sunny couldn't believe the cat was in real danger.

Trehearne tried to reach up and grab Shadow, but the height of the wall left the cat just beyond his grasp.

"How about climbing up on one of the bags?" Cale pointed to the luggage that had just been unloaded with the de Kruks.

"Yes! Please! Just get it!" Augustus didn't sound much like an emperor. He was begging.

Looking dubious at the whole process, Trehearne lugged a large hard-sided case up to the wall and hoisted himself on top of it. As soon as he began to draw level in height, Shadow strolled casually along the top of the wall, keeping slightly more than an arm's length away. Sunny could have told the security chief how this was going to end. Instead, she bit her lip as Trehearne stretched after the cat, who remained just tantalizingly out of reach. She could hear muttered swear words as the man reached a precarious balance at the edge of the bag. He stretched yet again, ramming an angry hand more in a punch than a grab at the cat, who responded by hissing and arching his back. That didn't deter Trehearne, who leaned back and then suddenly lunged to catch Shadow, apparently intending to grab the cat and make a landing.

Instead, Shadow hissed and met Trehearne's groping hand with a set of claws. With a yell of pain, Trehearne jerked his hand back, sufficiently distracted enough to blow his landing and collapse in an ungainly heap at the foot of the wall. Trehearne got himself up on his hands and knees to find the cat in almost the same pose above him, yowling cat curses down.

Staggering upright, the security chief got out his radio. His face was brick red from exertion and fury—and embarrassment over the smothered laughter from some of the onlookers. The last thing he wanted to do was call in reinforcements over a cat. But he had to admit the need for them, especially with Augustus de Kruk sobbing and shouting for cat blood.

Several black-jacketed security men arrived in response to his call. They moved with military precision to surround and subdue the intruder. One team advanced on the wall with a ladder. Another climbed onto the wall where it was lower, proceeding along the top on foot. A third force blocked the way to the house and advanced from there.

Sunny began to take the situation seriously enough to consider what kind of plea she'd have to make to keep Trehearne from wringing Shadow's neck. But just as the forces of humanity closed in for the capture, Shadow moved like greased lightning. He jumped down onto the head of the security man on the ladder, slid down his back, and bounced off the guy steadying the ladder. In an instant he was on the ground, breaking into evasive maneuvers on the run.

The man on the ladder nearly toppled off after making a belated grab, much like Trehearne. Augustus de Kruk let out another howl as Shadow darted past, about five feet away from his expensive shoes. With the glare Lee Trehearne sent after the cat, Sunny was surprised the lawn didn't burst into flames.

The whole welcome event dissolved into chaos. Magda, Augustus's latest blond wife, half-supported him as he tottered toward the house. She was quickly joined by Carson and Beau, who got the elder de Kruk inside and into a chair. Beau had a hand on the older man's chest and then checked his pulse. "Are you short of breath?" he asked in his best emergency room manner.

"He should be okay now that the cat is out of sight,"

Carson said. Apparently he'd seen his father react like this before.

"Augustus has this very strong reaction to seeing cats," Magda explained. Her accent made the "this" sound like "zis," and "cats" became "catza." She patted her husband on the shoulder. "Many famous people have had it: Julius Caesar, Shakespeare, Napoleon, even your President Eisenhower."

"Ailurophobia," Sunny muttered to herself. Having done some research on the subject, she wasn't exactly surprised that Mrs. de Kruk had skipped over a few of the other famous historical sufferers—like Genghis Khan, Hitler, and Mussolini. She recalled a story about Napoleon being found in a room, pale and trembling, stabbing into a wall tapestry with his sword. When the guards arrived they found a kitten hiding behind it.

Obviously, his brush with Shadow had been a shattering experience for Augustus. He no longer looked like a bold bald eagle, but more like a hoot owl caught in strong daylight. His piercing eyes blinked, he shivered, and his face was covered in sweat.

The Senator simply stared, lost for words—in fact, completely at a loss as to how to deal with his guest. After all, Augustus de Kruk was a master of the universe. How did one talk to him after seeing him dissolve into gibbering, irrational terror?

Luckily, the Senator's wife stepped into the breach. "I think after all this confusion, a little rest is called for," she said gently. "We can show you to your room now."

"Are you sure, Julia?" the Senator asked.

"Yes." Her voice was definite. "I believe we can wait on supper for a little bit, until our guests are settled."

Carson and Beau helped an almost pathetically grateful Augustus up to the guest bedroom.

Sunny took advantage of the intermission to go outside. Maybe she'd be able to spot Shadow. Maybe he'd come back. He had to have seen her.

But when she came out the door, she saw black-jacketed security guys all over the compound, searching for the renegade cat. Her heart squeezed a little. *Oh, Shadow, what have you gotten yourself into this time?*

Her worried thoughts were interrupted by muted laughter. Cale Kingsbury sat on a lower part of the wall, disregarding any threat to his good suit. He looked up at Sunny, his bad-boy grin threatening to split his face. "Un-be-lievable!" he chortled. "The all-powerful Emperor Augustus, brought low by a pussycat! You should have been using your camera, Sunny. A guy like de Kruk would pay through the nose to keep that meltdown off the Net. A couple of pictures, and you'd be set for life."

Sunny gave an uneasy nod. "Frankly, I'm more worried for the cat."

Another voice joined the conversation. "He seemed like a nice cat." Yardley Neal came out to stand beside Sunny. "I saw him earlier today. I just thought he was a neighbor-hood cat wandering around. He visited over at the pool this afternoon. He didn't like the water and the splashing, but he wasn't at all hissy with me."

"I bet you didn't try to grab him," Sunny said.

"No, but he let me pet him." Yardley smiled. "We had kitties all the time I was growing up. Pumpernickel and Daffodil. Daffodil liked flowers. I have no idea how Pum-pernickel got his name. Anyway, that cat had good manners.

He didn't stick his nose into things. I fed him some cold cuts from our sandwiches."

Well, at least that means he ought to have plenty of energy to escape Trehearne's Raiders, Sunny consoled herself. "I'm going to take a walk," she said. Maybe she could find Shadow. But then what would she do? Wrap him up in her jacket and smuggle him to safety? Where would safety be?

*

Shadow ducked into the cover of a flower bed, lying low among the greenery as another pair of two-legs went by. They wore the same black as the Clumsy One who'd tried to grab him, the one he'd marked with his claws. Maybe that made them all mad at him. Certainly, they seemed to be looking for him. But they didn't know how to hunt or stalk. Their feet made crunching noises on the little rocks in the paths, and they talked—or those boxes on their shoulders talked. A cat would have to be deaf not to know when they were coming.

The only problem was, he couldn't go back to try and find Sunny. He'd seen her there among the other two-legs when the Howling One had started in. That had brought the Clumsy One. At first Shadow thought he was trying to play the keep-away game, where Shadow stayed just out of reach. But that last attempt would have hurt if he'd gotten hold of Shadow, and Shadow had let him know it. He hadn't expected all this excitement, though.

What really worried him, though, was how Sunny had stayed quiet while the Clumsy One came after him. Shadow knew she'd seen him, but she didn't come to him or even say anything. It was as if she were pretending she didn't even know him. That hurt, and the feeling began to turn to anger.

He'd also caught traces of the made smell while he'd stood on top of the wall. Did Sunny ignore him because she was with the one who wore that scent? Shadow silently snarled, stretching his paw so the claws slid out. He'd mark that one, too. But not Sunny, of course. He'd never do that to Sunny. But he'd remember. *She'll have to do a lot before I forget how she deserted me,* he promised.

Yes, he'd make her pay—as soon as he found her. But where could he do that? He headed back to that odd-smelling house where she seemed to be staying.

*

Sunny zigzagged across Neal's Neck, looking for places where a cat might hide. She tried the pool area, since Shadow had successfully mooched a meal there. But he wasn't in the cabana. So she strolled on, paying special attention to plantings and shrubs. Shadow always surprised her with his ability to scrunch down and blend his tiger-striped body with the stems and leaves, especially in failing light. But she didn't find much in the way of animal—all vegetable.

She remembered her dream from earlier, seeing Shadow in her bedroom window. Or had it really been a dream at all? At the time, she'd thought Shadow was still home. Now she knew he was here.

That's why there was cat hair on my clothes, she realized. *He didn't roll on them in a snit, he stowed away in my bag!*

On a surge of hope, Sunny set off on the path back to

the guesthouses. Maybe Shadow had gone back to her room.

She'd almost reached the edge of the compound when she heard shouting ahead. Sunny picked up her pace, afraid of what she'd find. Black-jacketed security men were dashing around the house where she was staying. One of them brandished an old fish-landing net, like an oversized butterfly catcher.

Sunny broke into a run. She reached the edge of the house to see Lee Trehearne and six security guys pounding after Shadow, who dodged and evaded. The man with the net tried to snag him, but Shadow wasn't there when it landed, hitting the ground so hard that the wooden handle broke.

Shadow leaped away into the street, legs flashing.

Trehearne charged headlong after him, so focused on the cat that he almost crashed into the roadblock sawhorse when Shadow darted under it. The security chief skidded to a halt, suddenly aware of the state troopers staring at him . . . and of the photographers across the street. Shadow swerved to check on his pursuers, saw that he wasn't being chased anymore, and slowed his pace to romp away at a trot, his tail held high.

Sunny had to hold a hand over her mouth to keep the laughter from coming out. The whole episode had looked like some sort of cartoon. But she felt a chill, too. *Better be careful if you come back, Shadow,* she aimed the thought at the retreating cat. *Because now Trehearne might well try to shoot you.*

That wasn't the end of the incident, however. One of the troopers—Hank Riker, Sunny realized—walked over to the wrecked net, poking at it with his toe and talking with the security man who'd been carrying it. Then he spoke into the radio unit on his shoulder.

The amusing episode suddenly took on a more ominous tone, though Sunny couldn't quite put her finger on what had changed the mood so quickly, and she didn't feel confident enough to presume on Hank's friendship with Will to just walk up and ask. But she got an answer about an hour later, when they'd all reassembled for dinner, and the Senator was called away to respond to unexpected guests. Sunny quickly excused herself too and left the dining room in time to see Lieutenant Ellis Wainwright heading up the stairs with a couple of troopers. Hank Riker stood at the foot of the stairway, obviously positioned to prevent anyone from following. The Senator was nowhere to be seen.

Sunny looked around, and saw they were alone. "Can you tell me what's up?" she whispered to the trooper. "I saw you checking out the fishing net."

"That was enough for Wainwright to get a search warrant," Riker replied in an undertone. "We found the Nesbit murder weapon left in a storm drain. A very expensive fishing knife. Turns out Lemuel Kingsbury, the Senator's late son, was a big fishing buff back in the day. The net was part of his old fishing tackle. So the Lieutenant figured it was worth looking into."

"Priscilla's dad?" *Not to mention the father of Governors Lem and Tom,* Sunny realized.

Riker nodded. "According to the Senator, the tackle box was still kept in his son's old room."

Sunny frowned.

Where Lem Junior and his wife are staying now.

A moment later, Wainwright appeared on the upstairs

landing, not looking happy. "The knife is gone, but the gear's all scattered," she overheard him say as she stepped back out of his sight. "Whoever went to get that net must have been in a hurry. I think his are the only prints we're likely to find."

Sunny tried to edge even farther back, when she heard someone behind her and turned to find that she wasn't the only eavesdropper. Thomas Neal Kingsbury, former U.S. Senator, stood scowling at her.

The Senator couldn't call her out for doing what he himself had been attempting, especially not within earshot of the state police homicide investigator. But he obviously wasn't happy with a reporter knowing about the latest development in the case; one that implicated his own grandson. Neither he nor Sunny enjoyed the meal after they returned to the dining room.

As the diners broke up, the Senator gestured for Sunny to join him, causing a lot of people to glance at her in surprise. That certainly didn't untie the knot in her stomach.

For once, though, he didn't launch into oratory. "I suppose I can't fault your instincts," he said. "But this has been difficult enough without having our name further splashed around."

"I'm a guest here, sir, and I'm aware that involves obligations," Sunny told him. "I'm not here to break any sensational stories."

Sunny's conciliatory manner seemed to placate the Senator. For now, at least. But just because she wasn't putting out the news on her blog or the *Courier*, that didn't mean Sunny intended to keep it all to herself. She headed off to the guesthouse and the privacy of her room, got out her cell phone, and called her father. "Hi, Dad. Just checking in."

"With everything else that's going on, I've been debating whether to call you," Mike said. "The furball has disappeared—apparently right after you left. You know how he takes off sometimes for a few days. I didn't want to worry you."

"No worry," she assured her dad. "Turns out, he followed me here—stowed away in my bag, no less. You won't believe the trouble he's caused."

"Oh, I'd believe it," Mike replied in a dry voice. His relationship with Shadow definitely had its ups and downs. "Have you gotten hold of him again? Should I drive over with the cat carrier?"

"Right now he's still on the loose, but I'll do my best to try and coax him." Sunny shook her head at the mental picture of trying to get Shadow into the carrier against his will. "I don't think we have to worry about transporting him yet. How are you doing?"

"Enjoying a cat-free house." As Mike replied, Sunny heard a female voice speak in a scolding undertone. Mrs. Martinson?

Don't ask, don't tell, Sunny decided. She chatted for a moment more and then hung up. But she didn't put the phone away, instead dialing Will Price's number.

"Can't really talk, I'm busy crime busting." He must have recognized her caller ID, because he was doing a perfect Dudley Do-Right impersonation.

Sunny laughed. "And where are you pursuing this crusade?"

"They've got me patrolling the interstate through

outlet-land," he replied. "No demon speeders rushing to get last-minute bargains will avoid the long arm of the law."

"Sounds wonderful," Sunny said. "But when you finish your righteous work, maybe you can come by and talk to me. There's been a development."

Will dropped the voice. "You think you've got something?"

"I think Lieutenant Wainwright has something," she responded, "and I think we should talk about it. There are a couple of things to consider, and I think two heads are better than one."

"All right," he said. "I'll call you when I'm up there."

Sunny closed her phone and then debated what to do. Maybe a quiet stroll through the nearby streets to see if she could get in touch with the feline avenger . . .

That thought got interrupted by an almost timid tap at her door. Sunny opened it to find Cillie Kingsbury and Carson de Kruk outside.

"Can we talk?" Cillie was almost whispering.

Sunny motioned them inside and closed the door.

"I saw that my grandfather spoke to you after supper," Priscilla said. "I hope he wasn't—too much. But you have to understand, this can be embarrassing."

Murders often are, Sunny's snarky alter ego silently wisecracked.

"It's just that everybody knows how my father is on TV." Carson fumbled for words. "I hear how people call him Emperor Augustus and even make fun of him. He hates being laughed at, but he can live with it. That's just his TV image. But this thing about cats, it's beyond his control. I don't know if you're a cat person . . ."

Priscilla might have found out when she visited. But Sunny remembered that she'd cleared the living room of Shadow's toys. And Shadow had been his usual standoffish self, not putting in an appearance when company came calling.

"I know we asked you here," Cillie rushed in, "and you are a reporter and all, but do you think you could keep that part private?"

Carson's eyes were pleading. "Dad's not as impervious as he seems, and if this got out, it would really crush him."

It took Sunny a moment to switch gears, understanding what they were concerned about. But she said, "Nobody's going to hear about that incident from me—that's a promise."

The couple gave a simultaneous sigh of relief.

"But," she warned, "there are probably tons of pictures and maybe film of Lee Trehearne and his security crew chasing that cat off Neal's Neck. Some newspeople may begin asking questions."

She decided not to reveal what the Senator had actually discussed with her, the discovery of where the murder weapon had come from. The prospective bride and groom had enough on their minds.

And Wainwright would probably kill me for letting the cat out of the bag, Sunny thought.

When they asked her to join them downstairs in the living room, Sunny didn't see any polite way to refuse. She was soon roped into a game of Scrabble, which Beau opted out of, dozing in an armchair. They did teams again. Peter Van Twissel performed a lot better than he had at beer pong—and a lot less belligerently.

By the time the scores were totaled up, a glance at her watch told Sunny that Will was probably on his way. While the rest of the group headed upstairs, Sunny went outside to sit on the fieldstone porch.

If this were a movie, I'd look over and find Shadow sitting on the railing, she thought. But when she turned her head, the railing was empty. Sunny shook her head. *He never was a cinematic cat.*

Her cell phone began bleating. Sunny opened it and put it to her ear.

"I'm here," Will said. "A little down the road from the usual place."

Sunny got up, walked down the steps, and past the road-block. Instead of a blue Kittery Harbor police cruiser, there was now a white sheriff's department vehicle parked there, with a guy in a forest green uniform behind the wheel. She walked past him and turned the corner. Will's black pickup sat about halfway down the block.

"Let's just sit here quietly," he suggested, opening the passenger door for her. "So what did Wainwright find?"

"You may have heard already," Sunny said. "They found the murder weapon in a storm drain."

"The only thing I've heard was a lot of standard-issue radio chatter," Will told her. "Ingersoll wants me as far from this case as possible." He looked tired after his shift, but his eyes gleamed with interest. "So what was the weapon?"

"A fishing knife," Sunny began, but she was interrupted by a thump in front of them.

Sunny let out a stifled yelp, and Will went for his gun. But this wasn't the mad murderer who went after people sitting in their cars. They turned to find a familiar figure sitting on the front hood of the pickup. It was Shadow, regarding them with enigmatic, gold-flecked eyes.

Shadow sat looking in the window, his tail twitching back and forth. After being wakened from his new sleeping place, he'd thought the go-fast thing rolling to a stop looked familiar. Then he saw Sunny's He come out. And what happened then? Sunny herself turned up.

Finally!

He watched as they talked, creeping closer as they got into the vehicle. He listened, too. The good thing was that they weren't making any loud noises or hitting at one another. But as he spied on them, Shadow noticed their heads weren't close together, either. And she and the male two-legs sounded serious rather than happy as they sat together.

For a wild moment, he'd hoped that maybe Sunny had gotten into the go-fast thing to go home. But she wasn't carrying anything, and she'd taken a lot of things with her when she'd left her place where the Old One lived.

Shadow gathered himself for a leap and landed on the front of the go-fast thing. Sunny and her He both jumped as he landed to confront them. Shadow sat very still, staring at them while his tail lashed around. He was angry at Sunny—for leaving, for pretending not to know him when she saw him before, for raising his hopes now when she obviously wasn't actually coming home.

It wasn't the kind of thing he could settle with hisses and claws. But he could show Sunny how he felt. *She's not the only one who can go away,* he thought.

"That cat is worse than your dad," Will burst out. "He shows up whenever we're alone in the dark. But how did he manage to do it a half hour's drive from your house?"

"He followed me here," Sunny explained, stretching out a hand to the windshield. But Shadow didn't respond with his usual paw against the glass. "Or rather, he stowed away in my bag. Shadow was pretty upset when I left. And he caused a pretty big stir today." She explained about Augustus de Kruk's reaction to seeing Shadow and the ensuing pursuit.

"Well, I can't say I'm thrilled to see him turn up here." Will took a long, deep breath. "What are you—we—planning to do about this?"

"I don't know," Sunny admitted. "After all that happened, I can understand him being skittish. But now he's Public Enemy Number One on Neal's Neck. I'm afraid he's going to get hurt. And even if they only catch him, what am I going to do? Say, 'Oh, that's my cat,' and take him away? I don't think that will cut much ice with the de Kruks, Trehearne, or the Kingsburys, for that matter."

She stared at the cat still sitting on the hood, and gave him the evil eye. "Problem is, I don't think Shadow's just going to go back home quietly."

"I suppose we should try to catch him," Will said. "Try and get your hand on the door handle without letting him see it."

Sunny groped over, keeping her eyes on Shadow. "Got it," she reported.

"And I've got mine," Will said. "We'll go for a count of three. I'll take the left side, you take the right, and with luck we'll have him surrounded. One, two . . ."

When Will yelled "Three!" Sunny flung her door open, jumped out, and went for the hood. She saw a wild-eyed Will on the opposite side—but no cat.

"He must have ducked under when he saw us coming out." Will returned to the pickup, coming back out with a flashlight. "I'll see if I can spot him—"

"There!" Sunny pointed as Shadow streaked out from under the pickup and disappeared into a stretch of roadside underbrush. The circle of light from Will's flashlight was about a second behind him.

"It's hopeless to try and find him in that jungle." Will gave Sunny a sidewise glance. "He must be pretty peeved with you."

"He must be." Sunny couldn't keep the forlorn tone out of her voice. "One of the members of the wedding party gave him something to eat today. But heaven knows how he's getting along."

"Knowing Shadow, he'll manage to land on his feet." Will changed the subject. "Tell me more about this knife."

"Seems it belonged to Priscilla Kingsbury's father, Lem,"

Sunny said. "He was quite a fisherman before that landslide caught his campaign bus. Anyway, there was a big chase scene where Lee Trehearne and his security people tried to run Shadow down. One of the guys was carrying a fisherman's landing net, and your friend Hank Riker saw it. Lieutenant Wainwright came with a search warrant to look at the late Lem's tackle box and came down saying that the gear had all been disarranged and the knife was gone."

Will frowned in thought. "So what does this tell us?"

"Going by MOM, Beau Bellingham is still a possible candidate for the first murder," Sunny said. "He had a nasty fight with Eliza Stoughton—motive. She was strangled, and he's a big guy—means. And he has no alibi other than sleeping alone, which leaves him open on opportunity. None of it's a slam dunk, but he's the likeliest suspect."

"But now there's been another murder, and Beau had no known beef with Sheriff Nesbit—no motive." Will took up the line of reasoning. "Unless I suppose Nesbit found out something about him that the rest of us haven't. He left your beer pong tournament early, which again leaves him open on opportunity. But means . . ." His voice trailed off, then came back. "You'd need a very sharp knife to slit someone's throat like that, and a knife used to gut fish would be ideal. And if it had been sitting around in a tackle box for years, that knife probably wouldn't be missed, unlike grabbing something from a kitchen."

"The question is, how would Beau even know about the knife?" Sunny argued. "It's his first visit to Neal's Neck."

"It *is* hard to explain. He'd have had to pump Priscilla or somebody else in the family pretty thoroughly to get this information. On the other hand, the drinks were flowing pretty freely the day before Eliza got killed. Priscilla or one of the others may have mentioned something in passing. Did Beau spend much time with Caleb Kingsbury? He'd probably be a font of information about the quirks of the property—and the folks who lived here."

"Not that I saw," Sunny said.

"The use of Lem's knife does suggest someone familiar with the house and property. What about your friend Caleb?"

"I think everything bad in his life has already been spread out for media inspection," Sunny replied. "Since Sheriff Nesbit died, I've had to reconsider Randall's theory. Maybe we're looking for a person with a secret so dirty, they're killing to keep even the suggestion of blackmail away from their name. That sounds like somebody with a very public profile."

"Like a governor, maybe," Will suggested. "Governor Lem and his lovely wife have been bunking in his father's old room. Lem—the young Lem—boy, this is getting confusing. Anyway, the Lem who's still alive—did say he knew Nesbit in that blog post you put out today."

"You read that?" Sunny said in surprise.

"Of course. I wanted to see how you were doing." Then Will shrugged, his face twisting in annoyance. "And thanks to Ingersoll, you're practically my only source for information out of Neal's Neck these days. But forget about that." He quickly shook his head. "We've got to use your position as an inside person to learn more. Ask about family history, without going into specifics about things like Lem Senior's fishing. And the property itself—any oddball things there? Did Caleb or Priscilla ever sneak out of the compound? Could they have mentioned how they managed to pull that off to someone else?"

"Oh sure," Sunny said glumly. "That sounds easy enough to slip into a casual conversation."

She and Will spent a few more minutes searching the shrubbery for Shadow, then Sunny told him she'd better head back. She walked past the roadblock, skirting the trooper, and into the guesthouse. As Sunny opened the door to her room, she half expected to find Shadow curled up on her bed, but there was no sign of him.

Just as well, I suppose, she thought as she got ready for bed, but she had an uneasy feeling that she'd be paying for her current relief in other ways soon enough.

*

By the next morning, there were other things to talk about. All of the guests were awakened at the crack of dawn by Priscilla's brothers, who requested them to come to the big house. Once there, the whole family sat together watching one of the Sunday morning news shows. The comedy highlight for the day was the video footage of the Keystone Kops chase scene across the lawn yesterday. Augustus de Kruk stayed in the dining room for the whole scene. Apparently, he couldn't even bear to see a cat on television.

Deborah Kingsbury, Lem Junior's wife, winced while watching the attempt to trap Shadow with the net. "I'd seen that thing hanging around for years in our room. And when I suggested it might actually be useful—" She rolled her eyes in annoyance. "Your people just about tore the closet apart and made an enormous mess," she complained to

Lee Trehearne, who sat through the whole thing looking like a volcano on the verge of erupting.

The scene ended with Shadow scampering off. Sunny thought he looked pretty good on TV. Unfortunately, Lee Trehearne looked even bigger and more red-faced than in real life when he next appeared on screen, explaining that he and his people had been trying to retrieve a guest's pet.

It fell to the Senator to ask everyone to go along with the harmless deception.

"Fine," Beau Bellingham said. "But whose cat is it supposed to be?"

"I'll volunteer," Sunny spoke up quickly. "I'm local, so it's not impossible that the cat could have come along with me. And since I'm media, I'll be able to handle any questions."

Lee Trehearne looked as if he'd accidentally swallowed a razor blade, but he didn't say anything. Priscilla and Carson thanked her warmly, the Senator less so. Even the Emperor Augustus unbent enough to express his appreciation when he rejoined them.

"Thanks," Sunny told him. "Maybe you could do something in return and let me quote a few nice words from you about the area here. I know it's not like the sort of resort that you're used to visiting, but maybe you could say something about the fresh air and talk about how much you enjoyed the unspoiled scenery while flying in, and so forth."

The Emperor Augustus wasn't thrilled, but he suggested that she work something up and he'd look it over. That was enough of a win for Sunny. It would tickle Ken Howell and offer Ollie Barnstable a nice plug for the area that they could also co-opt for use on the MAX website.

Sunny was working on a draft of the statement to show

de Kruk when her cell phone rang. When she answered, she heard Ken Howell's voice. "Well, the boys in Levett have made their move, and it's a doozy. I just came out of the press conference."

"About what?" Sunny asked.

"About who's going to go on the ballot in place of Frank Nesbit," Ken replied. "Don't you know what's going on?"

"To be honest, I'm a bit isolated up here," Sunny told him. "So who's the September surprise? What did they do? Name a party stalwart?"

"Even worse," Ken said gloomily. "They named Lenore Nesbit—the old 'vote for the widow' trick. And it seems to be working. Nobody had the gall to ask her any hard questions, not even me. I think Will is up against it."

Considering that Ken was one of the founding members of the breakaway Kittery Harbor faction with Mike, this sounded pessimistic indeed. "How does my dad feel?" Sunny asked.

"I'm trying to figure out how to break it to him," Ken responded. "I mean what with his heart and all."

"Oh, he can stand a little bad news," Sunny told him. *At least Shadow isn't around for him to try to kick,* she thought. "I just hope the furniture can take it."

The rest of the day Sunny spent watching and listening. She decided to have lunch with the older crowd and see how they were dealing with the situation. It was another buffet setup, but outdoors on a fieldstoned terrace behind the house. Tom and Lem Kingsbury appeared with damp hair and shiny faces, apparently having taken quick showers after a morning's workout on the tennis court.

Sunny paid special attention to Lem Junior, who'd risen

on her personal suspects list. He'd certainly known about his father's tackle box, a handy source for a sharp knife. He had easy access, since he was staying in the room where the thing was stored. And for a governor with presidential aspirations, a bit of blackmail was easy to imagine turning into something to kill over.

On the other hand, Lem didn't seem to be under any strain. He ate a hearty lunch and chatted amiably with the members of his family. He even joked a bit with Augustus de Kruk, who told him that if he put as much effort into politics as he did into tennis, he'd have been president already.

Lem took it good-naturedly. "I guess that's the problem with this family. Politics is our sideline. Tennis is the business. If you're up for a game, maybe Cale can be persuaded. He's not as bloodthirsty as Tom or I."

"It's been a while since I even held a tennis racquet," Cale told Augustus. "I'm not sure what kind of a game I'd give you."

Maybe he should challenge the Emperor to beer pong, Sunny's irreverent side suggested.

"We'll see," Augustus said. "Maybe later in the afternoon."

Deborah Kingsbury put a fond hand on her husband's shoulder. "Anything to interrupt the unending marathon between you and Tom."

She looked as cool and unruffled as ever–if she'd been helping her husband hide two murders, she certainly wasn't showing any strain. *Although she was the one who drew attention to Lem Senior's fishing tackle,* Sunny thought. *Did she do that innocently because she didn't know about the knife? Or was it a more devious maneuver, ensuring a lot of fresh fingerprints would appear on the tackle so that her husband's wouldn't be so obvious?*

Sunny took a sip of chilled white wine. *Deborah even complained about what a mess the security people made. So if Lem's prints appeared somewhere they shouldn't, he'd have a perfect explanation—they're the result of him trying to tidy things up in a room where they've always slept.*

"Some more wine?" Cale gestured with the bottle, scattering Sunny's thoughts.

"No, thanks," she replied. The problem was, all these politicians and their families had plenty of experience in not letting their true feelings show. Even with her reporter's instincts, Sunny was having a hard time getting a read on them.

So either I need a little more white wine, or they need a lot of it, she thought with a wry smile.

Since neither possibility was likely to happen, Sunny decided to return to Priscilla and her friends after lunch. She did, however, make Cale promise to send word if he actually was going to meet Augustus de Kruk on the tennis court. Cillie Kingsbury laughed when she heard about it. "That would be worth seeing," she teased Carson. "Your dad, working up a sweat?"

"Oh, he doesn't mind getting worked up," the younger de Kruk told them. "Usually for money, but Dad would be okay going for a little glory, too."

Genevieve Kingsbury, Tom's wife, appeared sometime later with the news that battle would indeed be joined. The brunette looked a little envious of the young people lounging around the pool. They weren't all that much younger than she was, and with her lively eyes, Genevieve didn't seem the type to spend all day being a spectator.

Priscilla and Carson headed off to go and watch the game, and of course so did Sunny. Tommy Neal also decided to join the viewing party, while Peter, Beau, and Yardley stayed put.

As they walked over to the tennis court with Genevieve, Sunny said, "I'm still looking for some background to set the stage in my blog. The big house is so beautiful. Are there any interesting stories about it I could share? I heard about your great-grandfather trying to shoot the wasp, but that may be a bit too colorful."

Cillie laughed. "I guess the problem is that all the good stories are Neal stories, not Kingsbury ones. Like the widow's walk." She pointed in the direction of the big house. "You can't really see it unless you're flying overhead, but Great-Grandfather Neal added a platform on top of the house. It's got a great view out to sea, the highest point on Neal's Neck. He'd have somebody up there with a lantern, signaling the rumrunners when it was safe to deliver. It was a big deal to get up there," she added. "You had to work a catch on a secret door. Tom showed me when I was ten years old."

"He showed me, too, the first time I visited here." Genevieve's voice was tart. "It sounded very mysterious and exciting, but what it came down to was a ten-by-ten deck, and the wind off the water was freezing."

"Maybe you should tell Sunny about the copse," Priscilla said with a naughty look.

"The cops?" Sunny repeated. "You mean the security people? The troopers?"

"No, C-O-P-S-E," Cillie spelled it out. "It's a little thicket of trees out by the point, probably the wildest spot you'll find around here." She gestured at the manicured lawns around them. "There used to be a gazebo in the middle, but it lost most of its roof the year I was born. So now it's a romantic ruin, a bower—"

"Inspiration point," Tommy Neal put in. "Every teenager's dream: quiet, secluded, and yeah, I guess romantic. Just remember to bring a thick blanket along. That old wood can get splintery."

"Very practical," Priscilla scolded him. She waggled her eyebrows at Sunny. "It may not be the grotto at the Playboy mansion, but in our family, it has . . . history."

"History that Sunny won't be sharing on her blog, I hope." Genevieve tried to sound like the adult here, but Sunny noticed a faint blush on her cheeks.

Looks as if Genevieve visited the copse at some point, too, Sunny thought.

"That's the wrong kind of romantic past I'm looking for," she assured them. "I'm doing the blog for a family paper, not *Eagle Eye*."

They arrived at the tennis court, and conversation switched to the upcoming match.

"Dad might surprise you," Carson said to the group. "He plays a darned good game of tennis. The competitive streak in him, you know."

"But Uncle Cale is younger," Cillie said to Carson. "And he's in pretty good shape."

"We'll see."

Augustus de Kruk arrived in a set of tennis whites, prompting Sunny to wonder what other wardrobe items he traveled with—white tie and tails? A scuba outfit? And while he wasn't as svelte as Lem or Tom, his legs, exposed in shorts, were muscular. So were his arms.

Cale looked a little uncomfortable in what looked like borrowed whites from one of his nephews. They were a little tight, especially at the waist, but his legs were tanned and brawny, and his arms were ropey with muscles.

He must get a lot of exercise hauling the sails on his boat, Sunny thought.

They squared off, and Augustus asked, "Shall we spin the racquet to see who serves first?"

"Since you're the guest," Cale replied, "I'll let you make the choice."

Augustus chose to serve, and they were off. The Emperor had a strong serve, and Cale's response to his shots was always just a hair too late. His returns were rushed, not going where he aimed them; it was clear to Sunny that he just wasn't quite in the game. He'd battle back a little, but then Augustus would quickly regain the upper hand.

Sunny maintained the silent decorum that tennis required, even though she was more used to rowdy softball games where raucous comments from the sidelines were the norm rather than the exception. Several times she was tempted to holler at Cale to get the lead out . . . and then she noticed something. Cale wasn't even breathing hard.

She leaned over to whisper in Priscilla's ear. "Is your uncle throwing this game?" Cillie turned from the action on the court to give Sunny a knowing look, whispering, "Augustus has made a couple of nominal donations to the foundation, but Uncle Cale wants to hit him up for something more substantial."

Sunny smiled. *What better way to loosen the purse strings than to lose gracefully?*

In the end, Augustus enjoyed a handsome victory, not

too easily won, and accepted the congratulations of the bystanders with a satisfied smile.

Old Cale might not be fighting for reelection, but he's as much a politician as anyone in the family, Sunny told herself. Looks like a case of o*nce a Kingsbury, always a Kingsbury.*

Sunny, Cillie, Carson, and Tommy headed back to the pool and some late afternoon sun. The evening meal offered the usual buffet plus a rehash of the tennis game between Cale and Augustus. Sunny was glad to have a little time to herself afterward. Scarcely getting out of the property for days was beginning to feel a bit too claustrophobic for her taste. Sunny left the compound for a good reason, searching for Shadow. But, even though she worried about what kind of predicaments he might get himself into, she found herself enjoying fresh air without the need to wear a mask of decorum. She just about pounced on her cell phone when a text message came in from Will:

DUG UP A LITTLE, WANT 2 DISCUSS. WILL CALL.

By the time Will called, Sunny had circled around to the block where they usually met, arriving well ahead of him. She spent the time looking around in the bushes but found no sign of her trouble-causing kitty. As Will pulled up, she waved and quickly climbed in, asking, "What did you find?"

"I did some checking up on Lee Trehearne," Will said. "He served in the army—Iraq—and when his enlistment was up, worked for a private security firm there. Not to say there weren't good men in those companies— "

"But they have a reputation for acting like cowboys,"

Sunny finished. "And a lot of money disappeared from the supposed nation building after the war. Was there any hint of something Trehearne could be blackmailed over?"

"Not that I found," Will began, but that was as far as he got before a white sheriff's department cruiser screeched around the corner in front of them, and a similar vehicle pulled in behind, effectively boxing them in. Captain Ingersoll got out of the rear car, stalking over to Will's pickup and gesturing that the window come down.

"Perhaps I didn't make myself clear, Constable Price." Ingersoll's hoarse voice grated out the words. "When I said you were relieved of your duties here, I meant that you were no longer connected with this case. So you had no reason to go searching into the military records of the chief of security at Neal's Neck, much less turn up here. Perhaps the sheriff was willing to turn a blind eye to these little personal projects of yours"—he glared at Sunny as if this were all her fault—"but the new administration will not tolerate failure to obey orders. So let me put this in words you can understand, Price. You are off the Stoughton case. You are off the Nesbit case. I do not want you interfering in the ongoing investigation. I don't even want to see you on the streets of Wilawiport. You get that now? I hope like hell you do. I'm told you're a good officer. Don't make me fire you."

16

Shadow crouched in the underbrush, feeling his disappointment turn to anger. For a moment, he'd let his hopes rise again. Maybe this time, Sunny was going home with her He.

But then the noise had started, not from Sunny and the male, but from those white go-fast things, and that Fat One hollering. Shadow crept closer to catch a whiff of the shouting two-legs. No trace of Smells Good. That was a relief. If Sunny had gotten involved with a human like that, there was no hope of staying with her.

Sunny got out of the black go-fast thing, and her He drove off. The Fat One got into his vehicle and zoomed away, too.

Only Sunny was left, standing by herself. She looked very lonely there in the darkness. For a second, Shadow wanted to go charging toward her, pounce on her foot, make her laugh, and just be with her. But Sunny had ignored him when he needed a two-legged friend, when the others were chasing him. And then she and her He had tried to grab him themselves.

Right now, Shadow wasn't certain he could trust Sunny. What if he came to her and she grabbed him? Or worse, pushed him away? No, his heart would surely break.

So he stayed at the side of the road, just watching her.

Finally she started walking back to that place where she was staying. Silently, Shadow followed. He couldn't trust her . . . but he couldn't leave her, either.

*

Sunny lay in bed, eyes open, for a long time, going over the facts she'd gotten from her interrupted conversation with Will and his subsequent phone call. Given the outlines of the career Will had sketched out, there was certainly the possibility that Lee Trehearne had something worth blackmailing in his past. And who better to put the squeeze on during a big event than the head of security?

Taking it a step further, why couldn't Trehearne be the Taxman? Sure, he was way out on the fringes of society, working for the Senator. But if he'd used information he discovered from the Kingsburys as a start, and then expanded his operation . . . That might even explain the Taxman's business model, using former victims to lure new ones into his web.

On the other hand, Trehearne hadn't looked much like a criminal mastermind while in bumbling pursuit of Shadow. Although Shadow had a way of driving even the most competent people to a hair's breadth of screaming craziness.

Including myself, Sunny had to admit ruefully. But blackmail victim or perpetrator, Trehearne had the physical ability to do unpleasant stuff like strangling girls and slashing sheriffs. He also had the knowledge of Neal's Neck, where the surveillance cameras were and how to avoid them, probably even what junk was stored where.

You can make a case against him, Sunny had to admit. *But you can make a case against most of the guys stuck behind the security perimeter here. That doesn't narrow things down. What I need is provable evidence.*

Unfortunately, that, like sleep, seemed in short supply.

*

The morning was well advanced by the time Sunny pulled herself out of bed, feeling droopy. She'd lain awake way too long but had finally dropped off sometime in the wee hours. She found herself at the late sitting for breakfast, joining Beau Bellingham and Tommy and Yardley Neal at the table. It wasn't a comfortable meal. Everybody seemed a little stir-crazy.

"If I have to sit around that pool again today, somebody's going to get drowned." Tommy snarled as he stabbed his knife into a jar of preserves. A little belatedly, he realized how his words might sound and sent a suspicious glance over at Sunny.

"To tell the truth, I'm feeling the same way myself," she admitted. "Maybe I'll talk to Priscilla and Carson about arranging some kind of outing. There are lots of non-touristy things we could do."

"If we don't mind being followed by a bunch of paparazzi." But she'd started Tommy thinking and his sour mood lightened a bit. "Maybe we could talk Cale into taking us out again on the *Merlin*," he said. "I wouldn't even mind hoisting all the sails as long as it got us out of here for a while."

With this plan in mind, they set off for the swimming pool, where they found Carson and Peter involved in a card game.

"I'm afraid Priscilla's not here," Carson said as he tossed his cards down. "She and Caleb left early this morning on some foundation business. She'll be back for lunch—or rather, hors d'oeuvres, since we'll be tasting some sample wedding cakes. "

"Probably too late for us to get out on the water." Tommy explained his idea, scowling. "Unless," he suggested, "I could take the wheel."

"You really want to take Uncle Cale's pride and joy off on a little unauthorized sail?" Carson asked skeptically. "He'd never forgive you."

"All right, all right, you've got a point." Tommy flopped down onto a beach chair.

Sunny noticed that Beau hadn't paid any attention to the conversation. He'd just arranged himself on a lounge chair with a baseball cap shading his eyes, and in moments, his chest was rising and falling in easy sleep.

I wish I could do that, Sunny thought jealously.

"Feel free to join our card game," Peter invited the others.

"I only play for money, Van Twissel," Tommy replied. "And that's something that neither you nor Carson has got." He rose from his seat, shrugged off the loud Hawaiian shirt he'd been using as a cover-up, and jumped into the pool with a lot more violence than necessary, showering Sunny with spray.

"Tommy!" Yardley called after him in a scolding voice.

"Don't worry about it," Sunny told her. "It'll get even wetter when I jump in later." She undid the towel from around her waist and ran it over her hair, leaving it around her shoulders. "Would you mind another poor person at the table?" she asked.

They spent the morning playing all the most ridiculous versions of poker they knew, wild cards, baseball, even something Carson called "Indian poker," where players had to hold their cards up on their foreheads, seeing what kinds of hands other players had, but not their own.

Between crazy games and crazy bets, Sunny had won a lot of imaginary money by the time Deborah Kingsbury appeared at the gate. "The Senator thought it might be nice to have everyone present for the cake tasting." Lem's wife didn't have to add that whatever the Senator thought to be appropriate had the force of an order.

*

This is a *stupid place,* Shadow thought as he crept along the wall of the house. He was in a bad mood; things had not gone right since last night. Sunny had walked back to that place where she was staying, and Shadow hadn't been able to sneak in after her. So he'd left her and gone back to his sleeping spot next to the planter. But when the sun came up, loud people with even louder machines had come to do things, and Shadow had run for his life.

After that rude awakening, he'd quickly become aware of an unpleasantly empty feeling in his middle. He'd tried another backyard visit to the place where the nice two-legged woman had fed him the other day. But he was out of luck. No kind human, just that stupid white cat being all unfriendly and brave behind the safety of the glass.

He'd tried foraging around, but all he encountered were the scents of large, dangerous animals apparently already hunting in the area. Not just biscuit eaters, but the nasty-black-masked critters.

Feeling a little desperate, Shadow went toward the big water, hoping to find something on the beach. But there, large white birds kept swooping down at him, screeching.

So, still hungry, he'd headed back through backyards toward the place where Sunny was. There was a wall barring the way, higher than he could jump, but Shadow had already found a spot along the base where some of the soil had washed away and a determined cat could squeeze in.

Maybe it's better that I was empty before I tried that, he thought as he barely managed to squirm through.

He quickly darted to the side of a house and made his way through flowers and plants until he faced a large open area. Keeping a wary eye out for the aggressive two-legs in black, he made his way from bushes to flowers to trees, doing his best to keep out of sight. They might not be able to catch him, but he'd hate to have a meal interrupted because those ones happened to come along.

As he came to the place with the splashing water, Shadow heard human voices. He used his best stalking moves to slink up, peering suspiciously around the metal post that held a gate. Another disappointment—all he saw were a pair of male two-legs bent over a table. Nothing to eat, and the friendly female who'd fed him wasn't there. He wandered on still in search of a meal.

At last he came to a big, big house. Shadow moved even

more cautiously. This was where the Clumsy One had tried to grab him. It might not be a good idea to meet that one again. He had been angry, very angry, when Shadow got away.

Using every bit of cover he found, Shadow made his way around the house, following his nose. The breeze was coming toward him, and it held a touch of that slightly rancid tang that came from food the two-legs had thrown away. Well, sometimes a cat could happily fill his belly from what the two-legs didn't want.

The scent grew stronger as he advanced, until at last he found the source—another disappointment. Shadow could clearly smell the old food, but there were only traces left on the stony ground beneath his feet. He couldn't eat traces, and the food itself was sealed away in heavy metal containers that were too hard to break into and too heavy to knock over.

It was enough to bring a faint mew of frustration out of him.

Then he heard voices again, and scrunched down to make himself as inconspicuous as possible. But the voices didn't come his way, so he went to investigate.

That turned out to be an excellent idea, because as he drew closer to the voices, he also smelled food. Good food. Shadow poked his head around something that couldn't make up its mind whether to be a window or a door and found a room the two-legs used for messing around with food, making it hot or mixing it up together. Sunny and the Old One often worked in a room like this. It was also where they fed him.

But this room was much, much bigger, and there were several people in there, clattering pans and talking. It reminded him of places he'd sometimes seen in his travels, somewhere a cat might find a meal. Sometimes a cat might even try to make friends and get a really good meal. He'd learned, though, not to go inside. That would only mean trouble, loud voices, and someone in white chasing him away.

So he'd held back, watching the busy humans, until finally they started coming outside carrying very large plates. This seemed odd. Were they going outside to eat? Sometimes Sunny and the Old One did that, but they usually brought food to the thing that made smoke. And he didn't smell smoke now.

Shadow waited for a chance to follow one of the two-legs and came to a table. A long white thing came over the sides and down to the ground, and Shadow quickly hid under that. But he peeked out from under it, watching many feet come and go. Then they stopped, and he decided to take a risk and come out from hiding. Shadow craned his neck and stretched as high as he could, unable to see the top of the table but taking in the smells that wafted down.

He could distinguish several kinds of food that he knew— and many more he didn't. It was enough to make a cat's mouth water. Shadow gathered himself for a jump to the top of the table. But then voices came from the other side, and he darted to the cover of the white stuff again, crossing under the table and peering out from under the far side.

Feet again! This was getting monotonous, not to mention annoying. His stomach growled from the good smells. Shadow poked his head out to see what the two-legs were up to.

He caught a wave of made smells and saw humans in bright colors talking loudly. They were clinking glasses and eating little things. . . .

That's what must be on top of the table! He slunk out, but no one noticed him. He tried to sit and watch, to wait for his chance. He waited for a long time. Seconds, at least.

The smell of food was making his head swim. He couldn't help himself—he had to have some!

Crouching low, Shadow sprang up and scrambled to the top of the table. Yes, there were the big plates, covered with all kinds of little foods. Ignoring everything else, he followed his nose, greedily trying everything he came across. Some of it tasted odd, some of it he spit out. But lots of it tasted good . . . *very* good.

*

Sunny looked in her closet, trying to mix and match an outfit into existence for a so-called casual lunch. Deborah had mentioned that the meal would be outdoors, so Sunny figured a top and slacks should be appropriate.

The problem is, I've worn most everything I've brought. Remembering all the bags the de Kruks had unloaded didn't exactly cheer Sunny's mood. She finally chose a pair of khakis and the blouse she'd worn under her cinnamon suit.

When she got downstairs, Sunny found Tommy and Yardley Neal dressed as if for an afternoon at the country club. Yardley wore a white linen suit, while Tommy wore a raw silk jacket over a polo shirt and dark gray slacks.

I guess this is how it feels to be the poor relation, Sunny thought gloomily. *Of course,* she comforted herself, *when we get to the big house, we'll probably find the present Mrs. de Kruk wearing a diamond tiara, and Emperor Augustus in a golden crown.* She really wished Cillie

Kingsbury were there to lighten the mood, but she wasn't around, apparently having gone straight to the big house.

When they met up with the rest of the guys, Carson had on a light blue linen-weave jacket over a white collarless shirt, Peter wore the jacket from his blue suit over a green T-shirt, and Beau had recycled his oatmeal-colored jacket over a tan Henley shirt. *At least half of us look like fashion casualties,* Sunny's alter ego commented snidely.

Perhaps because it was a command performance, the Senator—or more likely his wife Julia—had tried for a more festive atmosphere. The younger group arrived at the terrace to find the Kingsburys and de Kruks with wine-glasses in their hands, nibbling on hors d'oeuvres.

Fiona Ormond stepped onto the terrace like a general commanding her troops. Indeed, she had a single file of people carrying covered trays behind her. "Ladies and gentlemen, our cake candidates!" she announced.

The folks with the trays marched to the serving table, placed their burdens down, and removed the covers.

The cakes came in a wide range of varieties, some in small round tiers, others square. The frostings ranged from fondant to butter cream to cream cheese and even cannoli filling, decorated with spun-sugar blossoms or cunningly created leaves or petals, climbing vines, and in one case, what looked like a bunch of grapes dangling down the side. They weren't all white, either. Some bore designs in contrasting colors. One had stripes, which made the tiers look like stacked hatboxes to Sunny's eyes. Then there was one in delicate lavender with purple polka-dots. And one bakery had apparently decided to go completely nontraditional, with a chocolate ganache cake.

The cake servers themselves were an equally unusual assortment, from the thin guy in chef's whites (including a toque with a poofy top) to the the curvy girl in a shirt emblazoned with the legend, "LA PATISSERIE DE MAINE."

Sunny blinked when she realized who was wearing the sweatshirt—Robin Lory. Ben Semple's girlfriend was staring around so avidly that she almost missed the table when she put her tray down. She looked very disappointed when Fiona shepherded her and the others back to the kitchen.

La Patisserie's entry was more on the traditional side, a stepped set of round tiers ringed with pink frosting flowers, whimsically surmounted by a miniature bride and groom. *They've got serious competition,* Sunny thought. *But at least Robin had her moment as a waitress to the rich and famous.*

Apparently, Beau had a similar notion. "I'll be the bartender," he volunteered, heading for a sideboard with bottles of wine and aperitifs. Most of the crowd gravitated after him to get their glasses filled or freshened.

I suppose I might as well play waitress, Sunny thought. She headed for another table which held platters of various finger foods.

But as she edged around the crowd and got a full view of the table, she froze.

Standing on one of the platters was an all-too-familiar figure, happily scarfing down all the snacks.

Shadow!

Holding her breath, Sunny advanced on the table. *That crazy cat isn't even looking up from the stuff he's gobbling,* she thought with a stab of annoyance. *He had people chasing him all over the place. Doesn't he know how dangerous this is?* Then she thought, *He must really be hungry, usually he doesn't like to fool around with people food.*

Sunny was right beside him now. She gave out a low "Pssst!" to get Shadow's attention.

He looked up from licking something off a cracker, saw Sunny, and his ears went back. They stood for a moment, and then Sunny heard a commotion breaking out behind her.

Sounds as though Old Augustus has noticed Shadow again, she thought.

"It's back!" she heard the big man's voice quavering. "Get rid of it!"

As if on cue, Lee Trehearne came hustling out onto the terrace. His eyes took on a maniacal gleam when he spotted Shadow. But the cat saw him, too, launching into a leap for the table with the wedding cake samples. He skidded a little, upsetting La Patisserie's entry. The tiers collapsed, sending the bride and groom under Shadow's paws.

The security chief was beyond noticing or caring what else was on the table. After playing Elmer Fudd to Shadow's Bugs Bunny, he saw a chance to recover his self-respect—not to mention to catch that rascally cat.

Trehearne went into a dive, squishing more cakes under his bulk as he went for the cat. Still distracted by Sunny, Shadow clearly hadn't expected such an extreme assault until it was too late and Trehearne actually had his hands on him. Trehearne reared back, lifting Shadow like some sort of victory trophy. He had traces of at least six cakes smeared down the front of his Windbreaker, but he didn't care. His face was a mask of lunatic glee.

"Gotcha, ya little—" The security man tightened his grip on the cat's midsection.

Not the best move, Sunny thought as she came around the table to try and take Shadow. *Obviously, he hasn't eaten in a while. All that strange, rich food on an empty stomach. And now you put the squeeze on him . . .*

She was too late. Shadow made a husky, rasping sound, and then all the food he'd been gorging on came back up. The stream caught Trehearne right in the face and dribbled down, half-digested and undigested, to join the mess he was already wearing. Fiona Ormond screamed, whether from repugnance or because of the destruction of her carefully presented tasting, Sunny couldn't tell. Other guests gasped and turned away from the spectacle.

Trehearne himself made a loud, involuntary sound of disgust, and his hold on the cat slackened.

That was all Shadow needed. In an instant, he'd twisted loose, dropped to the table, and streaked away again, leaving Trehearne pop-eyed, his face red and distorted, disgusted . . . and disgusting.

*

Shadow ran full out, even though his ribs hurt and his throat felt raw. But the part that hurt the most was his feelings. *How could Sunny do that to him? How? How?* The thought pounded in his head in time to the pounding of his heart. *She caught my eye and kept me staring until the Clumsy One could sneak up and grab me. What a nasty trick!*

He didn't even want to think what was wrong with him to let a noisy two-legs stalk him successfully. But he decided to blame that on Sunny, too.

This was bad, bad, bad.

Shadow finally took cover in some bushes and lay low

to get his breath back. He put down his head and hissed. *To let some stranger come up and grab me—to help them.* . . . He rested his chin on his paws, trying to call up his anger again. But it was gone. His chest felt empty.

So did his stomach. All that nice food, gone. Although it was almost worth being sick to see the look on that big, red, mean face.

That's another thing Sunny owes me, Shadow thought. *She made me lose a meal.*

17

Nothing like an ailurophobic breakdown and cat barf *to start things off with a bang,* Sunny thought as she looked at the strained faces around the table. They had moved indoors, away from the dreaded cat, after the tasting debacle. Augustus de Kruk was reduced to weak tea and toast after this second visitation, and Fiona Ormond ate nothing, zombie-like after the catastrophic outcome of her big show. And Lee Trehearne had gone off to wash up and cool down after his latest misadventure.

Julia Kingsbury, Priscilla's grandmother, made a valiant effort to carry on some sort of conversation, but her efforts fell flat when no one else seemed able to join in.

Sunny herself just wanted to leave, but she didn't want to be the first to go. The food tasted like ashes in her mouth, and all she could think of was Shadow, wandering around Neal's Neck with Trehearne ready to go full Elmer Fudd on him, shotgun and all.

I've got to find him. The thought kept running through her mind. *I don't know what I'm going to do when I get him, but I've got to find him.*

Beau Bellingham's emergency room training overcame his reticence. "Are you sure you're okay, sir?" he asked Augustus de Kruk, who sat toying with one of the toast slices. "That was another really nasty shock for you. Maybe you should—"

"I don't take medical advice from a kid with hair like a goddamned sheep dog," the Emperor roared, as loudly as on any of his TV appearances. "An *unclipped* goddamned sheep dog."

Carson tried to come to his best man's defense. "Dad, he's got a hell of a schedule—"

But Magda de Kruk obviously paid more attention to what Beau had said. "Maybe it would be better to go upstairs," she suggested in her slight accent. "We could rest in bed." Augustus let himself be persuaded, and that was pretty much the end of lunch. Sunny waited until the de Kruks rose from the table and headed for the stairs before she made a move toward the French doors that led to the outdoor buffet.

That's where I last saw Shadow, she thought. *Although God knows where he's gotten to since.*

"Um, Sunny?"

She turned as Beau Bellingham came over to her, running an embarrassed hand through his blond thatch.

"That's the second time Mr. de Kruk nailed me for my hair," Beau said. "You're local. Can you suggest a place where I could get a decent trim?"

When she didn't answer immediately, he only got more embarrassed. "I know I haven't been all that sociable. I'd ask Priscilla, but she and Carson are going up with Augustus."

"It's not that, I'm just trying to sort out a place for you," Sunny explained. "I've got a troublesome head of hair, and not everybody does a good job. It took a while for me to find a good stylist, but she's in a women only salon and day spa."

She thought a little more. Will went to Harbor Barbers, not too far from the MAX office. They were fine for buzz cuts and the sort of hair styles a police officer might want, but Sunny shuddered at what they might do to Beau's mop. Where could she send him?

Finally, inspiration struck. She dug out her cell phone and pulled up the number for MAX. Nancy answered on the second ring. "Maine Adventure X-perience. How can I help you?"

"Hi, Nancy, it's Sunny. Everything going okay?"

"We're getting a lot of calls and e-mails about apple picking," Nancy reported. "Otherwise, no excitement. How about you?" Her voice got more animated. "I love your blog posts—those presents were hilarious! Have you figured out whodunit? Can I help with a clue?"

Sunny quickly cut off that line of discussion. "What you can help me out with is that a fella here needs a haircut," she said firmly. "He has to look presentable, and he's got very thick, curly hair. Can you check our local business database and find a place nearby with good recommendations?"

Nancy muttered for a moment, and Sunny heard the clack of computer keys. "Okay. The top of the list is a place called Wilawi Cuts, on Wilawi Wharf Road. Twelve reviews, all of them positive. One guy even said it's the only place that doesn't make him look like a poodle."

"A ringing endorsement if I ever heard one." Sunny repeated the address Nancy gave her to Beau. "Wilawi Wharf Road is a major business street in town," she told him. "I'm sure that any of the security guys here will know how to find it."

Getting back on her phone, she thanked Nancy, was reassured again that there were no office problems that couldn't be handled, said good-bye, and cut the connection.

Beau still stood in front of her, looking pretty impressed. "Can you do that with anything around here?"

Sunny grinned. "Anything legal."

"I better get going," Beau said, heading out the French doors and circling around, aiming for the path that led back to the guesthouses. Sunny took the same route, but much more slowly, stopping to check out every clump of brush or flowers for a hidden cat. That turned out to be wishful thinking, though. She didn't find a trace of Shadow.

Then, up ahead, she heard loud orders squawking over radios and saw security guys converging at a run. Sunny's heart squeezed into a little ball. *This is it,* she thought. *What are they going to do with him? Turn him over to Animal Control? Will they spot the little tag with my name and number on it?* In the excitement of Shadow's earlier brushes with security, she hadn't even thought of that before.

A second later, she sighed with relief to find it was a false alarm. It turned out to be a large, fat squirrel that went scampering up the trunk of a tree to disappear into the foliage. The security men dispersed, and Sunny continued with her solitary search.

Somehow, I don't think walking around saying, "Here, Shadow-Shadow," is going to work. Even with only herself as an audience, that thought fell flat in the humor department. Sunny had a sinking feeling that if Lee Trehearne had his way, Shadow would wind up in a bag full of rocks flying off the end of the point—or maybe get made into a hat. Almost unconsciously, she began to walk faster. *I've got to do something. Trehearne and his men in black are really on Shadow's case.*

Her hunt took her past the pool, where she saw Carson, Peter, and the Neals already reinstalled on the lounges. Unfortunately, Shadow wasn't there mooching anything from Yardley.

Sunny continued to work her way toward the guesthouses, one hiding spot at a time. At one point she knelt, trying to pierce the shadows in a lush planting by the path, and was startled by the sound of a car horn behind her. She scrambled to her feet and out of the way as one of the ubiquitous town cars rolled past. Beau Bellingham leaned out of the rear window, running a hand through his tousled curls. "You can say good-bye to them," he said with a grin. "I've already got an appointment!"

Laughing, Sunny waved him on, watching as the car passed the troopers and the roadblock. Her eyes went from the disappearing car to the guys' guesthouse, and her mood got more thoughtful.

Carson and Peter are at the pool, she thought. *With Beau going off to get shorn, that means no one's home. Maybe I can snoop a bit somewhere Lieutenant Wainwright can't get a warrant.*

Trying to look casual, she strolled across the private

road to the fieldstone steps that led to the front door of the other guesthouse.

Here goes, she told herself. *I just hope nobody's looking.*

*

From his hidey-hole under the porch, Shadow watched Sunny approach. This wasn't a good sleeping place—it was too cool and damp. But with bright sun coming down, it was a good place to keep out of sight, while keeping a lot in view. He'd watched the big, black go-fast thing come rolling past. And now here came Sunny, apparently heading straight for him!

Had he been wrong all this time about her? Was she able to track him by scent?

No, she turned to go up the steps to the door. Shadow rested his chin on his paws and thought. *This isn't Sunny's place. Her things are in the house across the way. Why would she come here? This place only has males. . . .*

A horrible suspicion dawned. A female visiting a house full of males. Was Smells Good in there somewhere? Was Sunny going to see him?

Shadow almost flew from his hiding place, scrambling up the stairs. Sunny was quietly opening the door. She seemed to be looking around a lot, but not down on the ground where Shadow was. He slunk through the space between her feet, careful not to touch her, and rushed down the hall, casting around for a trace of scent.

It was much like the other house, many dead smells from a place shut up too long. Some interesting aromas came toward his questing nose on a puff of breeze from the rear, probably from the room of food. Some of them smelled like food going bad. There was also a strong odor of that sour stuff the two-legs liked to drink, the stuff that made them get silly.

No made smells here, although some of the more pungent stinks wafting down from upstairs could certainly cover the more delicate fragrance he was searching for.

Sunny seemed to agree, because she started up the stairs. When she reached the hallway above, though, she stopped as if she wasn't sure where to go. As Shadow stealthily crept after her, he caught traces of male and female scents from one of the rooms. But Sunny merely peered into that room and went away. She stopped at another room that smelled as if no one had been in there for a long, long time. Shadow could tell that, even from his spot crouched by the wall. Couldn't Sunny scent anything at all?

She continued across the hall. The next room had some interesting smells that Shadow had never come across before, some of them nose-twisting, some of them metallic. For a second, he considered slipping past her to investigate.

But what happens if she closes the door? That thought held him in his place, keeping watch. Besides, Sunny didn't go in there either. She continued to the last room, the one where the strongest stinks came from.

Shadow charged. Is that why Smells Good covered himself in a made smell? Was his natural scent too strong? Shadow came through the doorway ready to unsheathe his claws and draw blood, to punish the interloper who had stolen his Sunny.

But she stood alone, pulling out furniture drawers.

The rest of the room reminded Shadow of some male

places he'd seen. The bed things were rumpled and hanging down to the floor. Old clothing also lay around. Shadow couldn't help himself from sniffing at a sock rolled up on the floor. Yes. Very male indeed.

What he didn't detect, though, was any trace of the sweetish, spicy scent he'd caught on Sunny. This wasn't the place of Smells Good. What did Sunny want with this other He?

Shadow went over to the bed to see if there was anything to find there. A rumpled green shirt hung half on, half off, clinging to a blanket. He stretched up for a sniff and recoiled with a mew of surprise.

There were traces of blood there.

*

Normally, Sunny might not have heard the faint sound. But she was standing alone in an empty house, and the noise hit her ears like a small explosion. She whirled guiltily around from the dresser she'd been searching to find Shadow staring up at her.

"Shadow!" She knelt to scoop him up in her arms, but by the time she reached for him, the cat wasn't there. He'd bounded onto the mattress, although it was heavy going for him through the tangled bedclothes.

Sunny pursued, calling his name, pleading with him. "Everything's okay, I'm not angry with you, I want you to come home!"

Shadow didn't seem to pay much attention. He seemed more intent on evading her, although he didn't turn to the more drastic tactics he'd used on Lee Trehearne. There was no spitting, no clawing. He just dodged when she grabbed. Sunny managed to head him off when he reached the head of the bed, keeping him from leaping off and hiding under the bed frame.

But he darted back, somehow worming his way between the mattress and the headboard. Sunny hesitated over the bed, trying to figure out where Shadow would pop up next.

Instead, something else popped out. As Sunny knelt, completely distracted by the object on the floor, Shadow disappeared under the bed and then rocketed out the door.

It was a small plastic bag, with one of those resealable zip tops, the kind Sunny used for storing leftovers. Except in this case, the bag was half full of pills. Most of them were white tablets with a score line on the back. They reminded Sunny of one of her father's heart medicines.

But there was also a blister pack of other pills. Sunny could see them through the little plastic bubbles. They looked pink and crumbly. She jumped up and searched around for something she could use to turn the bag over without letting her fingers touch it. Finally she found a pencil. With a couple of careful pokes, she managed to flip the bag and see the foil-sealed back of the blister pack. There was something printed there, but not in English. It was in an alphabet she didn't recognize.

A sudden crash brought her to the room next door, where she found a screen on the floor and a cat's rear end disappearing out the window. By the time she got there, Shadow had made a death-defying leap into the shrubbery below, promptly disappearing.

There goes any hope of catching up with him, Sunny thought as she returned to Beau's room and the other problem she faced.

Frowning, she tried to decide what to do. For all she knew, this little supply of pills could have been jammed in place years ago. Just because Beau was a medical student, working in a hospital, it didn't necessarily mean these drugs were his. *Though if this is Beau's stash,* she thought, *taking it will alert him that someone has searched his room.*

Sunny pondered possibilities for several minutes, and finally brought out her cell phone. She activated the camera and began taking shots of Beau's room, including the bag on the floor. Then she knelt over it and focused several close-ups.

Finally, wrinkling her nose, Sunny used the top of one of the socks on the floor to pick up a corner of the bag and wedge it back into its hiding place. She left the room—and the house—much more quickly than she'd gone in.

But as she came down the steps to reach the private road, she slowed down, trying to fit what she'd found into what she knew.

I guess a supply of pills might suggest why Beau seems zonked out all the time, Sunny thought. *Does the fact that he's using drugs add anything more to motive, opportunity, and means?*

The answer seemed to be "not really." Despite ticking the most boxes as a suspect, even at his worst, Beau seemed grumpy rather than murderous. Peter Van Twissel, on the other hand, came off more dangerous while under the influence.

Once safely on her side of the street, Sunny sent a text to Will: THIS CLD BE EVIDENCE, and attached photos of the plastic bag. Maybe this was just a distraction from her search for Eliza's murderer. It could even be a dead end. But she had to follow it.

Beau looked like a new man when he returned from town and came up the path to the pool. The hairdresser hadn't just trimmed off the shaggy bits of his mop, he'd given Beau a haircut sculpted to complement the shape of his face and his features. He'd gone from looking like a frat boy gone to seed to the young medical professional he was aiming to become.

Sunny caught up to him just before the gate to the pool. She'd been watching for him, trying to devise some sort of a plan. Finally she decided this was the place to brace him, just out of earshot but within view of the other people around the pool. Hopefully, the presence of witnesses would keep Beau from trying anything drastic.

"You look good. How do you feel?" Sunny asked.

"Lighter." Beau ran a tentative hand along the back of his neck. "Have I got a tan line back there now?"

"No, you were smart enough to spend most of your time sleeping in the shade," Sunny told him. She decided to jump right in. "Speaking of which . . ." She brought out her phone and showed Beau a picture of the bag of pills. "Is this how you manage to stay so calm and rested?"

For a moment, Beau seemed to loom over her, his face gone blank. Then, as if he'd developed a sudden leak, he deflated. "It's not what it looks like."

"It looks like a supply of pills," Sunny said. "Of course, some people say that's almost a required accessory for med students."

"And they might be right," Beau shuffled his feet, kicking at the gravel in the path. "It's pretty hard to stay sharp when you're averaging about four hours' sleep a day. I got some . . . chemical help. Something to pep me up. Thought

I could keep a handle on it, but I couldn't. It sounds about as stupid as I feel, but . . . I got hooked."

Sunny stared at him, thinking of Beau's constant drowsiness. "If those pills are supposed to pep you up, I don't think they're working."

"You don't understand," Beau said. "Those pills aren't uppers. They're supposed to help me get *off* the uppers. I knew I was getting messed up. This time off would be my only chance to stop using. If I took this stuff, it would help me detox with minimal withdrawal symptoms."

He gave Sunny a rueful, mirthless smile. "Unfortunately, there's a side effect that affects a very small percentage of users, so I didn't worry about it. But some people taking this stuff suffer lethargy and extreme tiredness."

Sunny nodded. "And you're one of the lucky ones."

"It's like I'm making up for all the sleep I lost in the last year." Beau looked embarrassed. "I even dozed off in the barber's chair."

"So I presume that explains all the white pills," Sunny said. "What about the pink ones?"

Beau's expression suddenly became guarded, but Sunny pressed. "Are they an emergency supply of uppers in case your do-it-yourself detox didn't work?"

"Look—please." His voice was strained.

"You've come clean this far," Sunny told him. "Why not go all the way?"

Beau's big shoulders slumped. "It's true. You know my secret now . . . but so does someone else. I was blackmailed."

Sunny struggled to keep her expression neutral, while internally she thought, *Hot damn—looks like Randall might be right!*

Beau's face became relaxed as he unburdened himself. "When I got the demand, there wasn't much I could do. Residents with drug dependency issues usually don't become doctors. And it was supposed to be a one-time payment—a hefty one, but I managed to scrape it together and wire it off."

A one-time payment, Sunny thought. *That fits.*

"Why would you trust that there'd only be one payment?" she asked.

"It's not like I had a choice." Beau shrugged his heavy shoulders. "Besides, Carson and some of our other friends knew other people who'd gotten similar demands. I heard them talking. Bits and pieces, rumors and gossip. But the payment seemed to work. There were no more demands for money."

His voice ran down, but Sunny knew there was more. "The problem was, you still owed a favor."

Beau jumped as if he'd been stung. "How do you know?"

"I've heard bits and pieces, too," she told him. "So the pink pills are the favor you owe?"

The big guy didn't so much nod as drop his head. "Rohypnol."

Sunny stared. "The date-rape drug?"

"I was told to get a supply, something untraceable, from out of the country," Beau said miserably, still hanging his head. "Nowadays the legit stuff has an additive that turns drinks green if you drop the pills in them."

"What—?" Sunny began, but Beau quickly cut her off.

"I don't know. I don't know what was going on." The words almost tumbled out of him. "All I was supposed to do was pass them on to Eliza Stoughton. Whatever was going down with her, I have no idea. Guess we weren't close enough to share our really big secrets."

"She was being blackmailed, too, I hear."

"I figured as much, the way she started going off on everybody." Beau let off a long breath. "I was supposed to lie low until she contacted me. The thing is, even though she was always screaming at me, she never asked for the pills. And then she wound up dead." He shuddered. "I really wanted to keep my head down after that." Beau looked at Sunny pleadingly. "How do you think that Wainwright guy would react if I told him the same story I just told you?"

"Better than you might think," Sunny said, keeping her reporter alter ego's harsher opinion to herself. *Or he may just stamp "case closed" on the file and ignore all the loose ends.*

"And how about you? You're a reporter," Beau said, remembering that a little belatedly. "What are you going to do?"

"For now, I've got to think about it," Sunny replied. "You have to know this may be connected with the deaths."

Beau stared miserably at his feet. "I had nothing to do with either of them."

"If I can keep you out of it, I will." Even as she made it, Sunny wondered if that was a smart promise.

The minute Will hears about this, he'll want to turn it all over to Wainwright, and to hell with Beau, she thought. *Is that the right thing to do? Beau's getting clean. And I believe him when he says he's not involved.*

Sometimes, she had to admit, her reporter's truth radar could be fooled. But Beau had been forthcoming about his drug use and the blackmail. And as for not knowing what Eliza Stoughton was up to, that rang true to Sunny as well.

On the other hand, if I'm wrong, I've just warned a killer that I'm onto him, she thought as a chill ran through her. Sunny hated to admit it, but the blackmail angle actually made things look worse for Beau. If Eliza was supposed to contact him, that meant they both knew that the other was being extorted. Sunny had a further uncomfortable thought. *What if Sheriff Nesbit, armed with Randall's blackmailer theory, had raised the subject in a quiet meeting with the prime suspect—Beau? I could end up like Eliza, or Nesbit. As part of his surgical training, Beau would know his way around a knife.*

Pushing that thought from her mind, Sunny asked, "How did the blackmailer contact you?"

"Text messages that disappeared from my phone," Beau replied. "Pretty freaky."

Sunny decided she needed a bit of time to try to digest this new information. She sent Beau off to his friends at the pool and set off on a walk around the Neal's Neck compound. Not the most reassuring of considerations after getting old Beau to open up. It certainly piled more into the boxes for motive and means. Opportunity, though . . .

Lee Trehearne's cameras still placed Beau inside the guesthouse when the murders occurred, a definite alibi. Unless he'd managed to climb up to the roof and grow wings to commit his crimes, Beau had been, if not asleep, then at least in the house. Possibly he could have figured out how to avoid the cameras, but how would he have even known about them? This was his first visit to Neal's Neck.

Rather than avoiding the cameras, it might be possible to fool them, Sunny thought. *You'd just need the technical skills.*

That suggested Peter Van Twissel, the computer genius

with the strong-looking hands. His alibi depended on the cameras, too. And then there were the disappearing text messages—another bit of techno-magic. Could Peter be the mysterious Taxman? A poor boy lifting money and favors off the rich?

Not to mention an unpleasant drunk. Sunny scowled. *Was he the sort of criminal who'd screwed up his own plans? Everybody seemed to be drinking when I passed the pool party the day of the press conference. Did Eliza somehow tumble to the fact that Peter was the Taxman, and he eliminated her? And then did the same to Nesbit? For that matter, would he have been able to see straight enough to go after the sheriff?*

She continued to walk aimlessly. Peter could have been playing drunk—or drunker—to give himself an alibi. But Sunny had problems putting him in the middle of the Taxman's web. Randall said the extortion scheme had been going on for at least a decade, which would have made Peter a young teenager when it began. Where would a high school kid have gotten the kind of information required?

Or maybe, where would a good hacker get the information?

Sunny found herself passing the tennis court, and Priscilla's brothers' never-ending marathon of games. How about one of them? Could one of the Senator's grandsons be supplementing his governor's salary and influencing people through blackmail? Both were a bit older than Sunny—certainly more used to technology than any of the older generation. Neither had shown himself as a computer whiz, but maybe that was on purpose.

The knife that killed Frank Nesbit did *come from Lem*

Junior's bedroom, Sunny couldn't help thinking. *And the Kingsburys are surely more familiar with their own security systems than any of the visitors. In fact, aside from the whole technology aspect, Senator Kingsbury would fit quite nicely in the role of the spider running the Taxman's web,* she thought. *He probably knows where a lot of bodies are buried, metaphorically or literally. And since he got dumped by his old associates, he'd have motive to make them pay.*

The problem was, she was certain that he didn't have the computer smarts to pull off something as fancy as vanishing text messages and untraceable payments. *Of course, he could have hired out the work, but that would've meant a partner who could reveal all. And what would any of the Kingsburys want with Rohypnol?*

An ugly scenario suggested itself to her mind: Tommy Neal was an up and coming Wall Street type, distant relation . . . and spurned suitor? Robin Lory and others had suggested that Priscilla and Tommy had been considered as matrimonial partners, but he'd ended up marrying Cillie's best friend. What if he still wanted Priscilla—but wanted to make sure she wouldn't remember it? A date-rape drug would take care of that.

Sunny shook her head. *This is beginning to sound like one of those new nighttime soaps,* she silently complained. It certainly didn't help her to narrow down the circle of suspects.

She suddenly felt very alone.

I'd give a lot to have a friendly face around.

*

Shadow trailed after Sunny, not even sure why he was doing it. First she'd chased him and then ignored him, and then she'd sat watching for the big He to come along. Shadow could smell that He even from the underbrush where he'd hidden. There were made smells on him now, some of them pretty interesting. But underneath that was the same strong male scent that Shadow had detected in the room where Sunny had gone.

Whatever else, though, this one was *not* Smells Good.

Shadow gave a little quiver of annoyance. *I thought Sunny was happy enough with the Old One, her He . . . and me,* he thought. *Why has she started fooling around with all these other two-leggity males?*

He wasn't sure whether he'd find out, but he kept on her trail, even when she absentmindedly walked past the Black Ones who were searching for him. Sometimes he had to detour to stay out of their way. But he always came back to Sunny.

Shadow could tell she was troubled. He might not be able to climb into her lap and comfort her, but he could make sure he'd be nearby.

18

By the time Sunny had mentally worked her way through all the possible suspects, a glance at her watch told her she was about due to head back and get ready for dinner. She strolled along to the guesthouse just in time to see Priscilla emerging from one of the ever-present town cars. Cillie looked very serious indeed in a sage green suit. She waved good-bye to the car—Sunny realized that Cale Kingsbury was in the backseat, also wearing a suit—and waited until the vehicle had gone around a bend in the path. Then Priscilla raised her arms and did a little shimmy.

"My happy dance," she explained to Sunny. "I've been working for months on a project to create food pantries statewide using the 99 Elmet Ladies' effort as a test program. It took two meetings in one day, but we finally signed the papers and organized the funding. It's a go! The biggest thing I've tried to get off the ground, and now it's set to happen. I was so afraid something would gum things up when the wedding plans went into high gear, or for the honeymoon." She heaved a deep sigh and gave Sunny a big grin. "Okay. Now I'm ready to get married."

"I think you still have a couple of months," Sunny told her, but she joined in the smile. But then the idea of fouling things up before the wedding tangled with the Rohypnol she'd discovered. Almost before she knew what she was saying, Sunny asked, "Does anyone have a reason to create a scandal around your wedding?"

Priscilla's cheerful expression faltered. "You mean a scandal besides two people getting murdered on Neal's Neck?"

Sunny took a moment to search for the right words. None came—at least, none that didn't involve mentioning the date-rape drug. "I mean something more like a sex scandal."

Cillie got very formal, almost prim. "That's not something people usually connect with us Kingsburys."

"Except, I guess, for people who know about the copse," Sunny suggested.

Warm color rose in Priscilla's face, but her eyes grew icy. "That's kind of personal."

"You're right—I was out of line," Sunny apologized. But her interior reporter's antennae were quivering. There was something here, but she wasn't sure what it might be. She took a moment or two to switch the conversation to other subjects and smooth Priscilla's ruffled hackles, much as she sometimes did with Shadow's fur. When Cillie was smiling again, Sunny went into the guesthouse and headed upstairs. She only had one unused outfit left in the closet, her coral party number. After a quick shower, she let her hair dry and put on a little makeup before stepping into the dress and heading over for dinner. Then she came out into the hallway, where Cillie stood waiting.

"Wow! Very impressive," Priscilla said as she took in the outfit. "You make me feel dowdy in this suit."

"Spoken like a true politician," Sunny told her.

"Politician's daughter," Cillie corrected as they headed downstairs to join Yardley, who actually did look a bit dowdy in her usual beige. The guys didn't say much when Sunny and the other girls joined them outside, but they each gave her some pretty complimentary looks. And when they reached the big house, Cale Kingsbury greeted Sunny with a big grin.

"You should have led with this dress, Sunny," he told her after a slow survey. "You know how first impressions are the most important."

She waved off the flattery. "At the beginning of the summer, my skin burns to exactly this shade," she told him.

"Oho," he said, "the nude look."

Rolling her eyes but grinning, Sunny headed for the dining room. The experiment with alfresco dining was definitely over, although as usual, the meal was buffet style. Both sets of French doors leading to the terrace were closed, and the food was arranged on the sideboard in closed dishes.

Sunny had to hide a grin. *Full security in case of a commando cat attack,* her inner smart mouth quipped.

The meal was quiet, but Sunny got a lot of sidelong looks from the males in the room, including a couple from the Emperor Augustus. She began to regret having worn such a striking color. By the time dinner ended, she was glad for the opportunity to make an escape.

As Sunny was leaving the mansion, Priscilla appeared at her side. "I was thinking about what you mentioned earlier," she said quietly. "About scandals. The Neals were more likely than the Kingsburys to get involved in, um, adventures. But somebody else had to deal with a lot of gossip—Eliza."

Sunny stopped and stared. "What kind of gossip?"

"Look, she's—she was a friend, and now she's dead." Cillie bit her lip. "I don't know if I should tell you."

"Let me help," Sunny said. "Is it something she could've been blackmailed over?"

Priscilla's eyes went wide. "Maybe. She wasn't specific with me, but she was pretty frantic about a year ago, right when she broke off her engagement. There were rumors about a sex tape that her fiancé had talked her into—and then managed to lose."

That could put the kibosh on Eliza's wedding plans, Sunny thought, although she said nothing. *And in the right hands—like the Taxman's—it could also be a dandy setup for blackmail.*

"But I don't see how an indiscretion like that could've led to her getting killed." Priscilla's voice was so soft, Sunny could barely hear it.

"I don't know either, but it may tie in," Sunny said. "I'm still casting my nets as widely as possible. Then I'll try to see what facts fit together."

Priscilla nodded somberly, and they moved together in silence for a little while. But when Cillie made the turn to head for the guesthouse, Sunny shook her head. "I'm going to walk a little more. Try and sort out my thoughts."

She took a wide loop around the compound, along the paths nearest to the water. Blackmail. Scandal. Sex tapes. Rohypnol, which almost was synonymous with date rape. It seemed like a consistent thread, but how did it tie together?

She was almost to the tip of Neal's Neck, the headland that jutted out into the water like the prow of a vessel, when she spotted the copse, the only halfway-wild stand of trees amid the otherwise immaculately tended gardens and lawns. *That has to be it,* Sunny thought, spotting the ruins of an old shingled roof among the foliage. On impulse, she walked over. There was the barest suggestion of a path, overgrown with twigs that tugged at the hem of her dress. She zig-zagged deeper into the shadows and found the gazebo. Although the roof was pretty much gone, the base of the structure and the supporting posts had managed to survive. A few token flecks of white remained on the more sheltered sections, vestiges of an ancient paint job. But most of the bare wood had weathered to a silvery color.

Left to their own growth, the surrounding trees had spread up and out to create a green roof where the shingled one had been torn away. *In the summertime I guess that's pretty romantic,* Sunny thought. *What had Cillie called it? A bower?*

As a lover's rendezvous, however, it looked pretty Spartan. Blankets would definitely be necessary. And maybe some moonlight, too. Right now, the lighting was all wrong. The evening sun had turned the western sky a glaring red, as if a huge fire were blazing just beyond the horizon. That was quite pretty when viewed from the open. But it gave an infernal atmosphere to the shadows in here.

Well, Cale should be happy, Sunny thought, peering out through the screening brush. She tried to remember the poem Dad and his fishing buddies always quoted:

Red sky in the morning, sailors take warning.
Red sky at night, sailor's delight.

There was a whole scientific explanation for the folklore, something about atmospheric conditions foretelling the weather, Sunny wasn't sure. But for Mike and his pals, a sky like this evening's meant a pleasant journey for the next day's fishing. *Maybe we can persuade Cale to take us out on the* Merlin *again tomorrow.*

She was just turning to find her way out again when she spotted something that didn't belong: a box attached high up on one of the roof supports, smaller than a pack of cigarettes, but thicker—because of the lens. In fact, she might not have even noticed it if a breeze hadn't shifted the branches on the trees, letting in a shaft of sunlight that caused an orange reflection on the lens.

This was a camera. Sunny had been researching extreme sports for an article on the MAX website, things like BASE jumping, skydiving, and paragliding. Part of the fun for the participants was recording their particular death-defying stunts, so to meet the market, cameras like this one (small enough to mount on the adventurer's gear or helmet, and that used a Wi-Fi signal to send images to a recorder) were now widely available.

Somehow, Sunny didn't think this particular camera was part of the Neal's Neck security surveillance shield. That was supposed to be on the perimeter, aimed outward, not into a secluded rendezvous location. *But a camera like this would make a dandy addition to a blackmailer's bag of tricks,* Sunny thought as she slowly made a circuit around the ruined gazebo. Now that she was looking for them, Sunny spotted three other cameras, enough to capture all angles on the floor.

Rohypnol, sex tapes, and a young guy about to get married and maybe make a run for the presidency. It all created an unpleasantly clear picture to Sunny.

She left the gazebo and began pushing her way through the overgrown path. Then a flare of light ten times brighter than the setting sun exploded behind her eyes as sudden pain screamed from the back of her head.

And everything went black.

*

Shadow skulked in the underbrush around the big trees. It smelled different in here than around the rest of this place, more rank and wild. He wasn't sure he liked that, especially when Sunny pushed her way through the bushes. Unpleasant things could hide in places like this—like the time he'd investigated a thicket and found himself nose to nose with one of those masked critters with the big claws and teeth. It was a good thing that both of them had been surprised enough to back away. *That animal had been half again my size,* Shadow thought. *It would have been a bad, bad fight.*

He had another problem. In a confused place like this, he might wind up nose to nose with Sunny. What if she was playing a trick on him? She'd left him very confused, ignoring him, chasing him, ignoring him, and now sneaking into a wild place. So he'd decided not to follow, just to stay on the outskirts and wait for her to come out.

She won't stay long, he told himself. *There's no food in there—at least, nothing Sunny would like.*

That reminded Shadow of his own empty stomach, so he decided to try and find something *he* could eat. He ranged around the circle of trees, looking for something to stalk, sorting out the smells of wild growth and damp earth, scenting for prey. . . .

The wind brought a new aroma, faint at first, then stronger, becoming more distinct over the wild scents. This was a made smell, sweet and spicy. The scent of Smells Good!

Shadow retraced his steps, circling round the little forest, but when he got to where the scent was strongest, no one was there. He raised his head, sniffing. Smells Good had gone through the bushes! Had he come here to find Sunny? What would they do in this quiet place?

A thought came to Shadow and made him blink. Could they have come here to mate? It didn't seem like a comfortable place. Shadow considered human beds one of the best things they had.

But then, two-legs were always doing crazy things. He set off through the underbrush to investigate. There was Sunny's scent, and the stronger aroma of Smells Good. Up ahead, he suddenly heard an odd cry. Was it pain, or something else?

Shadow began shouldering his way through the brush more forcefully, not caring now if he might be heard. Any sound he made would be drowned out by the weird creaking noises that came to his ears anyway. He burst out into an open place, where wooden steps ran up to a platform— and where part of the floor had swung up. A two-legged male was carrying Sunny down into darkness, her head lolling on his shoulder.

He smelled blood!

Desperate, Shadow leaped into the opening, going down, down, down into the dark.

One thing he knew for sure. This was definitely Not Good.

19

Sunny's eyes fluttered open—to a blackness as complete as the one behind her lids. Consciousness brought pain and a feeling of dampness in the back of her head. She tried to raise an investigating hand, and found her wrists were joined somehow. When she tried to twist them apart, the bonds stayed stickily put.

She slowly made sense of it. *Duct tape? I'm tied up with tape?*

Sunny realized she was lying on her side, and there was tape around her ankles, too, which made things even more clumsy.

A second later, she felt something tugging at the tape on her wrists. Something biting at it. Instinctively, Sunny jerked away. Her fingers felt the brush of a large, fur-clad body, and a moment later it was back, saying, "Meow" before biting at the tape again.

"Shadow?" Sunny tried to sit up—an extremely bad idea. Her head suddenly felt like a giant gong, the kind they ring by banging big logs against them. The pain exploding from the back of her head made her feel giddy, and the meal she'd recently eaten made a sudden concerted effort to escape from her stomach. She couldn't keep it in, but Sunny at least managed to turn away so she didn't get sick on herself or Shadow. But the cat disappeared.

Great, Sunny thought, *Shadow gets to barf all over Lee Trehearne and that's fine. But when I get sick after being knocked cold, he scampers away? I guess it's a little late to say, "Lassie, get help!"*

She tried to worm herself away from the foul-smelling puddle she'd created, not easy in the darkness with her arms and legs bound and a head that still vibrated painfully at the merest motion. Taking a deep breath, she tried to call out, "Hello! Can anyone hear me?"

It came out as a low croak, more of a moan than words.

"Don't bother," Cale Kingsbury's voice came back. "We're pretty well soundproofed down here."

A glow in the darkness came toward her, resolving itself into the image of Cale with a flashlight in one hand and a plastic bottle of water in the other. He knelt, holding it to her lips. "Here. You can wash your mouth out."

Sunny swished the water around and spit the acrid taste away. "Somehow, I don't have the feeling that you're here to rescue me," she said.

Cale's usually insouciant face looked very serious in

the dim light. "I'm afraid not. Are you in any danger of puking again?"

She carefully shook her head with no worse effect than paralyzing pain. "No," she said.

"Good." He produced a roll of duct tape, tore off a piece, and slapped it over her mouth. "The next part takes us to a place where you might be heard."

Cale picked her up without any sign of straining at the job and carried her along what Sunny soon realized was a tunnel.

"Another of Great-Grandpa Neal's built-ins," Cale explained as he walked. "A rum-running tunnel that goes from the basement of the house to the pier—and also to the gazebo. That was probably an escape hatch. There was another tunnel leading off the Neck, but that one collapsed, so I don't know where it was supposed to go."

Sunny shifted uncomfortably. *Collapsed. There's a cheering thought.*

"But this section is sound," Cale assured her. "I made certain of that, just as I made sure the trapdoors in and out of here still work."

He apparently reached their destination, because he set Sunny down.

"Need both hands for this," Cale said, sticking the flashlight in his mouth. He approached a wooden section angled into the wall ahead and heaved. It took a couple of tries, but the panel finally gave way, rising up and revealing the blazing sunset.

Cale gathered Sunny up again and stepped outside onto the pier. Behind them, Sunny saw that a section of the stairway leading down to the wharf had swung up. Cale deposited Sunny in the rowboat tied conveniently nearby and then went to shut the secret door. "Now for a little cruise."

*

Shadow dodged back when he heard Sunny being sick. Then he heard footsteps approaching down a long, dark hallway. And far, far away, he saw light. A single sniff was enough to tell him that Smells Good was coming back.

Crouching in the gloom beyond the circle of light, Shadow tried to decide what to do. What he really wanted was to leap on this two-legs with his claws out. But the human was much bigger than he was, and strong. He'd carried Sunny as if she weighed nothing. From the times she'd rolled over on him in bed, Shadow knew that wasn't true.

And now they were stuck in this dark place. Even if he overcame Smells Good-Acts Bad, could Shadow free Sunny? The sticky stuff around her hands had resisted his efforts to bite it. And it tasted very bad.

When Smells Good picked up Sunny again, Shadow silently trailed along.

They walked for a while, until the male put Sunny down and pushed against a wall. It moved away, and Shadow caught the scent of salty fresh air. Maybe now was the time to strike.

But too quickly for Shadow to act, Smells Good had Sunny again, stepping out into the fading light. Shadow charged after . . . and then froze. They were on a long thing made of wood, with water all around. That's where the salty smell came from.

And the bad human was putting Sunny down into a

smaller wooden thing that floated on the water! Shadow didn't like this at all. Oh, he'd had times when he got caught in water. He'd been lucky enough to paddle with his paws and get out of the wet stuff. But Sunny's arms and legs were tied together, as if she'd been playing with string and gotten tangled. She wouldn't be able to swim.

He'd have to wait for a better chance.

When Smells Good went back to close up the opening he'd made, Shadow waited until the human's back was turned, then darted forward and leaped into the floating-thing. Sunny stared at him as he landed, her eyes very big over the sticky stuff covering her mouth. Shadow squashed his way behind her so that the bad human wouldn't see him.

Smells Good soon returned, climbing into the floating-thing and making it rock in a way Shadow really didn't like.

From his hiding place, Shadow couldn't see what the human was doing, but he could hear rhythmic swishing sounds and got the feeling that solid ground was getting farther and farther away. He nudged at Sunny to bring her hands within reach and again started gnawing at the disgusting sticky stuff. Then the rhythm changed, and they stopped, merely bobbing in place.

Shadow risked a look to see Smells Good's back as he used a very thick string to tie the thing they were on to— Shadow wasn't quite sure what this was. It was as big as a house, but it floated on the water. Why would anybody want to have a house that floated?

That's the problem with two-legs, he thought as he

dropped back into hiding. *They make some good things. But they're crazy.*

*

Cale deposited Sunny rather unceremoniously onto the deck of the *Merlin*—more like a sack of potatoes than the gentlemanly helping hand he'd given her the other day. At least he had the manners to apologize as he moved her over to the cockpit, not that Sunny felt like appreciating them. As Cale ranged around the yacht, getting it ready to sail, she was shocked to see Shadow jump up onto the deck. He returned to the job of attacking her wrist restraints. He'd managed to tear a couple of holes in the tape with his teeth, but it wasn't giving—it hadn't been weakened enough. When Cale returned to raise the anchor, Shadow disappeared beneath the hem of her dress.

"Now we'll just sail away. No engines, nothing to draw notice." Cale took the wheel, and the *Merlin* surged forward. After a while he leaned over and removed the tape from Sunny's mouth. "I'm really sorry about this, but I had my suspicions after I overheard you talking with Priscilla. And then when I tested the cameras and saw you in the gazebo, my hands were tied."

"I think that's my line," Sunny said. She looked at the rowboat trailing along behind them on a towline. "So, secret passages and a rowboat. That's how you were able to get around without anyone knowing."

"Yes. That much worked well at least."

Sunny nodded. "You're used to having things work well—as the Taxman."

Cale shot her a glance.

"You're a legend in certain circles," Sunny told him. "Mainly crime reporters."

"Crime." Cale repeated the word as if it had a bad taste. "I didn't set out to commit any crimes. After the accident, I was looking for a second act—that was what the foundation was supposed to be, why it's called Act Two. But people weren't willing to give me a chance. Well, if they wouldn't give voluntarily, I figured they'd have to be persuaded. I knew things, and I parlayed that into funding—seed money. No one I put the bite on was a saint, you know. At least now they were doing some good, even if they didn't realize it. Those first transactions were pretty crude. But when we began extending our programs to work in prisons and I discovered the hackers, I was able to route money in more indirect ways."

"So it was about the money," Sunny said.

"Well, sure, it started out about the money," Cale explained. "Seed money, like I said. But I didn't want to make a pig of myself, or draw attention. After a while, when we showed what the foundation could do, we had more legitimate donors."

"And then it became about the favors."

"In a way I guess I'm a victim of my own success." Cale sat for a moment with his hands on the wheel, then said, "My little projects went so well, I stopped planning for failure anymore. And maybe the old saying is true—you shouldn't foul your own nest." He started to laugh. "But look at the prize! If Carson actually becomes Mr. President, he'll owe my family. But I'll *own* him. The black sheep of the Kingsburys, armed with a presidential sex video. I'd be able to write my own ticket."

Sunny winced. *He told me almost the same thing about getting Augustus de Kruk's breakdown on camera—that I'd be set for life.* "So that's what this was all about," she said slowly, "a sex tape featuring Carson de Kruk? You planned to force Eliza Stoughton to act as the leading lady in your little production and even extorted a supply of Rohypnol to get Carson into a compromising position without him even remembering it. Except it didn't turn out the way you'd planned."

"I thought it would work perfectly. I'd even be on hand to deal with any last-minute glitches." Cale might as well have been discussing a repair project on his boat. "Bellingham would provide the drug, and all Eliza had to do was persuade him to bring her along. As for the rest, she'd been indiscreet in front of a camera before. But this time, for whatever reason, Eliza balked. Worse, she confronted me. She'd had her suspicions, it seems, and it all came to a head when she went for a late-night swim. Maybe I'd overreached, by setting it up to happen while we were all together up here. In the end, well, it went badly. She'd been drinking and started to make a ruckus."

"So you used your knowledge of the rum-running passageways to get into and out of the house unseen. It was just a short stroll from the gazebo to the point, where you tossed Eliza's body off the cliff and then vanished back down the gazebo hole. As far as anyone knew, you were in the house the whole time, with a wall of external surveillance cameras to back up your alibi." Sunny's voice was dry and tight as she spoke, but Cale just responded with a matter-of-fact nod.

"I planned to just step back and let the police follow

their routine. I was disappointed at having to scratch my project, and I realized that there might be some bad publicity for the upcoming wedding, but hey, the Kennedys have endured worse." His eyes flicked over her. "There was even the possibility of restarting when you turned up. Bellingham had enough doses for two people."

If Sunny could have gotten a hand free, she'd have gone for him. But, while the tape gave a little, it still resisted her best efforts. So she used her mouth instead. "What happened with Nesbit?"

Cale's busy eyes kept scanning the horizon, but his lips quirked. "We'd known each other since I ran for Congress," he said. "But Nesbit had me all wrong. He suspected that *I* was the most blackmailable person on Neal's Neck, so he started to ask me leading questions. I denied the whole idea, but I knew he'd keep digging—and worse, he'd probably tell other people. So I arranged a meeting, and came prepared. When I went off to get the supplies for that beer pong tournament, I considered buying a knife. But I couldn't risk some shopkeeper remembering." That bad-boy grin crept onto his face. "Then I remembered my brother Lem's old tackle box."

"You got the knife from there, used the passage to the dock, and set off for a quick row in the dark to make the meeting."

Cale nodded with a flicker of anger. "Nesbit thought he held all the cards; that he was dealing with some screwup who'd roll over and tell him whatever he wanted. He was so surprised when I slit his throat."

"Arrogant," Sunny said. "Like you."

Cale's face was expressionless as he turned toward her.

"What," Sunny burst out, "I should worry about what I say to you? I can pretty much figure how this twilight cruise is going to end. You'll come back short an extra anchor or something. But I'm not coming back at all."

"I thought we might be able to at least keep it polite," he said.

"Real life is a lot messier," Sunny told him. "People wind up chasing a cat with a fishing net, and the cops are put onto a box of tackle that nobody had thought of in years."

"Yes," Cale said. "That damned cat put quite a crimp in things, bringing attention back to the house." Then he broke off. "Excuse me a moment. The going gets a little tricky here." He reached over to a set of marine charts set up at the side of the wheel—and yelped in surprise to discover Shadow standing over them. "What the hell is that cat doing here?"

Shadow showed him, sending the charts flying as he left a set of bright red claw-marks on the back of Cale's hand. Quickly lashing the wheel in place with a one-handed knot, Cale lunged for Shadow, only to end with his fingers just inches short as the cat used one of his prime evasion moves.

Cale hauled himself out of the cockpit in pursuit. Shadow led him a merry chase back and forth, but Cale managed to slam the hatch that led below decks before Shadow could reach it. "I want you out in the open," the man growled. "When I catch you, you mangy little so-and-so, you're going for a swim."

They continued to play a vigorous game of pounce and skitter, but Sunny could see that Cale was driving the cat toward the bow. Sooner or later Shadow would run out of yacht.

Sunny frantically fought with the tape holding her prisoner. Shadow's teeth had managed to pierce the stuff in several places. It was sort of like a perforated line. But it took a lot of effort to tear it open. Pull, twist, pop a section apart. Then pull, twist, and pop the next.

Meanwhile, Sunny could only watch helplessly as Cale backed Shadow to the very bow of the boat. *Somehow, I don't think he's going to play "King of the World" up there,* Sunny feared.

"So now what are you going to do, cat?" Cale demanded. "I've got you—"

Shadow responded by going straight up, leaping past the dumbfounded Kingsbury to land against the bellying sail with his claws out. As Cale snatched after him, Shadow climbed up the sail and out of reach.

Swearing furiously, Cale started letting down the sail as Shadow kept climbing. Just as the cat was running out of room, the *Merlin* suddenly came to a jarring, grinding stop that nearly sent Cale off his feet.

Sunny could do the math and grinned savagely. *A boat that falls off to port plus tricky sailing equals running aground.*

Cale let rip with an even stronger expletive, abandoning the sail and stomping back toward Sunny.

Is this where I get off? Or is he going to start the engine and try to back away from these rocks under us? Sunny sincerely hoped he was going with Plan B, but Cale surprised her, coming up with Plan C. He rummaged down in the cockpit and came up with a pistol.

Barely giving Sunny a glance he set off for the bow of the ship again, apparently determined on a little target practice with Shadow. Cale Kingsbury barely got a few steps, however, before a powerboat came thrumming up, and a cheerful voice shouted, "Hey, there! Can we give you a hand?"

Sunny found herself speechlessly staring at Ben Semple's smiling face—and at Will Price already jumping for the deck of the *Merlin*.

Cale Kingsbury brought up his gun almost as a reflex action, but Sunny's reflexes were better. She tore her way through the last of the tape, braced her arms on the deck, and scooted forward, aiming both of her bound feet behind Cale's left knee. He stumbled forward directly into the roundhouse right Will was already unleashing. Cale flew back, his head smacking against the sail's boom, and he slithered to the deck, stunned.

After kicking Cale's pistol out of the way, Will knelt down, reaching into his back pocket. He might be out of uniform, but he'd come prepared, with his handcuffs at the ready. As soon as Kingsbury was safely restrained, Will turned to Sunny.

His lips turned in a sour smile as he used a pocketknife to get the tape off her ankles. "Part of a cop's continuing education is learning to identify the latest looks in illegal drugs. The stuff in the picture you sent me came from Thailand. We just recently learned it was coming on the market over here. So what was the deal, a sex scandal to stop the marriage?"

"No, a sex scandal to blackmail a possible president," Sunny told him. "Cale Kingsbury is the Taxman."

Will turned to stare at the groggy Cale. "Keep a careful

eye on this one," he shouted to Ben. Then his gaze came back to Sunny, the wheels obviously turning behind his eyes. "Sounds like you caught a big fish this time."

"More like a shark." Sunny shuddered. "He is a murderer, and he was going to throw me away like a piece of garbage once we got far enough offshore. That's what would have happened if you hadn't turned up."

"Well, we know he had you tied up while sailing out to sea," Will said. "But can you prove the blackmail scheme?"

"I found a bunch of cameras set up to record the scene. They have a wireless connection, and I suspect that when you trace the other end of that, you'll find a computer with lots of incriminating evidence. Cale was clever, but arrogant." She paused for a second. "But to do that, you've got to report to the police. How is Captain Ingersoll going to take all of this?"

"I followed his orders to the letter," Will replied with a grin. "He told me he didn't want to see me on the streets of Wilawiport." He gestured at the open water around them. "Does this look like a street?"

"That's not what I mean," Sunny said. "Although it is pretty clever."

"You mean *why* am I here?" Will put both arms around her. "That was pure luck. We were just arriving when I spotted the rowboat heading for the yacht. That orangey pink dress of yours caught my eye."

"Coral," Sunny told him.

"I always liked you in that dress. It's very pretty." He held her a little more tightly.

Sunny looked down ruefully. "I hope I can get it clean."

She relaxed in the circle of Will's arms—and then stiffened. "Shadow! No!"

*

Scrambling down from the big curtain on a stick, Shadow had an excellent view when Sunny's He arrived— and it was very good to see. Sunny kicked the bad Smells Good two-legs, and her He knocked him down. That was good. Even better, Sunny and her male friend stood very close together.

Maybe things will work out all right, Shadow thought. *Sunny and I will go back to live with the Old One, and her He can come and visit.*

He still had some business with Smells Good, though. *Chase me around, will you?* Shadow thought, strutting up to the helpless human who was just beginning to stir and mutter. *You like made smells? Well, here's one for you.* Shadow braced himself, thankful that he hadn't had a chance to relieve himself before this adventure. By the time he was done, Smells Good smelled very different.

20

By the time Sunny and Will got to Shadow, the damage had been done. A reeking Caleb Kingsbury was taken into custody by several state troopers coming out on the commandeered launch from the Neal's Neck compound. Ben Semple had been busy on the radio.

In the end, plenty of law enforcement wound up represented. Lieutenant Wainwright was there, and Captain Ingersoll, alternating between a slow burn at Will's insubordination and astonishment not only at Will's story, but how quickly it was proven—and how the story kept growing. Even the Maine Marine Patrol turned up to deal with the stranded *Merlin*.

Police technical types quickly tracked down Cale's computer. Apparently in his rush to get to the bower after spotting Sunny on camera, he'd left the system on. And her prediction proved true. They found plenty of evidence of previous "little projects," as Cale had called them.

Scenting a sensational story, the media responded in its usual voracious way. But Sunny left the law enforcement types to deal with that. By arrangement with Ken Howell, she only gave one exclusive interview, to the *Harbor Courier*—well, semi-exclusive, since Randall MacDermott participated.

"We wouldn't have gotten the lead on the Taxman if it weren't for Randall," Sunny explained to Ken, who grudgingly went along with her request. Will insisted on accompanying her for the joint interview.

I don't know why he feels he has to be here, Sunny thought as Will took a chair beside her in the *Courier* office while Ken and Randall set up their recorders. *Does he think Randall is going to throw me over his saddle and head off to New York with me?*

Of course, she realized, Will had just decked a guy—literally—who'd tried to run off with her, so maybe he was operating under an excess of testosterone.

She outlined the Taxman's extortion business in general and then gingerly made her way into the specific scheme that had led to murder. It wasn't easy. Ken and Randall were both proficient *Q* and *A* types who put her through an interrogation that would have made Lieutenant Wainwright green with envy.

Sunny fought to keep Beau Bellingham's pill problem out of the discussion, just vaguely referring to blackmail. What was the use of ruining his life? But the story of Eliza's sex tape had already surfaced, and she had to give some explanation of the plan to ensnare Carson. Neither of her interviewers was happy at her unwillingness to spill all the dirty details, but Sunny felt she owed that much to Priscilla and Carson. Sunny and Will had already warned them about the coming media firestorm as soon as they got on dry land, so it wouldn't hit the couple out of the blue. At last, realizing he wasn't going to get any more out of her, Ken turned off his recorder, eager to get going on the story and a new special edition of the *Courier*. Randall did the same, before rushing to his computer and getting the story down to New York before the *Standard* went to press. By the time Randall flew back to the big city, his front-page story would be hitting the streets.

But now, he hesitated. "I want to thank you, Sunny, and to apologize for those stupid comments I made about you not being much of a reporter anymore. You're a hell of a newsperson, digging up the facts, putting them together—"

"And nearly getting killed for it," Will put in, shooting an unfriendly glare at Sunny's former beau.

"Thanks, Randall." Sunny did her best to drown Will out.

"That's not all I'm sorry for." Considering that he was a guy who made his living with words, Randall seemed to have a hard time getting these ones out. Maybe it was Will's hostile presence. "If things had been different . . ."

"An old J-school professor of mine once told me that 'if' is one of the most treacherous words in the English language," she said gently, thinking, *so he's not eating crow in front of the Pulitzer committee, but it's a lot more than I ever really expected.*

"So is 'regret'—but that doesn't mean that even hard-boiled old editors don't feel it sometimes." Randall looked over at Will. "Good luck with the election." Then he looked back at her. "Good-bye, Sunny."

With that, Randall raced off to his keyboard. Will reached over and took her hand. Sunny wondered what kind of expression she must have on her face for him to look at her the way he was.

*

Soon enough, new scandals and disasters pushed the blackmail story into the category of old news. Augustus de Kruk's publicity machine remained remarkably quiet on the subject, but obviously the de Kruk-Kingsbury merger was on hold indefinitely—at least, that's what *Eagle Eye* had to say when the original wedding date came and went with no marriage.

Sunny knew that already; Robin Lory had told her. After her brief brush with the Kingsburys and de Kruks, Robin had a very proprietary feeling about the whole story.

So, Sunny, had to admit, did she—along with a very un-journalistic wish that Carson and Cillie might yet reach a happy ending after all. *Maybe all the negative stuff about Uncle Cale will scare both families away, and it will come down to what Carson and Cillie want,* Sunny thought. *I guess I can only hope.*

She killed the sound on the television set, turning to her father. "Do you think there's any place we can tune in for the election results?"

"Primary results," Mike corrected her. "And we'll be lucky to see something in tomorrow's paper. A sheriff's race isn't exactly big news."

He was wrong, though. When he tuned into the second half of the ten o'clock newscast, they had a brief blurb on how Lenore Nesbit had ridden a tidal wave of sympathy votes onto the ballot, which given Elmet County's voting habits, meant she had a lock on the election as well.

"I was afraid of this," Mike growled, glaring at the screen as Lenore waved to her supporters. "Even though Will did his job—and caught a murderer—it wasn't enough."

"Yeah, well, we kind of saw it coming," Sunny reminded him. "As political slogans go, there's a big difference between 'Keeping Elmet County Safe' and 'Catching Another Murderer.'"

The doorbell rang, and she found Will on the doorstep.

"Figured I'd come over to ask Mike when's the best time to concede," he said with a wry smile as he came inside.

Sunny put her arms around him, shutting the door. "And maybe get a little consolation-prize therapy?"

Will looked over her shoulder. "I dunno, it looks as though the chaperone is already in business."

Sunny turned to find a gray-furred face peering out at them from behind the cover of the archway into the living room. Slowly and mistrustfully, Shadow advanced toward them. But he came straight up, twined his way around Sunny's legs—and then did the same to Will.

"He's never done that before," Will said. Shadow sat back on his haunches as though he were regarding his handiwork.

"He does that on rare occasions with Dad, and I've seen him do it with Jane Rigsdale when he visits her at the vet's office. Looks as though he's marking you as one of his official people."

Will laughed. "Well, I guess that's one election I've won."

He was interrupted as the doorbell rang again.

"Kinda late for guests," Sunny said, going to answer. She opened the door to reveal Lenore Nesbit.

"Congratulations, Madame Sheriff," Sunny said.

"Forgive me for interrupting," Lenore said, "but a little bird told me you'd be here, Will." She made an abrupt gesture, as if she were erasing what she first intended to say. "I'm not here to crow. In fact, I'm here to make you an offer." She took a deep breath. "We both know how the election is going to turn out. In fact, the opposition candidate may just withdraw after my showing today. Here's the deal. After all the hoopla is over, I'd like to name you chief investigator for the sheriff's department. It would be equivalent to the rank of sergeant, and you'll get a raise."

She smiled at the startled expression on Will's face. "This did not make Dan Ingersoll overjoyed when I discussed it with him, but I think it's something we need to do. We have serious crimes to deal with, including crime that has affected me personally." Lenore was silent for a moment. "Times have changed, and we can't just ignore what's going on around us. As you said, we've got to be aware. I hope you can help us do that."

"I—I don't know what to say." Will stumbled over the words.

"Luckily, I don't need an answer right away," Lenore told him. "Think about it. Talk it over with your friends and supporters." She nodded toward the living-room arch, where Sunny's dad had appeared. "I hope, though, that you'll take the job."

As she spoke, the final member of the Coolidge household came forward, sniffing in fascination.

"Well, hello there." Lenore showed a familiarity with cats, bending over to offer Shadow a hand with the fingers curled under. Shadow immediately started pushing his head against her fingers, silently demanding a head scratch.

Well, Sunny thought, *this could be the beginning of an interesting friendship.*